The ties that bind may be the ties that kill as these extraordinary women race to beat the genetic time bomb that is their birthright....

Lynn White:
With enhanced senses and superspeed and strength, this retrieval specialist can breach any security— but has she been working for the wrong side?
DECEIVED by Carla Cassidy—January 2005

Faith Corbett:
This powerful psychic's secret talent could make her the target of a serial killer— and a prime suspect for murder.
CONTACT by Evelyn Vaughn—February 2005

Dawn O'Shaughnessy:
Her superhealing abilities make her nearly invincible, but can she heal the internal wounds from years of deception?
PAYBACK by Harper Allen—March 2005

* * *

ATHENA FORCE: The adventure continues with three secret sisters, three unusual talents and one unthinkable legacy....

Dear Reader,

You're about to read a Silhouette Bombshell novel and enter a world full of excitement, suspense and women who stand strong in the face of danger and do what it takes to triumph over the toughest adversaries. And don't forget a touch of thrilling romance to sweeten the deal. Our bombshells always get their men, good *and* bad!

Debra Webb kicks off the month with *Silent Weapon,* the innovative story of Merri Walters, a deaf woman who goes undercover in a ruthless criminal's mansion and reads his chilling plans right off his lips!

Hold on to your hats for *Payback,* by Harper Allen, the latest in the Athena Force continuity. Assassin Dawn O'Shaughnessy is out to take down the secret lab that created her and then betrayed her—but she's got to complete one last mission for them, or her superhealing genes will self-destruct before she gets payback....

Step into the lush and dangerous world of *The Orchid Hunter,* by Sandra K. Moore. Think "botanist" and "excitement" don't match? Think again, as this fearless heroine's search for a rare orchid turns into a dangerous battle of wills in the steamy rain forest.

And don't miss the twist and turns as a gutsy genius races to break a deadly code, trap a slippery terrorist and steal back the trust of her former CIA mentor, in *Calculated Risk,* by Stephanie Doyle!

Strong, sexy, suspenseful...that's Silhouette Bombshell! Please send your comments to me, c/o Silhouette Books, 233 Broadway Suite 1001, New York, NY 10279.

Sincerely,

Natashya Wilson

Natashya Wilson
Associate Senior Editor, Silhouette Bombshell

Please address questions and book requests to:
Silhouette Reader Service
U.S.: 3010 Walden Ave., P.O. Box 1325, Buffalo, NY 14269
Canadian: P.O. Box 609, Fort Erie, Ont. L2A 5X3

HARPER
ALLEN

PAYBACK

Published by Silhouette Books

America's Publisher of Contemporary Romance

Special thanks and acknowledgment are given to
Harper Allen for her contribution to the
ATHENA FORCE series.

 SILHOUETTE BOOKS

ISBN 0-373-51348-8

PAYBACK

Copyright © 2005 by Harlequin Books S.A.

www.SilhouetteBombshell.com

Printed in U.S.A.

Books by Harper Allen

Silhouette Bombshell

Payback #34

Silhouette Intimate Moments

Protector with a Past #1091

Harlequin Intrigue
The Man That Got Away #468
Twice Tempted #547
Woman Most Wanted #599
*Guarding Jane Doe #628
*Sullivan's Last Stand #632
*The Bride and the Mercenary #663
The Night in Question #680
McQueen's Heat #695
Covert Cowboy #735
Lone Rider Bodyguard #754
†Desperado Lawman #760
†Shotgun Daddy #766

*The Avengers
†Men of the Double B Ranch

HARPER ALLEN

lives in the country in the middle of a hundred acres of
maple trees with her husband, Wayne, six cats, four dogs—
and a very nervous cockatiel at the bottom of the food
chain. For excitement she and Wayne drive to the nearest
village and buy jumbo bags of pet food. She believes in
love at first sight because it happened to her.

Prologue

January

E-MAIL MEMO—URGENT & CONFIDENTIAL
To: Cassandras<Alexandra Forsythe, Darcy Allen,
Tory Patton, Samantha St. John, Josie Lockworth>
From: Lt. Kayla Ryan
Re: Lab 33 assassin Dawn O'Shaughnessy
Phys. Description: 22, 5'7", blonde, green eyes
Capabilities: Extraordinary strength, agility; possibly
other enhanced capabilities
Skills (partial list): Weaponry, martial arts, hand-to-
hand combat, stealth, B & E
Background: O'Shaughnessy conceived in vitro with
egg retrieved from former Athena Academy student
Rainy Miller, whose recent murder by Lab 33's Lee

Craig, code name Cipher, is being investigated by
the Cassandras. Retrieval conducted by Dr. Henry
Reagon under guise of an appendectomy. Actual
purpose: genetic manipulation experiment headed
by Dr. Aldrich Peters of Lab 33. Eggs fertilized with
sperm from Navy SEAL Thomas King, whose sperm
sample was stolen from a fertility clinic. Neither Rainy
nor Tom King were aware of procedure carried out
by Peters. Fertilized egg implanted in surrogate
mother; child taken at birth to Lab 33 in New Mex-
ico to be raised under Peters's supervision. Subject
has no knowledge of her true background; believes
her black-ops instructor, Lee Craig, is her uncle.
*Note: Subject actively working against the Cassan-
dras; must be considered extremely dangerous.*
Update: Subject has been told the truth about her
parentage. Her failure to kill Thomas King as per
Aldrich Peters's instructions and her elimination of Dr.
Carl Bradford to save Kayla and Jazz Ryan's lives in-
dicate that O'Shaughnessy is no longer an immediate threat. In fact, she has vowed to take down Lab
33 by herself. She will be given this memo and other
documentation in the hope that learning more of the
truth will encourage her to join forces with the Cassandras against—

The memo police lieutenant Kayla Ryan was holding—the memo she herself had written and securely
e-mailed to her best friends, the Athena Academy graduates known as the Cassandras, and that she had updated
only two days ago—had been torn in two at that point.
On the back was a handwritten note, unsigned, asking

Kayla to meet the writer at the Athena Academy gymnasium, which was usually deserted over Christmas break. Taking a deep breath, Kayla pushed open the double doors of the gym and saw a lithe figure pummeling the hell out of a workout bag.

She approached, noting the dampness darkening the honey-blond hair that had been secured into a thick braid, the sheen of exertion gleaming on the tanned midriff revealed between the low-rise sweatpants and the racerback top. The only thing impossible to see was what was going on behind Dawn O'Shaughnessy's gold-green eyes.

Kayla held up the scrap of memo. "You read this?"

A volley of punches slammed into the workout bag. Dawn stepped back. "I read it. It sums up everything you told me at your house a few days ago." She paused. "It's not every day a girl finds out her whole freakin' life has been a lie."

Kayla frowned. "You understand now why Samantha St. John had no recourse but to take down your uncle two months ago?"

"If I'd known then what I know now, I would have done it myself," Dawn replied. "And I'd appreciate if you didn't refer to Lee Craig as my uncle. He lied to me. He killed my biological mother. He let me go on an assignment to kill my biological father. What I felt for him is as dead as he is."

Kayla's gaze sharpened. When Kayla had told Dawn about her parentage three days ago, Dawn had shown no emotion. But now.... Unless she was mistaken, there were pinpricks of moisture glittering at the corners of those brilliant green eyes. *I knew Lee Craig as the Cipher,* she thought, *the world's most deadly assassin. But he was the only family Dawn had. Knowing he lied to her is tearing her in two—and until she deals with that conflict, she's a ticking time bomb.*

She kept her tone conversational. "There must be a part of you that wishes you could see him one more time, if only to ask him how he could betray you so terribly."

Without warning, Dawn faced the workout bag again and exploded into action, her gloved fists a blur. Kayla started when the bag split asunder, the sand it was filled with pouring out in a stream and the chain securing it giving way, solid steel links spilling to the floor like broken teeth. She'd hoped to get through to the woman, Kayla thought. Instead she'd set off a powder keg.

Dawn looked down at the destroyed bag. "Yeah, I'd like to see Lee Craig once more. Because it should be him lying here. If there were any justice, his death should have come at the hands of the woman he raised to follow in his footsteps." She backed away. "I'll have to content myself with going after my darling Uncle Lee's boss, Dr. Aldrich Peters...but for my own reasons, not the Cassandras'. I want payback."

Compassion filled Kayla. "Payback won't erase the pain. You should talk to someone—"

"No offense, Ryan, but I don't need advice on how to deal." Dawn's expression was shuttered. "You and your friends think you know everything there is about me. Want a demonstration of something that didn't make it into my file?"

Swiftly she reached down to her ankle. She straightened, and Kayla saw the small, snub-nosed automatic she was holding as Dawn flicked off the weapon's safety and jammed the muzzle against her upper arm.

"No!" Kayla grabbed for the gun, but too late. The shot's explosion echoed deafeningly. "Dammit—*why?*"

Even as the shocked question left her she was wrenching the weapon away and grabbing a nearby towel. "Stanch the blood with this while I get help."

"I told you, I don't need help with the healing." Dawn looked down at the wound. "Already reconstructing," she said, her smile oddly bitter. "Hurts like hell but that'll pass, too."

"Already recon—" Kayla's horror turned into bafflement. "Your body's knitting itself back together!" she gasped. "Your arm...it's as if—as if—" In silence she watched as the last traces of the wound disappeared, leaving only a few smears of blood. "It's as if you were never shot," she said unevenly. "We guessed that Peters was doing genetic experiments, but this is—"

Dawn's smile thinned. "Freakish?" she suggested. "When I believed my regeneration was a gift of nature, I thought it meant I was special. Lee Craig lied about that, too."

"I wasn't going to say that," Kayla denied hotly. "Your impressive demonstration aside, I still think you should seek help with the healing process. You'll never be able to move on till you do."

"I've already moved on." Dawn picked up a sports bag by her feet. "Like I said, I'm going to take down Lab 33."

"The Cassandras have another assignment we'd like you to consider first." She'd wanted to broach the subject less bluntly, Kayla thought, but from the start this meeting hadn't gone the way she'd expected.

"Find someone else. Aldrich Peters is my business. He has been since the day twenty-three years ago when he played God with my genetic makeup."

"Not only yours," Kayla retorted. "We believe there

was at least one other child born from Rainy Miller's egg. A baby girl. She was kidnapped at birth, possibly because Carl Bradford leaked Peters's plans to an interested party. Don't you want to find your sister before turning your attention to Peters?"

"A sister like me?" Letting go of the sports bag, Dawn gripped Kayla's arms fiercely. "Another woman who was manipulated by Peters the way I was?"

"We have no idea whether her abilities would be like yours," Kayla explained swiftly, shaken by the raw emotion in the younger woman's tone. "Or if she even has any. That doesn't change the fact that, if she's alive, she's your—"

"So I'm still alone." Dawn's arms fell to her sides. "I guess it was crazy of me to hope..." Her movements stiff, she started to pick up the bag again, but Kayla stopped her.

"Hope what?"

Dawn faced her directly. "That I'd found someone to share the nightmares with. When I was working for Lab 33 I told myself I was on the side of the good guys, but that doesn't change the fact that I was judge, jury and executioner. Lee was the only one who understood how I felt."

"The only difference being, he carried out every assignment Peters gave him," Kayla reminded her sharply. "He deliberately chose the dark side, Dawn."

"And so did Aldrich Peters." The younger woman's features tightened. "The Cassandras want me to find my sister before I turn my sights on Peters. Fair enough, but if you're hoping she'll be able to help me in this healing process you say I need, forget it. I heal just fine all by myself."

Without another word, she strode to the exit, her posture ramrod-stiff. Instead of following her, Kayla watched her go.

"That's just it, O'Shaughnessy, I don't think you will heal all by yourself this time," she said under her breath. "If you don't..." She glanced at the shattered steel chain, the destroyed workout bag. "If you don't, neither you nor the Cassandras have a chance of walking away from this alive. And from what I know of him, that's exactly what Aldrich Peters will be counting on."

Chapter 1

September
Status: twenty-one days and counting
Time: 0900 hours

Any second now the man sitting across the desk from her could give the order to have her killed.

Dawn smoothed her palms on the gleaming leather of the skintight catsuit she was wearing, but as Aldrich Peters leveled an emotionless look at her she realized her mistake. She schooled her face to blankness, knowing there was nothing she could do to control the triphammer beat of her heart. After a long moment he bent his head again and resumed his perusal of Lab 33's report on her.

Her few days AWOL from Lab 33 last December had stretched into nine months—longer than she'd anticipated, but then, her assignment for the women of Athena Academy had resulted in locating not one lost sister, Lynn White, but a second sibling, Faith Corbett, who had also been a victim of genetic manipulation and who'd had no knowledge of her true origins. Together the three of them had been introduced to the man who was their biological father, Navy SEAL Thomas King…a meeting she hadn't wanted to attend. *What was I supposed to say to him, dammit,* she thought as she waited for Peters to finish reading. *"Hey, now I know you're my dad I'm kinda glad I missed when I had you in my rifle sights a couple of months ago when I was working for the bad guys?"*

At the time she'd almost been glad she had the excuse of returning to Lab 33 to explain her hasty departure. But as the complex's steel doors had begun sliding closed behind her yesterday evening, cutting off her last glimpse of the arid New Mexican canyons and foothills, a sense of complete isolation had overtaken her. And with her first breath of the recycled air supplying the massive underground bunker, a Cold War emergency command center secretly built in the 1950s that had never been utilized, but for years now the site of Aldrich Peters's shadowy organization, her time away had seemed suddenly unreal.

For a moment she'd felt a terrible certainty that it *had* been unreal. There was no such group as the Cassandras; she hadn't found Lynn White and Faith Corbett, her biological sisters; she'd never learned the truth about her existence. She was a Lab 33 assassin. She answered to Aldrich Peters. She was in a nightmare where nothing had changed.

In near panic she'd whirled around with the half-formed notion of darting back through the closing doors. At her unexpected movement the nearest guard— a commander, as she'd noted from the dull red flashes on the collar of his field-gray uniform—had jerked his weapon up into firing position, at the same time scrambling clumsily away from her. Behind his face shield she'd seen his eyes, open so wide that rims of white circled his pupils.

They're scared of me, Uncle Lee! A long-buried memory flashed into Dawn's mind. *I wanted to play tag with them, but they shouted at me to go away. One of them called me a freak. Am I, Uncle Lee? Am I a freak like they say?* In Dawn's memory, the six-year-old version of herself felt arms scooping her close, smelled the somehow reassuring mixture of harsh tobacco and gun oil, heard a voice whose undertone of anger she knew wasn't directed at her. *They're the freaks, Dawnie. You're special, and don't you ever let the sons of bitches convince you otherwise. They're scared because they know you're stronger than everyone here, and I don't mean just lifting-things strong. Your strength comes from inside you. You understand what I'm saying?* Her sobs had subsided by then but she'd stayed in the circle of his arms, happy just to be held by him. *I guess. But you're stronger than the sunsa bits, too, right?* The arms around her had tightened. For a moment she'd thought the unthinkable had happened and Uncle Lee was mad at her, but when he'd answered his tone had been filled with such pain that she would have gladly traded it for anger. *Maybe once, Dawnie. Now I'm no better than they are. But I promise I'll always stay strong enough to keep them from owning you—even if staying strong costs me everything I care for in this world.*

Aldrich Peters laid aside a sheet of paper, the crackle as he did so sounding like a gunshot in the oppressive silence. Dawn didn't flinch. Her nervousness had disappeared in the past few seconds, she realized. She supposed she should be glad it had, but all she felt was anger.

When the hell are you going to stop falling into the same stupid trap, O'Shaughnessy? she berated herself. *Every memory you have of Lee Craig is tainted. Be glad you've got something truer than your memories of him to give you strength.*

She had payback. No matter that Kayla Ryan had seemed to think revenge wouldn't set things right for her. No matter that in the conversation she'd had with her sisters on the subject, Lynn and Faith had both agreed with Kayla. She had no intention of delivering Peters to justice. For one final time, she intended to be judge, jury and executioner herself.

She concealed a faint wince as the dull throbbing that signaled one of the headaches she'd recently been experiencing set up a low tattoo behind her temples. As if he sensed her momentary vulnerability, Peters slid the papers aside.

"You passed Section Eight's tests with flying colors." His austere features seemed carved in stone. "The lie detector, the bio- and neuro-feedbacks, the psychological workups by Drs. Wang and Sobie. Apparently you were telling the truth when you contacted me yesterday and said you wanted to take up your duties again."

A rush of triumph raced through her. Of course she'd passed their tests. She'd grown up here, dammit, and there wasn't a test invented that hadn't been run on her. By the age of eleven she'd known how to bend them to her advantage without even try—

"I would have been shocked if you'd failed," Peters added brusquely. "After all, if anyone could manipulate the results it would be you."

Dawn fought to keep her regard steady. She'd underestimated him, she thought tensely. Whatever his tests and his experts told him, Dr. Aldrich Peters preferred to rely on his own instincts...and those instincts were telling him she was lying. With seconds to revoke her own death warrant, she needed to go on the offensive—*now.*

"Maybe I'm being paranoid, but I get the feeling you don't fully accept my explanation for my disappearance from Lab 33 last winter," she said, allowing anger to creep into her voice. "At the risk of sounding more paranoid, I also get the feeling you're making up your mind as to whether I should even walk out of here alive. Am I right?"

The thin smile that appeared on Aldrich Peters's lips did little to soften the remoteness of his expression. "I don't call that paranoid, Dawn, I call that astute. You're right, I've got serious doubts about your story of going into an emotional tailspin after your Uncle Lee was killed. Lab 33's ultimate killing machine, the protégé Lee Craig was grooming to take his place, falling to pieces like any ordinary woman? I don't buy it."

"You don't buy it because you're forgetting one important fact." She stood abruptly, placing her palms flat on his desktop. "I *am* an ordinary woman in many respects—ordinary enough to feel pain when the only family member I've ever known is torn from me and ordinary enough to know that I haven't lived an ordinary life. I told you, losing my uncle was a shattering experience and I needed to come to terms with it."

She exhaled. "I needed time to come to terms with

who and what I am, too. As you just said, I'm not your usual twenty-two-year-old, am I? I'm a superwoman who's almost indestructible, trained to use my special talents to clandestinely further the best interests of my country as Uncle Lee did. After he died I felt it was time to ask myself if I really wanted to take his place."

"What conclusion did you come to?"

She answered him promptly. "That Lab 33's the only game in town for someone like me. And as Uncle Lee always told me, at least I'm working on the side of the good guys."

"Which leads me to my second question. Do you still believe we're the good guys, Dawn, or have you taken your allegiance elsewhere during these past nine months? After all, despite your orders, Kayla Ryan is still alive. Carl Bradford, whom I can assure you was on our side, is dead. Why is that?" Peters's tone held an implied threat. Slowly she let her palms slide from the desk and straightened to her full height.

"I told you. Bradford interfered with my assassination attempt. He kidnapped Ryan's daughter, made it a federal case. Then he tried to kill me. I had to take him out. And killing Ryan would have brought on too much heat. I'm certain she and the others are no longer a threat to us. I've dedicated my life to Lab 33. I've demonstrated my loyalty time and again, and you still feel you have the right to ask me that?"

This was it, she told herself as Aldrich Peters held her gaze. Either she'd allayed his suspicions or she hadn't— and if it was the latter, both of them would be dead minutes from now. Her plan of gathering as much information as she could over the next few weeks for the Cassandras before she made her move against him would have to be forgotten. But she wouldn't be able to stop him from hitting the emergency button on his desk that would bring the guards pouring in, and she had no doubt that they knew her Achilles' heel.

A woven-steel garrote had been part of the standard weapons issue for Lab 33 internal security for as long as she could remember…and for as long as she could remember, she'd instinctively known that particular weapon had been issued with only one opponent in mind. She could survive a bullet or a knife but, as she'd told Peters, she was an ordinary human being in some respects…one of which was that she couldn't survive without oxygen.

So be it, Dawn thought with deadly calm. *If I die, I die knowing I've taken him with—*

Without warning the throbbing shot through her head again. As fast as it had come it faded, and as her vision cleared she realized something had disconcerted Peters. His next words revealed what that something had been.

"The last thing I expected to see in your eyes when I questioned your loyalty was pain, but apparently the psych profile Drs. Wang and Sobie prepared on you was accurate," he said slowly. "This changes everything." He leaned back in his chair. "It seems I misjudged you, Dawn. Welcome home."

"It's good to be back." Her clipped reply betrayed nothing of the relief sweeping through her. *You did it, O'Shaughnessy!* she thought in fierce exultation. *You lied through your teeth to Aldrich Peters and the bastard bought it. Now nothing can stop you from—*

"Unfortunately, your little vacation couldn't have been more regrettably timed." Peters's composure was firmly back in place. "You're dying."

The man was a consummate manipulator, Dawn thought in disbelief, but whether he knew it or not his days of manipulating her were over. "Either I'm cleared for duty or I'm not," she said tightly. "But if you think I'm going to jump through any more of your psychological hoops, forget it. I've had enough of—"

"I broke it to you clumsily, but believe me, it's the truth." He shook his head with every appearance of regret. "To put it as simply as I can, your genes are breaking down. I've had my best people working on the problem for almost a year, but although we've isolated the triggering factor, we haven't been able to perfect the reversal process."

"Almost a year." Her mind still processing his stunning news, Dawn seized on the one detail she felt able to deal with. "You mean you knew about this before I went AWOL and you didn't inform me?"

"If I'd suspected you were thinking of taking some unauthorized R and R, I would have," Peters countered. "Be thankful that the medicals and psychological evaluations the doctors here have subjected you to all your life drew our attention to this as soon as it started to show up. Lab 33's always had your best interests at heart."

"Lab 33 has always had Lab 33's best interests at heart. And Lab 33's best interests include knowing the inner workings of their human lab rat," she answered flatly. "Spare me the hearts and flowers, Doctor, and cut to the chase. How much time do I have?"

"Worst-case scenario, twenty-one days. The degeneration of your genes is following a mathematically predictable time line that can be precisely charted." The well-tailored shoulders of his suit jacket lifted in a shrug. "We don't know exactly when the symptoms will start, but they should begin exhibiting soon. Unfortunately, we don't know what they'll be, either." He hesitated. "About the only thing besides the time line that we know for certain from our experiments is that your death will be painful. In effect, your body will turn on itself."

She'd taken on every conceivable enemy during her dangerous career. She'd gone up against those enemies, confident that she would be their final and ultimately unbeatable opponent. Was it irony or simple justice that her own final battle would be desperately waged and lost against herself?

Simple justice, O'Shaughnessy, Dawn thought bleakly. Justice was the only word that fit when the genes that had helped her become Lab 33's killing machine were the very ones that would bring about her—

Her thoughts came to a halt as a terrible realization filled her. Her mind went blank with fear before it grasped a possible glimmer of hope.

"You said worst-case scenario is that I have twenty-one days," she said through stiff lips. "What's the best case?"

Aldrich Peters steepled his fingers on the desk. "Your survival, of course. And there's a good chance we can achieve that, now you're on board with Lab 33 again."

It took the space of a heartbeat for her to comprehend what lay behind his smile. When she did, it took all her self-control not to jerk Peters's silk tie into a noose and end everything there and then.

"You know how to reverse the process and you deliberately let me think it was hopeless?" Her hands clenched into fists at her sides. "Enough with the games, Doctor. Let's get started with my treatment."

Because the sooner I receive it, the sooner I can get word to the Cassandras that Faith and Lynn are probably facing the same genetic breakdown, she thought. *Maybe I deserve to pay for my past that way, but they don't. And even if it means I have to push my own personal agenda back a little, I'm going to make sure they won't.*

She wasn't giving up the payback that was coming to her, but Kayla had been right—despite the fact that she barely knew them, despite the very different lives they'd led, her sisters were her first priority.

"Get one thing straight." Peters's voice was a whip-lash. "If I choose to make you sweat a little to bring you back into line after your irresponsible disappearance, you'll take it and like it. Yes, we can create a reversal serum, and yes, as a slap on the wrist I didn't immediately reveal its existence to you. But I agree, the tit for tat stops here…because you're leaving Lab 33 tonight on an assignment for me."

She shook her head decisively. "No deal. I get the serum before I take on the job."

"Getting the serum *is* the job." A wintry smile crossed his features as he dropped his bombshell. "Our scientists are missing the final piece of the puzzle that will allow them to formulate the reversal serum. In fact, there's only one man in the world who's possibly cracked the puzzle."

"Possibly?" she repeated blankly. "Dammit, you're not sure?"

"That's part of your assignment—to ascertain he's made the breakthrough we believe he has."

"Why not simply ask him?" she retorted. "Don't scientists practically fall all over themselves to publicize their findings?"

"Most do." Peters's lips thinned. "Sir William London's the exception, a paranoid megalomaniac who won't reveal anything until he's ready. He's also the greatest genius the world has ever known in the field of genetics."

"So I'm to break into the research facility where London works, steal his notes and bring them back for our people to use. Getting past a few security guards should be easy enough," Dawn said in defeat.

A simple B & E she could live with, she told herself edgily. At worst she'd have to temporarily disable a guard or two, but she'd make sure no one got seriously hurt.

And if it hadn't been a simple break and enter? If you'd been ordered to kill for the serum, would you have stepped over the line once more to save yourself and your sisters? The uncomfortable question came to her before she could thrust it away. She didn't know, Dawn admitted. She'd made a vow never to carry out Aldrich Peters's murderous orders again, but if the serum was all that stood between her sisters and a terrible death....

Pain spiked with sudden intensity behind her eyes. She fought against it as Peters pulled a sheaf of papers toward him with a frown.

"I should have made myself clear. Sir William is funded by the Defense Department in a joint venture with the British, and his laboratory's inside a compound in the middle of the Arizona desert. It's guarded by a crack team of military personnel headed by a certain Captain Des Asher—who's not only London's nephew, but a highly trained British Special Air Services officer. You'll pose as a research assistant and get close to London that way."

He held the papers out to her. "Study Asher's military bio. He's going to be your biggest obstacle, so assassinate him first."

Chapter 2

Status: nineteen days and counting
Time: 2300 hours

She was going up against Des Asher naked. She couldn't deny that there was a tiny ripple of excitement deep inside her at the thought.

With deliberate clumsiness, Dawn shifted the gears of the junker hatchback she was driving and was rewarded by the labored whine of an engine being pushed beyond its limits. She shifted again, this time correctly.

Of course, *naked* just meant without weapons. The most lethal piece of hardware anyone would find on her if she were searched was a nail file…and although she could remember an instance when, armed with little more, she'd taken out a couple of sadistic goons without even messing up the polish she'd been applying when they'd burst in on her, she didn't think a nail file would raise any red flags as far as Des Asher's people were concerned.

Especially not when it was being carried by Dawn Swanson.

"Swanson's never done the horizontal mambo, way I see it. I mean, repressed? Chick's a total man-hater, plus she's a dweeb," Carter Johnson had said with a grin two nights ago when she'd left Peters's office and reported to Lab 33's Identities Department. He'd extracted a glossy eight-by-ten photo from a file and passed it to her. "Check out your new hair, babe. Not that the big boss man told me any more than he had to, but with the rock-solid credentials I've created for you, I'm guessing this isn't a simple in-and-out assignment where a wig would be enough. After we're through here, you'll be scooting that fine butt of yours over to Helga for the works—a bad cut, an even worse perm and a mud-brown dye job." His grin widened. "I almost forgot the bottle-lens glasses we got for you to wear. Behind them your eyes look way magnified, but Carlos in Research and Development made them so they won't affect your vision at all. Man, I love this job!"

Carter was one of Lab 33's youngest employees, probably close to her own age. Much to the irritation of the older staff, he cultivated an indie-rebel air, wearing his hair in a spiky, bed-head style and using a skateboard to cruise up and down Lab 33's endless corridors. But Dawn wasn't taken in by his "Dude, where's my wheels?" manner. He worked here. That meant two things: one, he had to be the best at what he did, which was creating false identities and the documentation to back them up; and two, he'd willingly sold his soul to

Aldrich Peters—either for money or because of some crime he'd committed in the past that Peters had made go away.

Whatever the reason, Carter Johnson wasn't the boy next door. He was part of an organization that made the Mafia look like pussycats. To complicate matters, he'd borne a grudge against her ever since she'd told him, in no uncertain terms, that she didn't intend to date him until she had definite confirmation hell had frozen over.

She'd returned the photo to him. "Go back to the computer and reconfigure this. No perm. My hair stays the length it is. I'll go with a temporary rinse and wear it scraped into a bun while I'm undercover as Little Miss Repressed. When I walk out of here, I'll be Dawn Swanson, right down to the baggy science-geek sweat-shirt, but that persona's not going to come from clothes or a hairstyle, it's going to come from me. If you've got a problem with that, we'll go talk to the big boss, as you refer to Dr. Peters, together."

She'd won that round, Dawn reflected now as she deliberately clashed the hatchback's gears again. It hadn't been until she'd reached the motel where she'd stayed last night and read the extensive bio prepared for her— a bio she'd later burned before flushing the charred scraps down the motel room's toilet—that she'd realized Carter, with his own waspish sense of revenge, had gotten the last laugh.

Swanson lives, breathes and sleeps fruit flies and genetics, the typed pages had informed her. *Since seventy-two-year-old Sir William London is the world authority on her chosen passion, Swanson hero-worships him to the point of having a kind of crush on him. Several of the contacts we've blackmailed to supply ref-*

erences on our fictitious lab technician will mention the poster that supposedly hung above her bed at her college dorm—the famous shot of Sir William taken just before he won his first Nobel Prize in '58, when he was one of Oxford's "crazy young men."

In the margin, Carter had added a penciled note: *Who knows, O'Shaughnessy, you might get lucky with the old geezer. Here's hoping, girlfriend!*

"And here's hoping that when the Cassandras and I take down Lab 33, you spend the rest of your sorry life behind bars," Dawn muttered. She narrowed her gaze as the hatchback's headlights cut through the desert blackness to illuminate an unmarked secondary road up ahead. Although the slight rises and dips in the terrain made it impossible to see what lay ahead, the road had to be the turnoff to London's small but highly secure laboratory complex. She felt a surge of anticipation run through her. Since sound carried in arid terrain such as this, more so at night, her little maneuvers with the gears hadn't been premature. They'd insured that any sentry with ears sharp enough to catch the first faint sounds of a vehicle approaching wouldn't have heard Dawn O'Shaughnessy driving with her usual speed and skill, but Dawn Swanson, a woman who preferred to be surrounded by test tubes and petri dishes instead of behind the wheel of a car.

Live the lie, Dawnie. Unbidden, the tobacco-roughened voice of Lee Craig broke through her concentration, so clearly that he might have been sitting beside her in the dark. *That's the first rule of deep cover. Forget who you are and become the identity you've taken on. It's not always easy...but once in a while you might even find yourself wishing you didn't have to go back to being the real you.*

This time when she geared down there was no pretence in her mishandling of the car's controls. As she made the turnoff the hatchback veered dangerously close to the crumbling verge of the dirt road before she corrected its course.

"Don't worry, Lee," she said savagely under her breath. "I'm living the lie, just like you did, you bastard. And like you, when my cover's outlived its usefulness I won't forget who I am and what my real agenda is. You took down my mother. I'm going to take out Aldrich—"

Her words were cut off by a gasp and the hatchback swerved again. Her responses hampered by the intense pain behind her eyes, Dawn's corrective maneuver came a split second too late. She felt the rear end of the car slide off the road, felt the back tires fight for purchase on the sandy soil, heard them churning uselessly as they merely dug themselves deeper.

The hatchback stalled. The pain behind her eyes faded. Her hands gripped the steering wheel so tightly that her knuckles showed white in the greenish glow from the instrument panel.

It was time to face facts, she thought numbly. Lab 33's scientists might not know what the symptoms of her gene degeneration would be, but she couldn't fool herself any longer. She'd never had a headache in her life before now, just as she'd never caught a cold or contracted the normal childhood bouts of measles and mumps and tonsillitis. So the migraines she'd been experiencing with increasing frequency over the past few months had to be a first warning signal of—

Before her train of thought could reach its logical conclusion, she jerked open the driver's side door and stepped swiftly from the car. Striding toward the back of the stalled vehicle, she planted her hands on her hips and glared at the deep depressions in the sand where the rear tires were now embedded.

But standing still was a mistake. Unwillingly she found her mind completing the deduction she'd tried to thrust aside. If the loss of her invulnerability to common human ailments was the first symptom of her genetic breakdown, what else would be taken from her before she returned to Lab 33 with London's research?

In effect, your body will turn on itself. Peters's words had filled her with dread at the time, but only now could she fully comprehend the horrific possibilities of his prediction. Her sight—would it slowly dim or would she suddenly be plunged into a world of darkness? Or maybe it would be her reflexes that would desert her at the very moment she needed them, or her hearing or her strength or—

Her lips tightening, she bent to grab the rust-specked bumper of the hatchback. She took a deep breath and heaved.

Even for her, it was a near-impossible effort. She felt the muscles in her arms scream in protest, felt her balance shift treacherously as the sandy soil beneath her feet crumbled. Sweat beading her brow and running down behind the heavy horn-rimmed glasses Carter had provided her with, she set her jaw in grim determination and began pivoting the rear of the car toward the road.

There was a possibility that the security measures guarding Sir William London's laboratory included roving teams patrolling past the fenced perimeter of the facility. If even one of those teams came upon her now, not only would her Dawn Swanson cover be blown, but the enhanced abilities she'd always been so careful about revealing would be immediately exposed. She was taking an insane chance.

She didn't care. All that was important right now was that she accomplish the superhuman task she'd set herself.

"This is what you *are*." The barely intelligible words came from her in a strained grunt as she took another trembling step sideways, the tendons in her shoulders feeling as though they were about to pop. "No matter what you told Peters, you'll never be an ordinary woman—not like Kayla, with her unshakable integrity, or the rest of the Cassandras, who've found support in one another. Your strength and abilities may have come from a test tube, but they're all you have. And when they're gone..."

Through the soles of her sneakers she felt the more stable surface of the road. Taking two last shuffling steps, she set the rear of the hatchback unceremoniously down onto its tires. Slowly she uncurled her grip from the bumper, her arms and back feeling as if they were on fire.

She ignored the searing sensation and straightened to her full height. Behind the glasses her eyes squeezed tightly shut. "When the abilities are gone, what's left?" she asked in an uneven whisper. "Face it, O'Shaughnessy, *nothing*...and that's why you're terrified for the first time in your life. Not because of the pain you're going to suffer if this process isn't reversed, not because you could die, but because before the end comes you'll be revealed for what you are—a lab rat whose enhanced sight couldn't help her see the truth, whose strength only masked the weakness that allowed Aldrich Peters to manipulate her for so long, whose regenerative powers couldn't heal her destroyed soul. Any one of the Cassandras is more of a superwoman than you are. A mother working two shifts just to bring in enough money to keep her children fed is more of a superwoman than Dawn O'Shaughnessy ever was."

For a moment longer she stood there, her posture slightly bowed as if she were still carrying a crushing weight. Then she opened her eyes and thrust back her shoulders, becoming once again the implacable figure Kayla Ryan had confronted in the Athena Academy gym more than nine months ago.

"But of course, you're not Dawn O'Shaughnessy now, are you?" Her voice was no longer uneven, but harshly flat. "You're Dawn Swanson, and don't you forget it…because like Lee Craig used to say, sometimes all that's left is to live the lie."

She turned on her heel. Wrenching open the driver's side door, she slid in behind the wheel again, started the car and resumed the last few miles of her journey.

"I'm a biochem assistant. As long as the labs here aren't run with the same inefficiency as security appears to be, I'm really not interested in how your people screwed up the paperwork on me."

Dawn wondered if she was overdoing the pedantic monotone in her voice, but decided to keep going with it. Even if she hadn't recognized Asher from the photo in his file, the ID tag on his uniform would have told her she was dealing with the man whose suspicions she most needed to allay. *Just your bad luck he's a hands-on kind of guy,* she told herself, *who has standing orders to be notified by the gate guards whenever a new employee shows up. Even worse luck that someone here*

made a mistake over my gender—unless this is another
example of that little weasel Carter's sense of humor.

But even Carter knew better than to pull something
like this, she reflected. "William London certainly knew
I was a female when he hired me," she went on. "If
you've got a problem with my name being spelled
D-a-w-n instead of *D-o-n,* take it up with him. In the
meantime, I'd like to settle in and start work."

She shoved her glasses higher onto the bridge of her
nose and gave him a sullen stare in keeping with the persona Carter had chosen for Dawn Swanson, but behind
the lenses her belligerent gaze was unobtrusively taking a first real look at the man Aldrich Peters had
claimed would be her most dangerous opponent on this
assignment.

"Assassinate him first?" Thinking quickly, she'd
shaken her head in sharp disagreement when Peters had
issued the order in his office two days ago. "Sorry, Doctor, but when I'm working undercover it's my neck on
the line. That gives me a vested interest in the decisions
I make. I'll take out Des Asher if and when I feel the
action's warranted, but if I can complete the assignment without resorting to that, so much the better."

Peters had raised an eyebrow. "You sound like a woman
who's lost her nerve. Or at least her taste for killing."

"No, I sound like my Uncle Lee," she'd replied
evenly. "He's the one who taught me any thug off the
street can pull a trigger if he doesn't care about losing
his own life. A professional completes the assignment,
gets out safely, and lives to work another day. I'm doing
this my way."

Aldrich hadn't put up any further argument—most
likely, Dawn guessed, because with her as the best Lab

33 assassin, he was forced to recognize the merit of her argument. *So you owe me, buddy,* she thought as she assessed the fatigues-clad SAS captain who had abruptly walked a few feet away from her and was now conferring with a soldier in the guard shack by the facility's high barbed-wire gates. *I'm not saying you'd have been a cinch to take out, judging from what I've heard about the combat training you Special Air Services types receive, but in a one-on-one between the two of us, my money would have been on me.*

He didn't really fit her preconceived notion of a Brit, she thought with a frown as, impatience showing in every inch of his more than six-foot frame, he bent his head over a logbook a subordinate had handed him. In his late twenties or early thirties, he was deeply tanned, for one thing—a legacy, she supposed, of his recent service in the Middle East, which had been all too sketchily described in the bio she'd read. Peters had shown irritation at the lack of detail Lab 33's investigators had been able to dig up on Asher's military career, but Dawn herself had felt a private sense of relief. If Peters's people hadn't managed to uncover what assignments the SAS had given Des Asher, there was a good chance her own activities during the months she'd been AWOL would remain undiscovered.

But besides the tan and the heavy biceps straining the rolled-up sleeves of his fatigues, there were other incongruities that bothered her. So far he'd shown none of the famed politeness she'd always associated with the English. His manner, as he'd taken her credentials from her and then thrust them back, had been decidedly dismissive, and although she was unable to catch his low-voiced conversation with the soldier by the guard shack, at least twice he'd uttered back-alley curses loud enough for her to overhear.

He did't like his job. The revelation came to her with the conviction of absolute certainty, and behind the glasses her gaze narrowed. No, it was more than that, she thought slowly, taking in the tight set of Asher's jaw, the barely controlled anger displayed as he raked a hand through short-cropped, burnt-pewter hair. He *hated* what he was doing.

Which means we've got one thing in common, big guy, she thought as he handed the logbook to the guard and met her watchful gaze before she could avert her eyes. *Too bad we're working on opposite sides or I might have let you buy me a shot of Stoli and told you my reservations about this assignment before buying you a round of warm British beer and letting you fill me in on how you ended up in a dead-end job, baby-sitting your famous uncle.*

On second thought, she told herself as Asher nodded curtly to a younger officer who had stopped his jeep in front of the guard shack and was glancing curiously in her direction, maybe it was better having him as an opponent. His antagonism would keep her focused, and right now that was what she needed most.

Her headache had returned. This time she couldn't afford to give in to it.

"If the paperwork's screwed, my people didn't do it." Without pausing to talk to the young officer exiting the jeep, Asher strode from the guard shack and came to a halt directly in front of her. He continued, his manner barely civil. "I'd advise you to contact whoever sent you here and get them to resubmit your information. Until you do you're not getting past this gate."

The hand he clamped onto her upper arm was like a band of iron…or maybe it was just that her headache had progressed to the point that every nerve ending felt raw. This attack was ten times worse—*try twenty times,* Dawn thought with a sharply indrawn breath—than those she'd so far experienced, but judging from those previous ones it couldn't last much longer. All she had to do was ride it out.

Easier said than done, O'Shaughnessy, she told herself tightly. *And it's not ultrahelpful that Mr. Freakin' Special Air Services has his damn hand welded to my arm right now. If he'd just ease up for a second so I could concentrate on shutting down the jackhammer that's pounding away in my—*

His hard tone broke through the thin veneer of control she was trying to establish. "Letting strangers into a restricted area when their credentials don't check out isn't the way I work. On your way, lady."

Without warning, the pain soared to an unbearable crescendo inside her head, escalating its assault until it took all her energy just to stay upright. No one could endure this, Dawn thought in numb agony, no longer caring whether her face revealed what was happening inside her. She'd been trained to take pain, to resist pain, to rise above pain, and all that training didn't matter a damn. She wasn't going to get through this.

A long way away a voice was speaking, the low and deadly tones searing enough to dimly penetrate the haze of unconsciousness that was shutting down her senses. Faint hope stirred in her. Was the pain losing its grip? Was there still a chance she could win this fight? Drawing on reserves she'd thought were already exhausted, she focused on the voice with the desperation of a swimmer going under for the third time—*going under and hallucinating,* she thought hazily. *Because that voice sounds weirdly familiar, O'Shaughnessy—so familiar that if I didn't know better I'd say it was your own.*

"Call William London and get this straightened out, dammit! Because if you don't, I swear I'll—"

"Ash! Put the gun down! Lady, back away from him or I'll shoot you myself!"

The shouted commands came from the officer who'd gotten out of the Jeep. No longer standing by the shack, he was now only a few yards away and leveling his rifle at her, but as inexplicable as his actions were, Dawn barely registered them.

Her headache was gone. As instantly as if a switch had been turned off somewhere inside her head, the pain had simply stopped. Shaky relief filled her, but even as it did she stiffened in shock.

In her hand was a stilettolike piece of steel. The tip of it was pressed to Des Asher's tanned throat, hard enough so that it was making an impression. She couldn't even remember snapping the antenna off the hatchback behind her and lunging at him with it, but Asher had apparently reacted with almost the same speed as she'd displayed.

Because in his left hand was a heavy semiautomatic—a Sig Sauer P226, the weapon he would have been issued upon joining the SAS. The muzzle of the revolver was jammed into the space between her top left rib and her breast, aiming its load of nine-millimeter parabellum rounds toward her heart.

Glittering gray eyes stared down at her. "If you want to get out of this alive, put down that antenna and tell me again what you do for a living…and this time leave out the biochem assistant crap." The words were scarcely above a mutter, but with his mouth only inches from hers she had no trouble hearing them.

She'd blown her cover. The realization tore through the fog clouding Dawn's brain and icy clarity flooded in. What had happened just now? Why had she gone into attack mode for no good reason? She was a professional, dammit—she didn't make mistakes like this! Had she lost her edge, as Peters had suspected she might?

But the answers to those questions would have to wait. All that mattered at the moment was that she was going to have to abort the assignment and return to Lab 33 empty-handed. With no chance now of Aldrich Peters reversing her degeneration in time, she'd as good as signed her own death warrant.

Not only mine, but Lynn's and Faith's, she thought with corrosive self-recrimination. *Whatever's happening to my cells will be happening to theirs, even if they aren't displaying the same symptoms I've been experienc—*

She blinked, her mind racing. Slowly she lowered the snapped-off antenna she was holding, and saw the man in front of her warily do the same with his weapon.

That was it—the reason she'd gone ballistic just now, that she'd allowed herself to forget everything Lee Craig had ever taught her about her profession. Aldrich Peters had predicted her body would begin to turn on itself, but her guesses about how that would unfold hadn't gone far enough. Nothing she'd imagined could even begin to approach the horror of knowing that her personality—her impulses, her emotions, her very *mind*—was beginning to betray her.

She'd been raised to be Lab 33's killing machine.

She'd just seen a chilling example of what she could expect when the machine finally broke down.

Correction, O'Shaughnessy: you've just seen what'll happen if it breaks down, she told herself sharply. *Now that you know what the problem is, start acting like the professional you are and try to salvage the mission.*

For the second time in as many minutes, hope replaced despair as a plan took shape in her mind. It just might work but there was no time to waste—she needed to get back into the skin of prickly, abrasive Dawn Swanson right away.

"Don't you *ever* put your hands on me again." She forced flat hostility to her expression. "I didn't take seven years of self-defense classes just so I could allow myself to be manhandled, and I certainly didn't accept this position with the renowned Sir William London thinking I'd have to file a sexual harassment suit my very first day!"

Anger darkened the gray eyes watching her. "Nice recovery, lady. It makes me wonder who the hell taught you to be so bloody slippery. Come on, you and me are going to have a cozy little chat in a quiet room."

He had the height, but she had the superior agility. He outweighed her, outreached her and his Sig trumped her whiplike scrap of broken car antenna, Dawn thought—but *damn,* she'd like to take Des Asher on.

And you know what? she asked him silently, shifting her balance onto the balls of her feet and seeing him shift his in unconscious response. *I'll bet I could have you gasping for mercy before we were through. You're good—I knew that when you had your weapon out and ready for me so fast a minute ago. But I'm the best.*

She didn't allow any of her thoughts to show on her

face. Instead she turned to the younger man standing a few feet away, his weapon no longer at the ready but his tense posture an indication that he hadn't taken himself off full alert.

"Lieutenant Keifer?" She took her attention from the nametag on his uniform—an American uniform, she noted briefly, unlike Asher's British one—and met his eyes. He looked uncertain, she noted, which was good. "You heard what your fellow officer just said. I'll be advising my lawyers to take a statement from you to support the legal action I intend to take. A 'nice little chat in a quiet room'?" She turned back to Asher. "With no third parties present to monitor your behavior, I'm sure. Men like you who abuse their power to get their sexual ya-yas on would be pathetic if they weren't so disgusting!"

The revolted shudder was pure Dawn Swanson, Dawn thought. So was the pinch-lipped expression she was favoring him with and the stance she'd taken up. The persona Carter had created that had so annoyed her two days ago was now her only chance of explaining away her insane actions. She met Asher's narrowed gaze, her arms belligerently crossed over her baggy sweatshirt.

"I'm assuming ya-yas means shagging." His smile was sharklike. "Hate to break your bubble, but save your worries for what's going to happen after I'm through questioning you and I hand you over to the authori—"

"She's right, Ash," Keifer broke in. "Putting your hand on her was way out of bounds, and as for talking about shagging—" He lowered his voice. "A sexual harassment suit's the surest way to shoot your career down in flames. Maybe England's different, but that kind of thing is taken seriously here."

Asher's lips tightened to a line. "We've got rules about this in England, too. But when I attempt to escort an unverified visitor off the property and she comes within a hairbreadth of slashing open my jugular, all rules are off. After seeing the moves she's got, my guess is she's a bio-technician like I'm an interior decorator." He turned his attention to Dawn. "Too bad for you that whoever you're working for slipped up on the name. If we'd been expecting a woman, you just might have bluffed your way in."

"The slipup over the name, Asher?" Faint color rose under the younger man's tan. "I took the instructions verbally from Sir William. I just assumed—"

It was time for her to cut in, Dawn decided. "You just assumed the position had been given to a male. God, have I stepped into a time warp here?" She exhaled tightly. "Look—working with Sir William London is an honor I never thought I'd have the chance to experience. He's a great man and a personal hero of mine. In fact—" she allowed her voice to soften and hoped the dreaminess in her eyes wasn't obscured by the Lab 33 lenses "—when I was a student I used to have a poster of him over the bed in my dorm room. It was a picture taken in the 1950s, when he was one of Oxford's 'crazy young men.'"

"Not young anymore. Still crazy as a shi—" Asher didn't complete his muttered comment. He gave her a patently disbelieving look. "Even if I was fool enough to buy that, what's your lukewarm fantasy life got to do with this?"

"Ash—" Keifer sounded strained.

"My *admiration* for Sir William's got everything to do with this. I'm trying to tell you that I'd rather not have him associated, even slightly, with an embarrassing legal suit. Pick up the phone, confirm my credentials with him, and let me get started on the work I came to do. For Sir William's sake, I'll forget what happened here."

Without looking away from her, Asher spoke to the man beside him. "Do what the lady says, Keifer, but be sure you talk to the great man himself. If her story checks out, tell him from me that if he'd keep me in the loop like he's supposed to, maybe balls-ups like this wouldn't happen."

He waited until Keifer set off at a trot for the guard shack before going on. "Your story's going to check out, isn't it? Whoever you are, you're not amateur enough to suggest we talk to my uncle if you weren't confident he'd back you up."

Dawn feigned surprise. "William London's your—"

"Stow the acting," he interrupted. "It's just you and me right now, so listen and listen good. I'm probably going to have to let you walk past that gate, but I know damn well there's something wrong about you. The first tip-off was the bloody glasses, in case you're interested."

She injected a note of irritation into her voice. "My glasses? Is this another one of your insult—"

"I said stow it." He smiled thinly. "A girl I used to know wore the same thick kind of lenses. She never took them off unless she was in bed."

His tone was disarming and his manner more re-laxed than it had been since he'd first spoken to her. Dawn wasn't fooled. Des Asher was a dangerous opponent, and right now he was at his most dangerous. She opened her mouth to deliver a Dawn Swanson-type protest but he forestalled her.

"But you don't want to hear the down-and-dirty details of my sex life." His smile tightened. "Thing is, the gorgeous Maureen had been wearing heavy glasses for so many years that even when she took them off I could see a little indentation on the bridge of her nose. You've got a red mark where you keep pushing them up, but you don't have an indentation. If I had to guess, I'd say you put them on an hour or so before you arrived here."

She saw Keifer approaching, his face flaming. The Dawn/Don question had obviously been settled in her favor, she thought in relief. "With a man of science like William London as your uncle, you should know guesses are worthless without the proof to back them up," she said evenly. "I'd say your proof just flew out the window, Captain Asher."

"Hell, call me Asher. Sounds more friendly, seeing as how I just became your closest companion." His smile vanished and his tone hardened. "I know you're not who you say you are. Trust me, I'm going to be watching every move you make from now on, love."

Chapter 3

Status: eighteen days and counting
Time: 0330 hours

It was a whole new ball game, Dawn thought with a grimace. A few hours ago she hadn't felt the need to arrive here with a weapon that might be discovered in her luggage, but that had been then.

This was now.

"When I finally get my hands on Sir William's notes and need to break out of here, I don't want to be worrying that some recruit just out of basic training is going to be able to stop me because I suddenly don't have the strength to rip a wet paper towel," she told herself under her breath. "Since it seems to be a crapshoot as to how and when my abilities desert me, the sooner I level the playing field with a gun in my possession, the better."

Which was why, she thought in resignation, she was clinging to a cinderblock wall like a fly right now, peering down through the darkness to the ground forty feet below.

"Correction," she muttered, looking up for her next handhold. "A fly would have those handy sticky pads to keep it glued to this damned wall. Too bad when Aldrich was performing his Dr. Evil experiments on my genes he didn't think to give me those. Just because I'd survive a fall doesn't mean I want to have the experience."

Toeing a sneaker into a shallow line of mortar, she disengaged the fingertips of her left hand from the similar mortar depression they'd been gripping. Her body began to unpeel from the wall, but before the gap between her and the cinderblock could widen past the point of no return, her fingers were curling deftly into another hold. Without allowing herself to pause, she kept climbing.

She needed a gun. Soldiers carried guns. Ergo, she thought with determination as she felt her knuckles scrape against the slight overhang of the building's flat roof, it was only logical to go gun shopping in the one place where she could be sure of finding soldiers.

"A girl wants Manolos, she hits the designer shoe stores..." she muttered, suddenly pushing off from the wall with her feet. Her lower half swung out. As her legs reached the top of their arc she abruptly pulled her upper body as close as she could to the roofline before jack-knifing her arms out and thrusting herself straight up into the air. Immediately she folded into a ball, her head tucked and her arms wrapping around her drawn-in legs. The cool night air rushed past her as she tumbled once in midair, then twice, and as she completed the second tumble she quickly unfolded.

She landed lightly on the top of the roof in a half-crouch, her feet a few inches apart and all her senses on full alert.

"…and if a girl wants a gun, she hits a barracks—preferably at a time when she figures everyone's still asleep," she continued, rising from her crouch and briskly dusting mortar powder from her hands. "No matter how suspicious Captain Asher is, even he won't be expecting Dawn Swanson to go nosing around so soon."

After finally getting past the gate and being handed over to the lab's staff supervisor by an embarrassed Keifer, she'd barely taken time to unpack her suitcase in the room that had been assigned to her before putting her plan into effect. Aldrich Peters's Lab 33 was undoubtedly malevolent, she'd mused as she'd climbed onto the toilet tank in the small attached bathroom, but she couldn't fault its efficiency. Along with her fictitious bio, Carter had provided her with a thick sheaf of blueprints—the complete schematics for the research complex, which she'd committed to memory before destroying as she'd done the bio.

The bad news had been that the air ducts that served the combined lab section and civilian employees' living quarters didn't connect with those snaking through the ceilings of the military barracks and guardrooms. The good news was that the duct she'd wriggled into after sliding aside a metal grate in the ceiling of her washroom eventually joined up with a main artery that led to the roof. The barrack's ducts did the same.

Unfortunately, Dawn thought dryly as she saw the bulky silhouette of the second vent rising from the tar-and-gravel roof ahead of her in the dark, the reason the two didn't intersect at some point was that they were in different buildings. And although the buildings were only a couple of yards apart, the roof she'd needed to get to had been a good twenty-five feet higher than that of the civilian building—which was why she'd had to do her human-fly imitation.

"All the more reason no one would think to look for me in the military part, though," she told herself in a murmur as she lifted the screened cover and boosted herself onto its edge. "*If* they discover I'm not in my room, which they won't."

The journey through this duct was as hot and tedious as her maneuverings through the first, but whereas the one servicing the lab building had been spotlessly dust-free, that wasn't the case here. For the third time in as many minutes she found herself freezing to a halt as a sneeze threatened. Part of the problem was the baggy sweatshirt she was wearing, she thought in frustration as her nose stopped twitching and she allowed herself to breathe again. For a job of this type, normally she would wear something that hugged her like a second skin and didn't get in her way. But it would have been too dangerously out of character for the Swanson chick, as Carter had referred to her alter ego, to have packed a catsuit or even a tight yoga top and pants.

"Oh, no, Swanson wouldn't be comfortable unless she had something four sizes too large stirring up all the freakin' dust in here," Dawn muttered, her patience at an end as yet another sneeze tickled the back of her nose. As soon as it passed she wrenched the sweatshirt she was wearing up and over her head. A moment later the bunchy drawstring-waisted pants she'd had on were stripped off as well, leaving her clad only in a sports bra and formfitting boy-leg undies.

She could retrieve the Swanson duds on the way back, she thought as she continued at a decidedly speedier pace through the duct. Up ahead it branched into two sections, and without hesitation she took the left branch, which according to the schematics led directly to the enlisted men's sleeping quarters.

Maybe she was being sexist, but no way was she about to risk dropping in on a roomful of female soldiers, she told herself as she inched her way cautiously across the ceiling tiles, making sure she distributed her weight equally over several at a time, instead of putting undue stress on one and chancing the possibility that it might give way and fall into the room below. In her experience, women weren't only lighter sleepers but once awake, they came to total alertness a heartbeat faster than their male counterparts.

"Nice theory, O'Shaughnessy," she breathed, gingerly sliding aside a tile. "Guess you're about to find out if it holds water."

According to Carter's information, Asher had fourteen men and six women under his command—a far cry from the fifty battle-experienced soldiers he would have had in the SAS, she reflected, wondering again just how the man had blotted his copybook badly enough to end up here pulling down guard duty. But Des Asher's past foul-ups weren't her main concern at the moment, she reminded herself as she quickly scanned the double row of military-issue iron beds in the room below. Checking out how many of these beds were currently occupied and whether any of the occupants were awake was all she had to worry about right now.

The tight Dawn Swanson-type bun at the nape of her neck was secured with enough bobby pins to set off a dozen metal detectors. Sliding one free, she stealthily tossed it through the opening she was peering through.

The bobby pin bounced with a tiny *ping!* off a steel footlocker at the end of one of the beds. She held her breath.

Five of the beds were made up with military preciseness and were obviously empty. From the remaining nine came a muted chorus of snores. None of the blanket-covered lumps shot bolt upright, no one's breathing abruptly changed tempo, no opened eyes suddenly gleamed in the faint glow coming from the red-lit fire-exit sign by the door.

With an acrobat's agility, she dropped to the floor, immediately turning her landing into a head-over-heels roll that brought her to the shadowed side of one of the occupied beds.

At sixteen, she'd been as rebellious as any other teenager, Dawn remembered with a faint smile, although her acting-out against authority had taken a different form from a normal girl's. Once during a working trip to London that had left her sitting alone, bored and sullen, in a hotel room for too many hours while Uncle Lee had carried out a mission, she'd defiantly presented him with a Polaroid of herself standing in a vault at the Tower of London with a penlight clamped between her teeth and one gloved hand resting on the crown jewels of England. As if to make the point that she wasn't *that* different, a furious Lee Craig had punished her like any ordinary teen who'd come home late after a date.

He'd grounded her for two whole weeks. But after his death and before she'd come in contact with the Cassandras, she'd found he'd secreted the Polaroid as a memento in the hidden safe where he kept his emergency passports and contingency cash.

Past history, Dawn thought as she jammed the side-arm she'd retrieved from the footlocker—a Beretta M9 pistol, standard issue for a U.S. Ranger as she'd noted Keifer and the American contingent of William London's guards were—into the waistband at the back of her briefs. *All that little trip down memory lane proves is that I could have picked this padlock with my eyes closed and my hands tied behind my—*

Two things happened at once to cut off her thoughts. One was the bolt of agony that shot home without warning in her brain…and the other was the mumbled voice of the soldier whose gun she'd just appropriated.

"Angel?" His query was slurred and thick with sleep. Through the haze of pain that had descended upon her she saw him stir restlessly. "Angel…howzabout…you know, babe…"

The intensity of the pain eased off a little, but her limbs still felt weak and rubbery. She cast an alarmed glance upward at the telltale opening in the ceiling. Could she trust her legs to make the leap? And even if she could, did her arms have the strength to pull her all the way to safety?

Her head still throbbed and the nausea that accompanied the migraines made her feel as if she were trying to move through molasses. In a few minutes the symptoms would probably fade, but she didn't have a few minutes.

"Wassa matter, babe…don't you wanna play?"

Was it her imagination or did his voice sound less slurred, as if he was slowly coming awake? She shot another despairing glance at her unreachable escape route and made up her mind.

"Of course I do, lover," she murmured huskily, tiptoeing to the bed.

All she had to do was bring the edge of her hand sharply down on the precise point at the base of his neck that would insure his lapsing back into unconsciousness, albeit for a few more hours past reveille than he'd likely planned. *Not the way most women demonstrate they're not in the mood,* she thought grimly. *But I'm running out of time, so here goes.*

She took a deep breath and quickly brought her rigidly held hand down in a chopping arc that—

He turned his head and opened his eyes at her. A slow, sexy smile lifted one corner of his mouth. She froze, the edge of her hand so close to his neck that she could feel the heat coming off him.

"You're gorgeous, angel," he murmured softly. "One of these nights I'm not going to let you leave just as my dream starts getting interesting…"

His eyes closed. His breathing deepened and became once again regular.

Dawn felt a stab of illogical outrage. He was asleep, dammit! The man had actually had the nerve to fall asleep while she was half-naked by his bed!

Reason rushed back. *Thank your lucky stars Lover Boy did, O'Shaughnessy,* she thought as she moved with quiet haste to the foot of the bed. She reached for the fifteen-round magazines of ammunition she'd left beside the footlocker, and then paused.

A short tangle of pitch-black hair brushed his forehead. Thick, spiky lashes fanned against his cheekbones. Whatever his dream was now, it was causing a faint smile to soften his well-cut lips.

The man was gorgeous. And she'd been living like a nun for the past nine months, Dawn thought in frustration, turning away.

"Not that my sex life's ever been red-hot," she muttered ten minutes later as she hoisted herself out of the air shaft and ran lightly to the edge of the barracks' roof, the Dawn Swanson sweats tied in a bulky bundle around her waist. She removed the gun from her waistband before securing it and the ammo clips in the padding of clothing tied around her, and jumped. "There was that Roman god of a gardener last year in Milan when I was on the Italian job, and before him there was Alexei what's-his-name in Moscow, who could toss back vodka all night and still show a girl why he was nicknamed the Russian bear," she remembered, coming out of her landing roll. "Aside from them, the list is pretty skimpy."

But numbers weren't the point anyway. She made her way through the air shaft, her expression thoughtful. As fun as Alexei and the gardener had been, she had no illusions that they'd wasted any time dreaming about her after she'd disappeared from their lives. What would it be like to experience more than a one- or two-night stand with someone? What would it be like to know you were in his dreams, as the man she'd just left had drowsily asserted she'd been in his?

Pausing a few feet from the vent leading to her washroom, she shook her head decisively. "*Way* too much commitment. Still…it was kind of sweet to hear him say it."

She was almost sorry she'd chosen Lover Boy's footlocker to break into, she mused as she lifted the metal grate that overlooked the toilet and shimmied through the opening. She'd noticed a second sidearm in the locker, so hopefully he wouldn't feel duty-bound to immediately report a weapon missing and would assume its absence was part of a practical joke by a buddy. Balancing on the porcelain tank, she hauled down the bundle of clothing, first removing the Beretta and its ammunition and shoving them out of sight in the vent for retrieval later. She replaced the grate, stepped down from the tank and glanced at her watch.

The whole excursion had taken twenty minutes. There was time for a brief catnap before she needed to start getting ready to report for her first day of work in Sir William's lab. Stifling a sudden yawn at the thought, she lifted the unattractive brown robe that was part of her Dawn Swanson wardrobe from the hook where she'd hung it when she'd unpacked, wrapped it around her and unlocked the door to the bedroom. She took a step toward her bed and then stopped in shock.

The man sitting on the edge of it wore a shapeless sweater and a threadbare pair of gray flannel trousers. His bony feet, bare of socks, were jammed into odd-looking sandals with an assortment of straps and buckles. Half-moon reading glasses were perched on the end of a beaky nose, and his pure white hair looked almost as wild as Carter Johnson's funky bed-head style. He looked up from the notebook he had been scribbling in, his expression thunderous.

"What the bloody hell have you been doing all this time in the loo?" he barked. "And where's the damned poster of me I hear you keep over your bed?"

"You miss the point entirely," Sir William London snapped impatiently thirty minutes later. "Von Trier's ridiculous hypothesis aside, what's to stop the gene from mutating further under controlled conditions? Nothing!" He slumped back onto the pillows piled up against the headboard of Dawn's bed, the ergonomically molded soles of his sandals further disarranging the bedcover. "And yet it's as inert as a bloody pudding," he muttered disconsolately, "and I've already wasted two days trying to find out why."

The first stage of her agenda, after arriving here, had been to get close to the famed Sir William, Dawn thought, still finding it hard to believe the turn of events of the past half hour. It seemed she'd already accomplished that, and with barely any effort on her part.

"I've been unpacking and arranging my toiletries, Sir William," she'd replied to his querulous demand when she'd exited the bathroom and found him in her room. She'd walked unconcernedly to the bureau and picked up her horn-rims. "And although I used to have your poster over my bed when I was in college, I didn't think it would be appropriate to do so here. What can I help you with?"

"I need to pick someone's brains," he'd growled. "Since yours was the only room with a light showing under the door, I thought I'd pick yours. Why in God's name the rest of my staff need to sleep like logs all through the night when they know that's when I like to brainstorm, I don't know," he'd added in irritation.

Aldrich will be over the freakin' moon when I phone in my initial progress report later this week, Dawn told herself now. *If anything could reassure him that I'm still the best at undercover assignments, this will.*

She shut all thought of Aldrich Peters and Lab 33 from her mind and gave her attention to her unlikely companion. "More tea?" At his nod she walked over to the bed from the small desk where she'd been sitting, the battered thermos that Sir William had brought in her hand. Absently he held out a glass lab beaker, and she filled it before pouring some of the vile-tasting brew into a chipped mug for herself. "Of course there's nothing to stop the gene from mutating under controlled conditions," she said as she sat down again. "Since it hasn't, someone's obviously screwed up the conditions."

"A typically glib Yank answer." Under scraggly eyebrows, London's regard was sharp with annoyance. "Who the hell would dare to—" He stopped abruptly, his scowl deepening.

Who indeed? Dawn thought wryly. For starters, just about anyone, if this lab was anything like the one she'd grown up in. All scientists, in her experience, were prima donnas. All lab technicians were underpaid. All maintenance staff were overworked and cut corners where they could. At least at Lab 33 everyone ultimately answered to Peters, which kept them toeing the line, but that wasn't the case here.

A plan began to formulate in her mind. She pursed her lips Dawn Swanson-style, but before she could speak, London exploded. "That ass Hewlitt! He came to me straight from Von Trier's facility. The bugger's trying to sabotage my work!"

"Maybe." She kept her voice calm. "Then again, maybe not. Tell me something, Sir William—the supervisor who showed me to my room this evening, Roger somebody?"

"Roger Poole? What about him?" The scowl was back on his face. "Roger's been with me for years. He's as loyal as a beagle, so if you're trying to suggest he—"

"Loyalty's not the issue," she cut in. "Being a decent guy's probably his biggest problem. You need someone taking care of the day-to-day running of your lab who's not afraid to be disliked." She shoved her glasses higher up onto the bridge of her nose and leaned forward, her expression tentatively eager. "I hope I'm not out of line, Sir William, but any slip-ups that are occurring in your lab certainly can't be your fault. And you shouldn't have to take time from your groundbreaking research to correct these problems. I know I was hired as a lab tech, but it's obvious you need a pit bull a whole lot more than you do a beagle. Let me be your pit bull. Give me two days, and I promise your lab will be running like a well-oiled machine."

"She's not cleared for that kind of responsibility, Sir William." The door to Dawn's room crashed open and Des Asher, still in uniform, took a step across the threshold. His expression seemed carved from stone as he went on, directing his words at his uncle and ignoring her. "As head of military security here, I can't allow her to be given free access to this facility."

He turned to Dawn, his gray eyes cold. "You're good. It's only been hours since your arrival and already you've made your move. But I'm good, too. I've sent off top-priority queries on you to both Washington and Interpol, complete with your photograph. If you've ever gotten so much as a parking ticket anywhere in the world, I'll know it."

His smile barely lifted his lips. "If you have, you'd better hope it was under the name of Dawn Swanson. But I doubt it...because I'm beginning to think Dawn Swanson doesn't exist at all."

Chapter 4

Status: seventeen days and counting
Time: 0145 hours

As the angry whine got louder, Dawn spared a moment to gauge its nearness. She was cutting things a little fine, she judged, but her preparations were nearly in place. All she needed to do now was to splash the road with the volatile chemical she'd liberated from the lab earlier, make sure she had a match handy and then crouch down in the patch of sage that at this hour of night was nothing more than a slightly blacker shadow in the surrounding darkness.

Piece of cake. But she had no intention of telling Aldrich that. She didn't want him thinking he could set up these last-minute meetings whenever he felt like it.

Her mouth drew to a straight line at the thought.

Twisting the metal cap off the small glass container she held, she began sprinkling the gelatinous substance it contained onto the hard-packed dirt of the road. It took only a second to lay the wavering trail of clear jelly. When she'd finished she dropped the bottle into the hole she'd dug earlier in the soft earth by the shoulder of the road and then replaced the earth, taking care that no telltale trace gave away the bottle's newly filled in grave. The chemical itself would be totally consumed when it burned, Dawn mused as she brushed a few twigs over the settled dirt. If anyone investigated this incident, which was unlikely, they would assume that a leaky gas tank from an earlier vehicle had left just enough gas on the road to be ignited by a stray spark struck by a piece of gravel. She half rose from her burial detail and listened. The whine now sounded like a hornet in a bottle. Her shadow melting in and out of the moonlight, she ran across the road.

This was insanity. Either that or another one of Peters's tests, but whatever his reasons for insisting on a facc-to-facc progress report from her, they weren't good enough—not when they jeopardized her cover and especially not when her phoned-in report had given him all the information she'd been able to provide at this early stage of her mission. Or at least, all the information she was willing to give, she amended with reluctant honesty.

"Of course I did nothing to arouse Asher's suspicions!" she'd lied emphatically last night when, as arranged, she'd dialed the number that if traced would show as connecting to nothing more sinister than a bookstore specializing in used and out-of-print scientific volumes. She'd converted the anger in her tone to ice.

"Maybe when I was just starting out in this game six years ago you might have had some justification in asking me that question, Doctor, but now it's an insult. I told you, one of his people screwed up my cover name. He couldn't handle that, so he took it out on me. His attitude only got worse when Sir William overrode him and gave me the supervisor position."

That last was the mother of all understatements, Dawn thought, extracting a book of matches from her pants pocket before stretching out at the side of the road. She dug the inner edges of her sneakers into the dirt, kept her head down but her focus straight ahead and took her weight on her elbows.

It was the classic sniper position, and one that was second nature to her. She could wait like this for hours if she had to, but from the escalating decibels of the approaching whine the waiting would last only a few more seconds.

She didn't want to hurt the rider, whoever he was. She couldn't afford to damage the motorcycle. Precision was going to be key in this operation.

"When isn't it?" she asked herself in a mutter. "If Mr. SAS hadn't stormed into my room when he did yesterday morning, I get the feeling his uncle might have declined Dawn Swanson's eager offer and kept his old chum Roger on in the position of lab supervisor. But if they have nothing else in common, London and his nephew seem to share the same determination to get their own way. It couldn't have been more obvious that his insistence on giving me the run of his lab was just his way of jerking Ash's chain. And talking about jerking chains…"

Transportation was one of the pesky little details Peters hadn't seemed to consider when he'd insisted on this meeting tonight, she thought. Even though their clandestine rendezvous was to take place at a bar just outside the limits of the nearest town to London's facility, it was still a jaunt of twenty miles. What had he been thinking—that she would simply hop in the hatchback, wave airily at the man who'd already warned her he suspected she was an imposter and drive off into the night before returning again hours later?

She tilted her head and listened. For the past few minutes the unknown motorcyclist had been tearing like a bat out of hell down the ruler-straight road just before the curve where she'd stationed herself. Now she heard him gearing down rapidly in preparation for the hairpin bend, his engine revs red-lining as noisily as they had the previous night when the loyal Roger Poole had been showing her to her quarters.

She'd fixed a Dawn Swanson expression of irritation on her features. "I was under the impression this facility was located miles from anywhere, not right next door to a motorcycle speedway. Half the staff on this floor must be awake with the noise."

Roger had given an apologetic cough. She'd already learned that an apologetic cough was his one-size-fits-all reaction to most situations, and the thought had crossed her mind that he would be the perfect candidate to give lessons in being a real Englishman to Des Asher.

"I'm afraid we've just resigned ourselves to the racket. Really, it would be rude to complain." He'd raked a hand through thinning brown hair. "After all, the chap riding that infernal machine is one of the military guards protecting our research from falling into the wrong hands. He must be on day duty this week, because he's been roaring out of here for the past few evenings about eight and returning around now. I believe there's what you Yanks call a 'juke joint' in the next town? Ah, here's your room. Now, where did I put the blasted key?"

While Roger, coughing madly, had fished around in the pockets of his lab coat, Dawn had mentally filed away the information he'd given her. She hadn't realized she would be using it so soon, she thought now, but since she'd been put in a position where she had to, she owed it to the hapless biker to do it right.

Stripped down to the essentials, this particular operation was simple physics, as so much of her training had been. Except this time instead of calculating the trajectory and velocity of a bullet, she'd had to figure out the path an experienced motorcyclist would take after swerving his vehicle to avoid a sudden wall of flames. She'd remembered the hairpin bend from her own drive here two nights ago, but until she'd arrived with her rope and looked over the location carefully, she still hadn't known for sure whether it would do.

She'd been relieved to find the same dry and crumbling soil that had posed such a problem for the hatchback's tires when she'd run off the road the night she'd arrived. It wouldn't be like drifting into a feather bed but as a Ranger, the biker would know instinctively how to fall. Hopefully the worst of his injuries would be a bruised ego.

A single blinding headlight abruptly rounded the curve. Immediately emptying her mind of all else, Dawn focused on the swiftly approaching motorcycle. The biker, now that he had negotiated the turn and knew he had a straight run until the unmarked side road that led to his destination, wrenched back on the throttle to pour on more speed.

She struck the match she was holding and touched it to the chemical fire starter. Whoever he was, he was good. As the flames sprang up in front of him he reacted instantly, wrenching the Harley Sportster to one side with the obvious intention of going around the unexpected barrier. But as soon as the Harley's tires hit the loose dirt it began fishtailing, despite the unknown rider's efforts to keep it under control. "Dump it, buddy," Dawn muttered under her breath. "You're going to go down anyway, so you might as well choose your own moment."

As if he'd heard her advice and reluctantly agreed with it, the Harley's rider did just that. He'd long since eased off on the throttle and the rough terrain had further cut his speed, so the maneuver when he executed it was little more than a controlled stepping away from the falling bike. Jogging toward him, Dawn watched as he rolled like a paratrooper for a yard or so. He ended up on his hands and knees, shaking his helmeted head as if to clear it as she walked up behind him.

"But clearing your head is exactly what I can't let you do, buddy," she murmured regretfully as she stood over him. "I know I've already put you through the wringer pretty thoroughly, but…"

She slipped a stainless-steel cylinder from her back pocket as she spoke. As the biker began getting to his feet and pulling off his dark-visored helmet, she quickly twisted the cylinder into two parts. Reaching around him, she held the broken halves in front of his face.

The cylinder was one of Lab 33's more benign gadgets. Although if it had been found in her luggage when she'd arrived it would have been dismissed by a searcher as a slightly oversize fountain pen, when the seal that kept it in one piece was broken it released a sickly sweet cloud of gas, similar in composition and effect to chloroform but much more predictable.

The hapless biker sank to his knees again, his helmet falling from his gloved hands. Taking care not to inhale the remnants of the gas, Dawn eased him to the ground.

"Believe me, buddy, if I could have worked this any other way in the time Aldrich gave me, I would have," she told the unconscious man regretfully. "But you'll come out of your little nap in a few hours. By then I'll have returned your wheels and as far as you're concerned, you'll just have had a nasty spill that knocked you out for a—"

Instead of finishing her sentence, she inhaled sharply. Her mystery biker lay on his back, the moonlight shining full upon his face. Pitch-black hair brushed his forehead. His lashes were dense fans against his cheekbones. His breathing was regular and a faint smile softened his lips.

She felt a rueful answering smile tug at the corners of her mouth. On impulse she brought the tips of her fingers to her lips and kissed them.

"Wrong time, wrong place again, Lover Boy," she whispered huskily as she blew her kiss toward him. "Maybe one of these days we'll have a chance to get it right."

Her smile disappeared as she checked her watch. Briskly turning away, she grabbed up the fallen helmet and hurried for the Harley without looking back.

"I owe you an apologetic cough, Rog, old chap," Dawn muttered over the Harley's rumble as she rode the heavy motorcycle into the dirt parking lot outside a long, low building. Peeling purple paint covered the rambling structure and its entry consisted of a spring-loaded wooden door with torn screening, but its slightly sinister air was dispelled by the glittering strings of Christmas lights that festooned it. "I figured your command of American-style English was a little shaky but it was spot-on, as you Limeys say. This here's a juke joint, all right."

She cut the bike's engine and kicked its stand into position before using both hands to lift the full-face helmet off her head. She balanced it on the gas tank, shook her hair into some semblance of order and looked around her curiously.

The lot was full. Although there were some other motorcycles nearby, the majority of the haphazardly parked vehicles were cars, although not the usual run of modern sedans and SUVs. Pulled right up to the rambling wooden porch that ran the length of the dilapidated structure was an old black Buick. It had what looked like small chrome portholes along its sides, and the black metal visor protruding above its windshield must have been the last word in style some sixty or so years previously. A row over was a vintage truck, and beside it was—

"Oh my God," Dawn breathed, her eyes widening as she dismounted the Harley and walked closer. "A '55 Caddie ragtop. And she's cherry…original paint job, whitewall tires that look like they've never had a speck of dirt on them, lemon-yellow leather interior. Elvis may have left the building, but I think I've found his car." She tipped her head to one side as a blast of music started up from inside. A slow smile spread across her face. "And from the sounds of that wicked slide guitar,

I think I've found his blues roots. Uncle Lee only played that old recording of RL Burnside's 'Snake Drive' about a million times while I was growing up. He'd go nuts over this place."

"He did." Aldrich Peters moved out of the shadows and into the dim illumination of the lights. There was distaste on his aquiline features. One snowy-white shirt cuff brushed against the peeling porch railing, and he jerked his arm away as if he'd been burned. "What a dump," he said in revulsion. "Your uncle used to say it was the only place west of the Mississippi that reminded him of the dives he frequented in that poverty-stricken backwater he grew up in. Since he couldn't shake the Delta mud off his feet fast enough when he was given the chance to get out, I never understood the attraction." He shrugged. "Still, when I realized how near it was to London's lab I thought it would be a convenient contact location for us. Plus I learned that it's off-limits to the lab personnel and guards."

"Snake Drive" had ended. As Dawn walked slowly up the porch steps, she recognized the gritty growl of Reuben Glaser plunging into "Killer Blues," another of Craig's favorites, but this time recognition gave her no pleasure.

Too bad she couldn't regenerate her memory as well as she could her body, she thought stonily. If that were possible, she would cut out all the sentimental recollections and replace them with ones that were less likely to keep tripping her up. She suddenly wished that Peters had chosen anyplace else—a deserted factory, even a graveyard, dammit—for this meeting.

But he hadn't. He'd chosen this place, and if she knew him, he'd chosen it precisely because of its connection to Lee Craig. For some reason, he wanted her all misty-eyed and vulnerable, she thought with a cold inner smile. She could do that.

"I miss him, Doctor," she said with a slight throb in her voice as she reached for the rusty handle of the screen door. She held it open, but Aldrich impatiently waved her through first. "Oh, I always knew we were in a risky profession and that every time he left on an assignment he might not return, but I guess I never really believed he could be beaten. I was in denial for a long time while I was AWOL from Lab 33."

"Really?" Peters's tone was suddenly silky. "So was I. But eventually we all have to face reality and deal with it, don't we? Excuse me, waiter—could we be escorted to a table?"

His manicured fingers tapped peremptorily on the shoulder of a T-shirted man rushing by with a laden beer tray on one outstretched palm and a platter of ribs on the other. The man gave him a harried glance. "Sit anywhere you can find a chair, friend. Tell me now what your poison is and I'll drop your drinks off when I go by again."

Peters's lips tightened. "A Manhattan, I suppose. Perrier for you, Dawn?"

"We'll have two beers, whatever's coldest, no glasses," she said swiftly. "Those ribs as authentic as the music, mister?"

"Made to my dear departed mama's recipe," the man said and grinned. "Double portion?"

At her nod he raced off. Weaving her way through the jammed tables ahead of Peters, Dawn hoped the composure she'd assumed with the waiter had covered her sudden shakiness.

Aldrich Peters didn't make small talk. His exchange with her just before he'd stopped the waiter hadn't been idle conversation. She was as sure of that as she was that the jukebox was now blasting out Albert King's version of "Born Under a Bad Sign," but what she still needed to figure out was what had been behind his comment.

He'd admitted he'd been in denial for a time while she'd been AWOL. She was under no illusions that he meant he'd had trouble accepting Lee Craig's death, so obviously there had been something else that Peters hadn't immediately wanted to believe. But, as he'd just informed her, at some point during her absence he'd faced reality—faced it, and made plans to deal with it as expediently as possible.

Albert's whisky-dipped rasp was pouring out of the jukebox, informing the patrons around her that if it wasn't for bad luck, he wouldn't have no luck at all. She knew exactly how the blues singer felt, Dawn thought numbly.

Aldrich knew she'd gone over to the Cassandras. This meeting had to be a trap…and she'd walked straight into it.

Chapter 5

Status: seventeen days and counting
Time: 0230 hours

"**Y**ou eat like a farmhand." His manicured fingers beating a tattoo on the oilcloth-covered tabletop, Peters flicked an irritated glance Dawn's way as she finished the last of her ribs, then let his attention drift with seeming unconcern to the table next to them. Its occupants were leaving, but Dawn knew he wouldn't say anything of importance until he was positive there was no chance of being overheard. It was a cautious policy she herself would normally follow, but the music was loud enough that she wasn't overly worried.

She licked barbecue sauce from her fingers with assumed gusto and pushed her plate away. "You know I'm always ravenous. Besides, those ribs were fantastic."

Attitude was everything, she thought. Whatever Aldrich had planned for her, as long as he believed she didn't suspect him, she had the advantage. That had been why she'd plowed through the double order of ribs that, although as good as the waiter had promised, were now sitting in a lump in her stomach; why she'd listened to the music with every appearance of being completely absorbed by it; why she hadn't dared allow the slightest trace of edginess to show in her manner.

She needed to look like a woman who could be taken off guard. When she'd convinced her assassin of that, he would strike. She intended to be ready for him, Dawn thought.

He would either take her in the ladies' room, if she was foolish enough to pay it a visit, or he would wait until she and Peters walked out to the parking lot. *If it were my hit I'd choose the latter,* she decided promptly. *In the washroom, an innocent bystander might blunder in. In the parking lot the killer can hustle me into the shadows, maybe make it look like I had too much to drink and he's helping me to a car. So now the only question is, who did Peters pick to carry out this assassination?*

It wasn't just the only question, it was the million-dollar one, she realized after a momentary blankness. Lab 33 had plenty of covert operatives, a small army of guards, an indeterminate number of thugs whom Peters used for jobs that required little expertise, but there were only a few high-level assassins. One of those had been Lee Craig. Another was herself. She wasn't sure who the others were.

Who assassinates the best assassin? she asked herself in confusion.

"You lied to me. Did you think I wouldn't find out?"

Peters's harsh question broke through her racing thoughts with the explosive suddenness of a gunshot. She looked quickly up and realized that the patrons who had been seated next to them were now halfway across the room and heading for the exit. Peters followed her glance and then returned his gaze to her, his eyes coldly unreadable. "I'm waiting for your answer. Did you really think you could get away with it?"

Her first inclination was to buy time. It was on the tip of her tongue to ask him what the hell he was talking about, but even as she opened her mouth to say the words, she closed it again.

Buying time wouldn't work. There wasn't any left to buy.

"Honestly?" She arched an eyebrow and let a small smile lift the edge of her lips. "Yeah, Doctor, I guess I did think I could get away with it. But hey—can't blame a girl for trying, can you?"

Her flippancy had gotten to him, she saw with satisfaction. At the side of one of his elegantly silvered temples, a vein throbbed faintly and the manicured fingers that had been tapping impatiently on the table now curled into his palms like fists. Peters's steely control was one of his greatest weapons, Dawn told herself. She'd just disabled that weapon.

"So how'd I slip up?" She kept her tone light and lifted her beer bottle to her lips as she spoke, hoping to increase his anger. The tilted bottle had the added benefit of giving her the opportunity to swiftly scan the room, but nothing alerted her. She swallowed, then instead of setting the bottle back on the table, she casually kept her grip on it. "Did I say something that tipped you off when I contacted Lab 33? Or, wait—your suspicions were confirmed during that meeting we had in your office, weren't they? I thought they might be, but when you gave me this assignment I figured I'd managed to convince you." She shrugged, her expression wry. "So tell me, Doctor, why *did* you send me on this mission if you didn't trust me?"

"Enough!" One of Peters's clenched fists slammed down on the table and the pulse at the side of his temple sped up alarmingly, Dawn noted in cold detachment. *Don't go having a stroke on me, Doctor,* she told him silently. *My plans for you don't include you dying from natural—*

Her thought was cut short by a crash as the beer bottle slipped from her hand to the floor. She wasn't aware of it falling. She wasn't aware of Peters's quick frown or the knowing grins of the patrons close enough to have heard the bottle smash.

All Dawn was aware of was the pain.

It felt as if sharpened steel bolts had instantly shot home behind her eyes, locking her into a world of unrelenting agony. It couldn't even be called a headache anymore, she thought as she clamped her lips tightly shut against the screams that were rising in her. By definition, headaches were in a person's head. They didn't send piercing tendrils down every limb until it felt as if a cruel barb had been sunk deep into each fingertip and then hauled tortuously back. Headaches didn't claw their way through a sufferer's lungs, ripping and tearing until it wasn't possible to take the shallowest of breaths. They didn't feel like a knife-thrust to the heart, a jackbooted kick to the kidneys, vials of acid searing through every layer of skin.

This time the pain didn't ebb in a few moments' time.

Like an endless ocean it kept coming, each wave crashing onto her with more force than the last. She had to stay conscious, Dawn thought disjointedly. She couldn't remember why staying conscious was important, only that it had to do with some danger she was facing. She fought the blackness that was sucking her down.

"…were a fool to think you could keep up the lie. Worse than that, you jeopardized the security of Lab 33. I should abort this mission right now and deal with you the same way I've dealt in the past with others whose actions have verged on the traitorous. I'm giving you one final chance to tell me the truth—how long have you been experiencing the degeneration symptoms?"

The pain had gone. For a second Dawn could grasp nothing but that simple and miraculous fact—the pain was *gone,* completely and totally. Not even the faintest throbbing remained as proof that it had been tearing her apart only moments ago.

And Aldrich Peters hadn't discovered her connection with the Cassandras.

Was there a link between the two? *Maybe,* she thought rapidly, *because as soon as he spoke just now I was suddenly back to normal. Could stress be the trigger that sets the headaches off?*

But this wasn't the time to explore theories. Peters had suspected she'd been lying to him about her symptoms, not her loyalty. Had she said anything in this conversation that might have tipped him to the possibility that they were talking at cross-purposes?

You came close, O'Shaughnessy, she told herself with relief, *but your responses could have applied equally to either situation. You asked him if you'd given yourself away with the phone call—and although you meant the*

*call you made when you were ready to come back to Lab
33 after being AWOL, he obviously thought you meant
your phoned-in report from London's lab. When you
wondered if you'd slipped up during your meeting with
him in his office the day he gave you this assignment,
he assumed you were talking about inadvertently revealing your symptoms. So we're good here, right?*

Wrong. He was still angry. He still wanted to know
how bad the symptoms were. And if she told him the
truth, there was a more-than-even chance he'd pull her
from this mission rather than take the chance she could
endanger Lab 33. He would weigh his options, assess
the possible consequences and reluctantly decide to
shelve his plans of stealing Sir William's research.

*I prefer my earlier scenario of him hiring a hit man to
take me out tonight,* she thought grimly. *Whatever it takes,
I can't let him abort this assignment. Not only my life but
Lynn's and Faith's depend on receiving the reversal serum.*

"You're right, Doctor—I've been lying through my
teeth to you," she said flatly. She saw a flash of fury behind the icy gray eyes watching her, and knew instinctively that she was walking across a minefield. She went
on, realizing that a single misstep could cause everything to blow up in her face. "The symptoms started
when I went AWOL from Lab 33…shortly after the
time you say my blood tests revealed the first signs of
gene degeneration. I didn't worry about them at first—
they were just mild headaches, and although I'd never
experienced headaches before I certainly didn't jump to
the conclusion I was dying."

"No," Peters conceded coldly. "But after our meeting in my office last week you knew the situation. And
yet you continued to hide the facts from me."

"Because I didn't have a choice!" She let a trace of fear bleed into her tone. "Don't you understand, Doctor—I'm desperate! You'd just told me how vital it was that I retrieve London's notes so your scientists could complete the serum for me. What was I supposed to do? Tell you I'd have to pass on the assignment that could save my life just because I was getting a few headaches?"

She shook her head. "With Uncle Lee gone, I'm Lab 33's best assassin. As you said, Des Asher's a formidable opponent and at some point he might have to be taken out. I couldn't risk handing over a job of that magnitude to some yahoo with a forty-eight Special, dammit. I *won't* hand over this job."

She'd blown it, Dawn thought as she finished speaking and took a tense breath. Aldrich was studying her as he might study a specimen under a microscope—emotionlessly and assessingly, as if she had just revealed something fractionally interesting and he was wondering if it would be worth his while to pick up a scalpel and dissect her further. She'd had one chance to convince him to let her continue with the mission that would lift her and her sisters' death sentences, and she'd blown it.

The jukebox had been silent for the past few seconds. Now it launched into another number, but Dawn barely heard it.

"Give me Bach any day." It was the last thing she'd expected Peters to say, and she was caught unawares. She realized she was staring openmouthed at him, but before she could recover from her surprise he went on. "You really like this—this—" He winced. Reluctantly she helped him out.

"The blues?" She met his gaze. "Yeah, Doctor, I do. What's that got to do with anything?"

"Just that you're more like Lee Craig than I realized," Peters answered remotely. "Not only in the so-called music you like, but in your reaction just now when you fought to have the responsibility of this assignment. As I recall, that was the topic of the conversation I had with Craig before he left Lab 33 on what eventually proved to be his final assignment. I couldn't fault him then for his determination and dedication to the job and I suppose I can't fault you now for showing the same qualities."

"You're saying you trust me to be able to complete the mission?"

Peters frowned. "If you give me your assurance that these symptoms you've been experiencing won't interfere with your performance. You're sure you had nothing to do with Asher's suspicions of you?"

"I told you, the man's a control freak. The screwup over my name when I arrived made him look bad and he's trying to cover his ass by focusing attention on me." Dawn kept her voice steady. "The headaches are the only symptoms I've had and if I ever need to explain them, I'll just give Dawn Swanson a history of crippling migraines. There hasn't been anything else that might have aroused Asher's suspicions, I swear."

Unless you count flipping into assassin mode while I was trying to convince the man I was nothing more than a lab tech, she amended silently. *But since I'm pretty sure you* would *count that, Doctor, I don't intend to share that particular anecdote with you.*

"Very well." His nod was brief. "I must admit you've made good progress in the short time you've been at London's facility. If Sir William has taken a liking to you, as you say he has, it's possible you might not have to eliminate him to get your hands on his work."

"Very possible," she agreed woodenly. She had a sudden vision of William London as she'd seen him the previous night, his white hair wildly unruly, his still-bright blue eyes excited with the realization that his theory might not have been wrong, his insistence on sharing his container of undrinkable tea with her. Despite his irascibility, London had a childlike quality about him, perhaps because his whole life had been devoted not to gaining the money and awards that had been a by-product of his genius, but simply to the pursuit of pure truth.

It would be incomprehensible to Sir William that someone might want to kill him for that truth. But the man sitting across the table from her would see no problem in giving such an order if he deemed it necessary...which was just one more reason to feel relief that Peters hadn't chosen anyone else for this job.

"Well, then." Peters pushed his chair back, taking care as he did so not to touch the sticky tabletop. "I believe this meeting is at an end. I'm glad we straightened out our little differences, Dawn." He paused. "There is one last thing I should touch on. You asked me why I sent you on an assignment when I already had my suspicions about your capabilities. The plain and simple answer is that I had no one else to send."

"But I've reassured you on that point," she protested. "You know now that my symptoms won't get in the way of my doing my job, so—"

"I wasn't sure of that four days ago in my office. And during the months you were AWOL, I had no choice but to assume Lab 33 had lost its best assassin. I decided that's not a position I will risk being in again."

"You've chosen a replacement for me." *This* was

what he'd meant earlier when he'd said he'd been forced to face reality and deal with it, Dawn thought. It was a relief to know her fears that he'd set up a hit on her were wrong, of course, but something about his casual assumption that someone else could take her place with Lab 33 stung.

Which is totally insane, O'Shaughnessy, she argued with herself. *You hate the fact that you were Aldrich's favorite killing machine, so how do you justify feeling a sense of professional pique over his giving that title away?*

It didn't make sense. But she still felt an illogical spark of anger, and Peters's reply only fanned it.

"Not yet, but I intend to. I've drawn up a short list of qualified candidates and I'll be making my decision soon. None of them have your unique capabilities, of course, so I expect some of them won't return from the test assignments I've given them." He stood, his figure leanly spare in the immaculately cut gray suit. "But some are bound to succeed. Those who do will be the nucleus of Lab 33's newly formed assassination squad—a squad that will answer to you."

Dawn stood too, her legs feeling strangely rubbery. "I like the idea, Doctor," she said, forcing a smile. "And the test assignments are a practical way of weeding out the excess candidates. What exactly are their assignments?"

Peters's smile was characteristically brief, but for once it was shaded with real satisfaction. "Each assassin has been given the name of one of the Athena Academy graduates known as the Cassandras," he said as he stood aside for her to precede him to the exit. "Their missions are to kill their targets or die in the attempt."

* * *

The Cassandras had been warned, Dawn thought in relief an hour later as she waited for the feeling to come back to her limbs. She looked over her shoulder at the high-voltage fence she'd just scaled, still feeling the tingling residue of the electricity that had surged through her body and stopped her heart for a few seconds, but her thoughts weren't on her surroundings. Kayla Ryan herself had answered the phone when she'd rung the emergency contact number from a gas station pay phone, and Ryan hadn't wasted time in asking questions.

"I'll get the word out immediately," she'd said after a moment's stunned silence. "Some of the members deal every day with threats on their lives. Sam St. John once told me that she simply assumes that at any given time some creep somewhere in the world has a price on her head, and she never lets down her guard. But a few of the others will have to be provided with round-the-clock security."

"And my sisters?" she'd reminded Ryan, her tone curt with worry. "Aldrich may not know about Lynn and Faith yet, but we can't assume he won't find out and try to take them."

"I'll take care of it," Kayla promised. Her tone softened. "And you take care of yourself, Dawn. I know this is how you wanted to handle the Lab 33 angle, but ever since the other Cassandras and I agreed to let you play this dangerous double game with Peters I've regretted our decision—more so since he sent you on this undercover assignment. You're absolutely sure he doesn't suspect you?"

"Not absolutely sure," Dawn said. She sensed the other woman's apprehension and tried to lighten it. "But like my Uncle Lee always said when I was worried, if it's close enough for government work, why sweat it?"

She spoke unthinkingly. It wasn't until Kayla didn't respond to her that she realized what she'd said, and by then it was too late. She'd done it again, Dawn thought angrily. When was she going to stop remembering Lee Craig as if he had really loved her?

Before she could berate herself further, Kayla's voice came over the line once more. From her tone it was clear that she wasn't talking as a police lieutenant or a fellow Athena Academy student, but as a friend. "I told you once that Craig deliberately chose the dark side. I still believe that, Dawn. But I've also come to accept there was a part of him that he never relinquished to the dark. You were the part of him he kept separate."

"Still trying to help me heal, Ryan?" Dawn gave a short laugh. "I appreciate the thought, but as I once demonstrated to you, it's not necessary. If you really need to worry about me, worry about the damn SAS officer who's been on my case since I showed up at London's lab. Des Asher's proving to be one major pain in the butt."

"Really?" There'd been a smile in Kayla's voice. "In my experience, that's the only kind of man worth getting to know. After I deal with the current situation, I might just pull some strings and ask a contact of mine to fax me a photo of this Des Asher. I'd be interested to see what your major pain in the butt looks like, O'Shaughnessy."

Well, for starters, Ryan, he doesn't have pitch-black hair and a drop-dead gorgeous smile like Lover Boy, Dawn thought now as she slowly got to her feet. A reluctant grin tugged at the corners of her mouth. As usual, when it came to her, Kayla had it all wrong. If she'd been looking for a little R and R—*which I'm definitely not,* Dawn firmly assured herself—Mr. SAS would be her last choice. The man whose motorcycle she'd returned was much more her type, even unconscious.

Although he seemed to be coming around by the time I dumped the Harley by him and left, she thought, keeping to the shadows as she silently headed toward the dark shape of the lab and living quarters building a few hundred feet away. *That phone call to Kayla was vital, but it definitely shot my schedule all to hell. I'd planned to be safely tucked up in Dawn Swanson's bed by now.*

But the hard part was over. She'd breached the perimeter fence, had given her body several minutes to repair itself after taking the volts that had slammed through it, and now only had to cross the grounds that some obliging landscape architect had apparently designed with her needs in mind. Clumps of ornamental grasses were artfully dotted here and there like living fountains, massive boulder arrangements lent a solid contrast to the grasses, and desert-loving shrubs and cacti provided enough cover for a herd of elephants to sneak up undetected.

I bet Ash took one pissed-off look at this when he arrived to take command and promptly sent out a high-priority requisition to Washington to have the whole freakin' area bulldozed, she thought. *Too bad for him his requisition was obviously turned down. Getting out earlier this evening was a snap and getting back in is going to be just as—*

"It ever occur to you that you're letting this damned baby-sitting detail get to you, pal?" Dawn froze into position behind a boulder as the unfamiliar voice floated faintly through the darkness. Actually, it wasn't unfamiliar, she thought a heartbeat later. She'd heard it once before, a couple of days ago. She pictured the speaker— the Ranger officer whose boyish features had been tight with strain as he'd held his weapon on both her and Des Asher and who'd later sheepishly admitted to making the mistake over her name. She tried to recall his, but just then it was given to her.

"Yeah, Keifer, it's occurred to me." Asher's speech was different from his uncle's: harsher, less precise, and with a mid-Atlantic intonation to some of his words that implied he'd spent enough time in the past liaising with the American military that his accent had blurred. She realized he and Keifer were approaching her boulder as his voice gained in volume. "And I decided I don't give a flying—"

She heard his footsteps halt. Keifer's lighter step stopped too. "What's the matter? You hear something, Ash?" he asked in a low tone.

Dawn held her breath. She heard Asher's footsteps start up again, and exhaled in noiseless relief.

"I didn't hear anything." Wonder of wonders, there was an edge of wry amusement in Mr. SAS's voice, she noted. "But if you can believe it, I thought I smelled barbecue sauce for a minute. That's what I get for working through lunch and dinner, I guess."

Barbecue sauce! Her cupped hand flew to her mouth and she breathed into it. God, she *did* have barbecue breath, she thought, appalled. Just the slightest trace, but apparently the damn man had a nose like a bloodhound.

"Another example of letting this assignment get to you," Keifer said. "As the senior American officer here, Asher, I gotta tell you I think you're riding everyone too hard—yourself, the men…hell, even that poor dweeb of a lab tech you nearly blew away a couple of days ago. What were you thinking, man?"

"I was thinking that posing as a dweeb of a lab tech would be one smart way to infiltrate this place," Asher said shortly. "I was thinking that seven years of self-defense classes wouldn't teach her the kind of speed and ruthlessness she showed. I was also thinking that if you looked real close, she wasn't a dweeb at all. She was doing a good job of disguising her looks, but when the two of us were at each other's throats I couldn't help but notice."

"If you say so." There was patent disbelief in Keifer's tone, but Dawn wasn't reassured. This was bad, she thought tensely. Back at Lab 33 she'd assured Carter that her deception wouldn't depend on his efforts but through her own, and in the past that had always been true. Her knack for assuming an undercover persona had never let her down before now, but if Des Asher had seen through Dawn Swanson, then obviously that knack was one more skill she could no longer take for granted.

Aldrich Peters had said she'd made good progress so far. But it wasn't good enough—not when she had no idea which of her degeneration symptoms would next reveal itself, or how. She'd gotten close to Sir William, but she needed to get a lot closer if she was to find out where the obsessively suspicious genius concealed his research notes.

"…still say this latest idea you've implemented is taking things way too far." Keifer was speaking again, and she realized he and Asher were now directly in front of her boulder. Their footsteps stopped again. "You've got razor wire, an electrified fence, guards at the gate and doing perimeter spot-checks. Our people and the lab staff know they have to follow procedure if they want to leave the compound, and they also know that this area between the fence and the walkways is off-limits after dark. I don't see why you think you need—" He broke off abruptly. Dawn heard him exhale sharply. "That's them, isn't it," he said in resignation. "They've only just arrived and already you're putting the poor sons of bitches to work. Since I haven't been formally introduced yet, I think I'll just hustle my butt back to the unrestricted area, if that's okay with you."

Mr. SAS had a sexy laugh, Dawn thought in faint surprise. Too bad it was part of a package deal that included his crappy personality. Keifer appeared to be his one friend here, and even he seemed to have problems with Asher's tight-ass personality—a prime example of which was his apparent insistence on increasing his guard roster without giving the newcomers a chance to settle in.

He's going to have to walk them around the area, at least, she thought, sliding down into a more comfortable sitting position and crossing her arms over her chest in irritation. *Even he can't expect that all he has to do is snap his fingers and order them to get to work immediately. It's a drag, but I guess I'll just have to wait until he leaves with the poor—*

"Slasher! Ripper! *Come!*"

Even before Dawn heard Asher snap his fingers and issue the abrupt order, her eyes had widened in appalled comprehension at the sound of eight running feet on the crushed-gravel path. Keifer's description had been dead accurate, she thought hollowly as she peered far enough around the boulder to get a glimpse of the two black figures now sitting obediently at Asher's feet. The new guards were sons of bitches…literally.

Sons of *Doberman* bitches.

"Good lads." His back to her, Asher bent and scratched each dog briefly behind an ear. He straightened, and his voice took on an unmistakable air of command.

"Slasher! Ripper! *Hunt!*"

Chapter 6

Status: seventeen days and counting
Time: 0337 hours

The Dobermans leaped into action, torquing away from Asher's side so quickly that gravel spurted up behind them. They made straight for the boulder, their fangs bared and menacing growls coming from their throats as they went for Dawn.

She glared at them.

As if they'd suddenly thudded into an invisible concrete wall, the two dogs fell backward into each other. They scrambled to their feet, took a few snarling steps toward her again and then stopped. Right on cue, both of them started shaking at once. Their growls were now fearful, their formerly pricked up ears flat to their heads and their stubs of tails plastered to their hindquarters.

Very slowly, and without taking their eyes from hers, they began backing away.

Dogs didn't just hate her, Dawn thought resignedly. They really, *really* hated her.

Even Peters didn't have an explanation for her effect on them. Craig had given her a puppy for her fifth birthday and it had howled in despair for as long as she was in the room, only to revert to normal puppy behavior as soon as she was gone. The pup had been returned to the pet store, but the one that had replaced it had acted the same way, and so had the third. By then Aldrich's scientific interest had been aroused, and he'd run test after test with dogs of all breeds and temperaments.

Even the pit bulls had crouched in fear at her five-year-old feet, Dawn remembered. Deciding that the dogs could sense something different about her, although he never did pinpoint what it was that alerted them, Peters had finally given up on the experiments and Lee Craig had brought her home a kitten.

"Fluffy liked me," she muttered as she walked past the cringing Dobies and around the side of the boulder just as Des Asher came running toward it. He saw her and a look of alarm crossed his features.

"Slasher! Ripper! Stand *down!*"

"They already did," she informed him. She fixed a Dawn Swanson scowl on her face. "I don't see a bag in your hand. I suppose you thought if you walked your two mutts after dark you wouldn't have to stoop and scoop after them. If I step in something the next time I can't sleep and come out here to clear my mind, I'll certainly know who to blame."

Rule number one in bluffing, she reminded herself, was that no matter how outrageous the bluff, no matter how disbelieving the person you were trying to scam, you couldn't falter. Even if they presented you with proof positive that you were lying, you had to keep to your story.

Works for politicians, she thought. *No reason why it shouldn't work for me.* She began to walk past Asher's solid bulk, but he sidestepped with the same instantaneous reaction he'd shown two days previously when he'd drawn his weapon. He faced her, his features hard.

"No." His tone was flat. "We're not playing it your way this time. Instead of spending the next half hour going round and round the mulberry bush, you're going to cut the crap right now and tell me what the hell you're doing in a restricted area at this hour of night."

"What do you mean, a restricted area?" If there was one thing that pissed her off royally, Dawn thought in irritation, it was having to look up at a man. She was tall enough that the problem didn't occur often and in heels she could go eye to eye with just about any male under basketball player height, but right now she was wearing Dawn Swanson's scuffed runners and she was definitely having to tip her head back to talk to Asher. *Six-five,* she estimated. *But a well-placed jump kick brings even the big ones down to size, buddy.*

"You saw the signs. You would have had to walk right past them on your way here from the bughouse." His frown deepened. "The lab and staff quarters building," he corrected curtly.

She looked past him, ostensibly to search for the signs he'd mentioned but really to hide the fact that she'd nearly been startled into a grin. She'd overheard one of the guards using the term the day before, but hearing it come inadvertently from Asher was way better. She almost wished she didn't have to use his slip-up against him.

Almost.

"In case you hadn't noticed, I'm not wearing my glasses. I'm probably not the only one on staff who takes them off to give my eyes a rest when I'm not working, so I suggest that if you really want to keep this area to run your overgrown pets in, you edge it with a small ornamental fence or something."

His jaw tightened. "They're not pets, they're trained—"

"One more thing you should bear in mind, Mr. Asher," she cut in, deliberately omitting his rank. "You may not respect Sir William and the work he carries on here, but the rest of the world does, myself included. Despite the fruit flies we use in our genetic experiments and the somewhat eccentric behavior of some of the scientists working with your uncle, calling this place the 'bughouse' is offensive. If it happens again I'll have to lodge a complaint." She gave him a dismissive nod. "I'll try to watch out for the signs next time. Good night, Mr. Asher."

Just for a moment she thought her bluff was going to work. He'd lost ground with his bughouse remark—for someone like Asher who kept such a tight rein on everything and everyone under his command, being tripped up by his own tongue was galling, and being put on the defensive by her must have been even more so. *Perfectly executed feint and attack on my part,* she told herself with an inner smile. *Anytime you feel like losing another mini Battle of New Orleans with this here American, Captain, go right ahead and bring it on.*

She took two steps past him, heard whining behind

her, and knew her perfectly executed plan had just been shot to hell.

"What did you do to them?" His hand clamped around her upper arm. She felt her biceps tighten in reflex and quickly relaxed it, hoping he hadn't had time to wonder why a lab tech had muscles like iron. But Asher was preoccupied. "The dogs—what's the matter with them?"

Reluctantly she turned to face the animals. They'd found the courage to slink out from behind the boulder and were huddled at Ash's feet, their gleaming bodies trembling so badly they looked like two cans of midnight-black high-gloss being violently shaken in a paint-mixing machine. Twin pairs of canine eyes met hers. Slasher—or maybe Ripper—attempted a growl. It ended in a strangled whimper. The second Doberman just bared his teeth, lifted his muzzle and howled.

"If I find you poisoned them with something smuggled out of the lab, Swanson, I'll have you in lockup so fast you won't know what hit you," Asher grated. "And this time neither Keifer nor my gullible uncle will be able to save you. What did you give those dogs?"

Rule number two in bluffing, Dawn thought wearily, was knowing when rule number one wasn't working anymore. On the few occasions in the past when she'd reached an impasse like the one she currently found herself in, she'd had no compunction about resorting to a physical solution. *Not that I have any compunctions this time either,* she told herself. *But going* mano a mano *with Slasher and Ripper's master is out of the question, unless I want to kiss off any chance of getting Sir William's research back to Lab 33.*

She would simply have to Dawn Swanson her way

out of the situation yet again, she thought without enthusiasm. God, she was getting tired of this particular alter ego.

So go ahead and dump the Swanson chick, O'Shaughnessy. As soon as the reckless little voice inside her head offered the suggestion, it seemed overwhelmingly attractive. Not that she could abandon her cover persona, Dawn thought glumly. Going undercover meant staying undercover, not popping in and out of character on a whim. *That's the beauty part, though—it's not a whim, it's a double bluff!* the little voice argued. *And there's no freakin' rule against double bluffs, is there?*

Maybe there was in Aldrich Peters's book, but not in hers, she thought slowly. A spark of excitement flared in her. She was going to do it, dammit!

"I didn't give the mutts anything," she retorted with a shrug. "I'm just the dog bogeyman, for some reason. If you don't believe me, watch this."

She lunged at the Dobermans. In panic they backed into the boulder, and at that point they forgot the last shreds of their training. She turned to Asher as his canine line of defense ran off yipping into the darkness.

"They sense something wrong about me," she said offhandedly. "Dogs and SAS officers are supposed to be smart that way, right?"

He was staring after the Dobermans in disbelief, but at her question he turned back to her, his eyes narrowing. "Are you admitting that both the bloody dogs' instincts and mine are correct, Swanson?"

She scooped her hair back from her face with her hands, continuing the movement to lace her fingers behind her head. "Why not," she said carelessly, her voice losing the pedantic tone she'd been assuming. She rolled her shoulders to relieve the strain. "You guessed my big secret, Ash. I'm not Dawn Swanson, lab nerd—I'm the original femme fatale. Last I heard, I was rated one of the top three international assassins in the world, but I figure I got rooked. As far as I'm concerned, I'm in the top two." She drew her eyebrows together thoughtfully. "Except since the guy above me died last fall, I guess that leaves yours truly as number one with a gun."

His gaze was still on her. She returned his stare coolly, taking in the way the short spikes of his burnt-silver hair contrasted with the mahogany of his tan, and how the beach-glass aqua of his eyes couldn't be completely concealed even behind the denseness of his half-closed lashes. He wasn't in the same league as Lover Boy, she thought assessingly—one look at Des Asher and a woman's thoughts didn't veer immediately toward a vision of rumpled sheets and deliciously wasted afternoons. One look at him was enough to make any sane woman keep her guard up rather than let it down.

Even as the thought flitted through her mind, her guard fell completely away.

A few minutes ago she'd heard him laugh at something Keifer had said. His laugh had been surprisingly attractive; low with amusement and somehow giving the impression that it was a fleeting glimpse of the real man. So yeah, his laugh could be called sexy, Dawn thought dazedly. But his *smile*…

His teeth gleamed briefly white in the shadows. A corner of his usually grim mouth lifted. His aqua eyes were still half-hidden, but now instead of glinting coldly at her they seemed to draw her in.

She still didn't think of wasted afternoons when she looked at him, she told herself unsteadily. Her thoughts were running more along the lines of hustling the man into her bed this very night.

Bad mistake, O'Shaughnessy. Real bad mistake.

She snapped back to sanity as he spoke. "Number one with a gun, Swanson? You sure you're not just trying to impress the hell out of this poor Brit?" The laughter in his voice was reluctant, but it was still there as he continued. "Because I am impressed, love. See, I figured you for a small-time operator hired by someone a little higher up on the criminal food chain to infiltrate this place and report back on its security measures and procedures. I'll admit I was pretty shaken by your moves when you and I got it on a couple of nights ago at the front gate, but I had no idea I was dealing with the female equivalent of the Jackal."

Her instincts had been right, she thought in amazement…reckless but right. The truth was so fantastic that Asher found it easier to believe she was spinning him a story, and he'd been amused enough by what he saw as her outrageousness to play along. *You could keep this up indefinitely, O'Shaughnessy,* the daredevil voice inside her urged. *Come on, isn't it a whole lot more interesting playing 'catch me if you can' with the man rather than being stuck acting out the Swanson role?*

It *was* more interesting. It was more interesting because it was more dangerous, she told her inner daredevil repressively, fixing a scowl on her face and opening her mouth to revert to a Swanson-style put-down.

So it's more dangerous. Where's the downside to that?

Dawn closed her mouth without delivering the put-down. Slowly she widened her eyes at Asher. She let the corners of her lips curve into a smile, and when she spoke there was absolutely nothing of Dawn Swanson in her purr.

"What happened between us at the gate, Ash?" She let the faintest trace of disappointment color her tone. "Maybe that counts as getting it on where you come from, but to a red-blooded American girl like me it barely rates as a warm-up to foreplay. Not that I'm trying to scare you or anything," she added, examining her nails with assumed casualness.

This time his startled laugh wasn't reluctant at all. Looking up from her nails, Dawn saw a slash of humor crease a tanned cheek as he replied to her veiled dare. "Don't forget I'm SAS, Swanson. We don't scare easily," he informed her. "Know what our motto is?"

"Who Dares, Wins," she replied without hesitation. "Us international assassins know everything there is to know about our opponents. And since we're on the topic of what we know about each other, have you had any luck in getting that information on me you contacted Interpol and Washington about?"

He didn't answer her immediately. The crease of humor in his cheek disappeared, although a ghost of a smile still played around the corners of his mouth. Without appearing to have shifted his stance in any way, there was an instant stillness in every muscle of his body, as if he had sensed a slight movement of the earth beneath his feet.

Or as if he realized that although they were still playing a game, the rules had suddenly changed, Dawn thought, watching him intently. *They have,* she told him silently. *By asking about your inquiries into my background, I just confirmed there's something I don't want you to find out about me. Your response will tell me*

*whether you're going to end this now and act on that
confirmation...or play the game a little longer to see if
you can get anything more from me. The next move is
all yours, big guy, so are you going to fold and walk
away, or are you still in?*

Mr. SAS was going to fold, she decided with an ob-
scure feeling of let-down. The moment she'd asked
about his inquiries to the authorities he'd gone on full
alert...and with a man like Des Asher, full alert didn't
include playing games. Which was too bad, because
matching wits with him during her time here might have
been fun. She'd have won, naturally, but with his SAS
training in strategy and maneuvers he would have been
a worthy opponent.

She stifled a yawn, trying to work up enough interest to plan some sort of Dawn Swanson explanation for
her behavior. *A bad reaction to some headache medi-
cation? Delayed shock and fear from being set upon by
Slasher and Ripper?* she wondered without enthusiasm.

"Funny you should ask." Asher's voice broke into her
thoughts. She looked at him swiftly, but the same half
smile ghosted around his lips as it had a moment ago
and the same wary watchfulness was in his eyes. He
continued, his tone giving nothing away. "Until this
evening I hadn't gotten a single damn thing back from
either Washington or Interpol in response to my inquiries about you. Nothing. *Nada.* Zilch. At first I figured
I'd made a mistake about you."

"Weird." Dawn arched her eyebrows in astonishment
and was sure she saw a flicker of humor momentarily
overlay his wariness. "Because I'm beginning to think
I made a mistake about you. Maybe we both shouldn't
have been so quick to jump to conclusions."

"Maybe you shouldn't have," Asher replied. "But as much as I'd like to shelve all my unworthy suspicions of you, something tells me I'd end up regretting it for a long time. No, I've pulled some less-than-smart moves in my career, but trusting you won't be one of them. Whoever prepared your cover story slipped up, Swanson." He rubbed his jaw thoughtfully. "Not that Swanson's your real name, but I might as well keep calling you by it for now."

He was trying a bluff of his own, Dawn thought with an inward smile. For an opening move in this preliminary skirmish, it wasn't bad, either, but she doubted whether he expected her to fall for it. He was simply trying to get her off balance, plant a momentary worry in her mind that Carter might have overlooked a detail when he'd created Dawn Swanson.

But for all Carter's faults, overlooking details wasn't one of them, so she wasn't worried. It wouldn't hurt to let Asher think she was, though.

"What do you mean, they slipped up?" She frowned quickly and then just as quickly smoothed her brow, as if she hadn't meant to let him see her consternation. The shaky little laugh that followed her alarmed question was the perfect touch, she thought as she fixed an uneasy eye on her opponent. "An international assassin like myself wouldn't have anything less than the best backup team available. My people don't slip up, Ash." She paused long enough to nervously bite her lip. "But just for interest's sake, what do you think they did wrong?"

Even before she finished speaking, he was shaking his head. "You disappoint me, love. I'm in this game for the same reason you are—because until you drove up in that wreck of a hatchback a couple of days ago and tried to slice me open with a car antenna, I was going out of my mind with boredom. I'm used to operating behind enemy lines, taking on assignments that never get written up in the official reports, making HALO drops over occupied territory. This particular posting doesn't exactly compare—"

She couldn't help interrupting. "HALO?"

He shrugged. "An SAS term. High Altitude Low Opening parachute jumps. Essentially, dropping like a bloody rock right up until the last possible second, which is the quickest and dirtiest way to get from a plane five thousand feet up to the ground where the fighting is. But what I'm trying to say is that for a minute there I thought you were going to make things interesting. Then you started overacting like crazy, Swanson—biting your lip, opening those big green eyes as wide as you could. Hell, I haven't seen a performance like that since I was a five-year-old kiddie being taken to a Sunday afternoon pantomime by my dear old nannie."

Sheer outrage robbed her of speech. *Overacting?* Dammit, had she been overacting when she'd infiltrated a certain Middle Eastern potentate's palace dressed as a dancing girl and taken out the sheikh's murderously corrupt son before he could sign a deal that would destroy the balance of power in that part of the world? Had she been overacting when she'd posed as a nun in the godforsaken jungles of a tiny but violent South American country, had allowed herself to be kidnapped by the group of terrorist thugs that had been slaughtering foreign civilians, and had then coldly dispatched the whole band of killers, one by one, during the night? Had overacting gotten her the position as secretary to a Swiss money launderer, enabled her to get close to the Russian Mafia hit man who'd been jeopardizing one of Aldrich Peters's more lucrative operations, put her in place to carry out the half-dozen or more other assignments that had required her to play a part?

I don't think so, Dawn seethed. *And those jobs needed way more finesse than putting one over on Mr. SAS. He's just trying to piss me off by—*

By telling her the truth. Her outrage faded away, to be replaced by uncomfortable self-honesty. The man was right, damn him. She hadn't given it her best shot. Her performance a moment ago had been amateurishly halfhearted because she'd assumed she wouldn't have to work at conning him. She'd violated one of Lee Craig's cast-iron rules.

Act like every assignment is your first, or else it could turn out to be your last, Dawnie. Never let yourself forget that laziness and arrogance can kill someone in our profession faster than a bullet.

Des Asher had said she'd disappointed him, Dawn thought wryly. He might be taken aback to learn that an assassin who had gone under the code name of Cipher would have said the same thing if he'd been alive to witness his former protégé's most recent efforts.

She pushed all thought of Craig aside and concentrated on the frowning man standing in front of her. "Three things I want to get straight—firstly, I'm not real sure what a pantomime is, but I have the feeling I've just been insulted." She exhaled tightly. "Secondly, I probably deserve it. I thought I could get away with treating this as a game. But with you as my opponent, I should be treating it as a war game, right?"

"Going up against me won't be the walk in the park you seem to think it'll be," Asher agreed with a tight smile. "Even though I don't buy your international-assassin story, I'm willing to accept you've taken on the best, and won. But I'd lay good money you've never taken on the SAS and beaten us. Don't count on this being the first time, Swanson."

"I'd lay good money you've come out on top in most of the confrontations you've been in, too," she told him, her smile equally tight. "Ain't gonna happen that way with me, buddy. So we're on the same page here—bluff, counterbluff, no holds barred and may the best woman win?"

"Bring it on, love." Asher's tone was strained.

"You bet, sweetie." Hers was just as edgy.

For a long moment gold-green eyes locked with aqua, the tension between them so thick Dawn had the impression that if she'd had a blade in her hand, she could have sliced through it. This was what she'd needed, she thought, feeling her senses sharpen and the blood quicken in her veins. Try as she might, she couldn't completely eradicate her Lab 33 history and the training she'd received from Lee Craig, but in the months since she'd met the Cassandras and learned the truth about herself, the outlets that had in the past served as releases for her restless energy and instincts had been closed to her.

I guess you could say I've been itching for some real action, she told herself. *Something tells me I've just found it.*

"What was the third thing?" Asher's question pulled her abruptly from her thoughts. She blinked at him.

"The third thing?"

"You said there were three things we had to get

straight between us. I almost forgot to ask you what the third one was."

Her blankness disappeared, and with it went some of the rigid tension that had been gripping her. War games were still games, Dawn told herself as she let a slow smile curve her lips. Playing with Des Asher was going to be fun.

"The third thing was you admitting you'd had a nannie, Ash." She slanted a dubious look at him. "If I were you, I wouldn't make that public knowledge. Not unless you're totally secure in your masculinity, that is."

"Oh, but I am." Earlier in their conversation she'd injected a purring note into her voice and now he did the same; although with its undertone of roughness, Asher's purr reminded Dawn of velvet over concrete. *If I was a girly girl, I might even feel the tiniest hint of a shiver running down my spine at Mr. SAS's bedroom voice,* she decided. *In fact, girly girl or not, I believe that's* exactly *what I'm feeling right now.*

"But you understand that kind of security, don't you, love." His glance swept briefly over her, from her sneaker-shod feet past the baggy sweatpants and top to the mud-brown of her hair. "Only someone with supreme self-confidence would have no problem with posing as a dweeb, as Jeff Keifer calls you. That godawful shade of brown comes out of a bottle, right? My guess is you're a natural blonde."

"Wrong. Fiery red," Dawn said promptly. She might have weakened to the point of having a shiver or two down her spine, she thought ruefully, but she hadn't completely thrown all caution to the winds. She'd told him she was an assassin in such a way that she'd known he wouldn't believe her; offering an important identifying detail like her true hair color went against all her professional instincts. But Asher was shaking his head.

"You're too cool and controlled to be a spitfire of a redhead. You're definitely blond. Not as light as platinum, but not a dark blond, either." He studied her. "I'll go with the color of wild honey. Is this a money wager or not?"

"Not." Her reply came out more quickly than she'd intended. Dammit, the man had rattled her, Dawn thought in chagrin—*her,* Dawn O'Shaughnessy, who up until tonight hadn't known the meaning of the word. "It's not any kind of wager, for the simple reason that you'll never get the chance to know if you were right or not. Sorry, big guy, but that's the way it has to be."

"You sure about that, Swanson?" The velvet on concrete was back in his voice again, but she was ready for it.

"Abso-freakin'-lutely, Ash," she drawled. She glanced at her watch. "And now if you don't mind, I have to turn back into a pumpkin. Dawn Swanson has to be at Sir William's side again in two and a half hours, all bright eyed and bushy tailed and ready to crack the whip over his tea-swilling staff, so although it's been swell, I'd better haul—"

"Understand one thing—he's not part of your game, love." The easy endearment did nothing to warm the sudden ice in his tone, and all Dawn's senses immediately heightened. "My uncle may be a bloody-minded pain in the arse and being assigned to watch over him might be my idea of hell, but I have a certain affection for the old boy. He's the genius everyone says he is, but he's also childishly naive in many ways."

"A lot of geniuses are," she agreed curtly. "What's your point?"

"My point is that within the space of a couple of days, you've duped him into thinking he can trust you." Asher's jaw tightened. "I'm going to make sure that whatever it is you're planning, you won't pull it off, Swanson."

He moved quickly for a big man, Dawn noted dispassionately, but not quickly enough to take her unawares. As his hand shot out, she knew he intended to grasp her arm and she had time to react, but instead she let his fingers close over her wrist.

Maybe sometime in the future she would have to demonstrate her superhuman reflexes to Des Asher. To do so now would merely give him advance warning of what he could expect in a fight with her. But even if letting him trap her wrist was good strategy, there was no rule that said she had to be happy about it, she thought angrily.

"You've got ten seconds to say your piece and get your hand off me." She kept her voice even and her gaze steady as she met his eyes. "Ten. Nine. Eigh—"

"Ten seconds is plenty," Asher cut in. "Don't get me wrong—I'm not averse to adding some interest to our personal war by bending the rules a little. We're both professionals—we know how to handle ourselves. But Sir William's a civilian. If any harm comes to him because of you, I'll hunt you down, Swanson." He released her wrist as swiftly as he'd grasped it. "And although I've got a fatal weakness for green-eyed blondes, don't count on that stopping me from doing what I have to when I find you. Understood?"

He stepped back, as if he suddenly needed to put some space between them. "It probably would be smarter to take you in right now, and the hell with our strategic little game."

"What game?" His right hand was by his side, Dawn saw. The movement could have been unconscious on his part, or it could have been calculated to put him within closer reach of his sidearm, the heavy Sig Sauer he'd drawn on her once before. It didn't matter one way or another. This encounter was nearly at an end. "We never had this conversation, Ash. I was never here. Dawn Swanson's been safely tucked up in bed for the past five hours, and if you try to say different, I'll simply deny it." She gave him a thin smile. "You're already on shaky ground where I'm concerned. Keifer wasn't too happy with the way you reacted at the gate when I arrived, and your dire warnings about me to Sir William got you nowhere. Maybe if your inquiries to Interpol and Washington had resulted in anything more than a big fat zero, your suspicions might be taken more seriously, but as it is…" She let her sentence trail off, but just as she was congratulating herself on having made her point, the crease she'd seen earlier reappeared in one tanned cheek.

"Who said my inquiries resulted in a big zero, love?" he asked softly. "I told you that up until this evening I hadn't found anything on you. As of about two hours ago, that situation changed."

"Changed?" Without glancing sideways, she let her peripheral vision widen to include the shadowy expanses of grounds to either side, but her reaction was mere reflex. Escape wasn't an option. What she'd told Asher was true: she needed to be back in the persona of Dawn Swanson. As dreary as her alter ego was, being her for the next little while was the only way of remaining close enough to Sir William to find the notes she and Lab 33 needed.

"Remember having to submit to being fingerprinted

before you were given your lab pass the night you arrived?" Asher's grin was tight. "Dawn Swanson made her indignation bloody clear, as I recall."

"I remember," Dawn said shortly. "Indignant or not, I wasn't worried about being printed. I'm not on file anywhere."

"Dawn Swanson isn't. But two years ago the Swiss police obtained a partial thumbprint of a certain Donna Schmidt. Seems Fräulein Schmidt was the personal secretary of a murdered Zurich banker who was later learned to have been into cartel money laundering in a big way. That's probably why the Swiss weren't as zealous in finding his murderer as they might have been…and why they didn't pursue their inquiries into Fräulein Schmidt when they found she'd dropped out of sight immediately after her boss bought a bullet." His focus on her suddenly sharpened. "But you know what I found most interesting about Donna Schmidt? The minute portion of her thumbprint that Interpol has on file is a dead match for yours."

"Which doesn't mean squat or we wouldn't be having this conversation," she answered with a shrug. "A partial print? Minute portion? Depending on how small it is, it could match up with half a million other prints in the world. You're fishing, sweetie, but you won't catch anything with bait as puny as that."

"And it's just a coincidence that Donna Schmidt and Dawn Swanson both sound like aliases for the same woman?" At her nod, frustration crossed his features. Then he gave a reluctantly brief smile. "Like I said, cool and controlled. For what it's worth, I sent a reply to Interpol saying you couldn't be Schmidt, that I had solid confirmation you'd been in the U.S. during the relevant time period."

Although she'd kept her composure during all his other revelations, this latest one caught Dawn totally off balance. "But you don't—not if you think my whole résumé's a clever fabrication. Why didn't you simply drop a dime on me to the Swiss authorities?" She saw his confusion and realized with irritation that she'd used a Lee Craig-ism. "Rat me out," she elaborated. "Turn me in to them."

The aqua eyes holding hers showed momentary amusement before they hardened again. "Because I don't give a tinker's damn that a money launderer for the cartels was executed or that you might have been the inside contact for his killer. I just give a damn about what you're doing on my turf…which is why you're coming with me now to the guard's office where Keifer can witness my official interrogation of you. You still haven't told me what you were doing out here, Swanson, and—"

The quiet of the night was suddenly shattered by the raucous sound of a motorcycle's engine. Asher glanced with a frown in the direction of the main gate as the cycle's throaty rumble was abruptly cut off, to be replaced by raised and furious voices.

Lover Boy had just arrived and was catching hell for coming in so late, Dawn realized swiftly. But as far as she was concerned, his timing was perfect.

"That bloody Reese and his motorbike. This is the second night this week he's broken curfew and whatever his excuse is this time, he's going on report," Asher muttered as he began to turn back to her. "This place is supposed to be run along military lines, dammit, not—"

Already moving at top speed through the shadows, Dawn allowed herself a small smile. From the darkness behind her came an angry explosion of swearing. Mr. SAS certainly had an impressive command of basic Anglo-Saxon curse words, she thought as she heard his reaction to her disappearance. Any moment now he would realize he was wasting time and turn his efforts to something more productive, like making straight for her room, but by the time he arrived she would be in bed and feigning sleep.

As she'd told him, he wouldn't be able to prove she hadn't been there all along. She didn't have to worry about any repercussions from tonight's escapade.

All she had to worry about now was the fact that her partial fingerprint was apparently on file with Interpol. Which was odd, she told herself grimly...because four days ago her prints hadn't been on file at all.

Chapter 7

Status: fourteen days and counting
Time: 1607 hours

"Marmite sandwich, Miss Swanson? They're awfully good."

Drop that last adjective and your assessment's probably more accurate, Rog, Dawn thought with a mental shudder as Roger Poole eagerly thrust a dried-out triangle of two layers of bread encompassing a thin and gluey brown filling practically under her nose. Unwillingly she plucked it out of his hand, gingerly holding it between her thumb and middle finger.

"I'm a vegetarian," she lied. "Sorry and all that, but—"

"How simply wizard, so am I!" Behind his taped-up glasses, Roger's brown eyes goggled in kinship at her.

"Then you'll love the taste of this. It's a yeast product. Very popular back home, you know."

With a Dawn Swanson frown, Dawn handed the sandwich back to him. "Yeast is a living organism. I'm not the kind of woman who bends her principles just because they're inconvenient." Her own sandwich was on the cafeteria tray in front of her. As she picked it up and sank her teeth into the ham and cheese on rye she saw him look dubiously at her. "All soy," she explained inelegantly, her mouth full. "Tastes just like the real thing."

His dubiousness vanished, to be replaced once more with the puppy-dog adoration that Dawn Swanson apparently engendered in him. In fact, Dawn mused, most of the scientists and technicians sitting in the cafeteria right now were throwing similarly besotted glances her way. For some reason, the Swanson chick's abrasive personality and determined dowdiness had the male contingent of Sir William's lab vying for her attention.

They're probably all picturing me in leather with a whip, she thought, washing her mouthful of sandwich down with a swallow of milk. *Or maybe as a stern schoolmarm, with them as the bad little boys who haven't done their homework. Oh, well, whatever floats their boats.* She took another bite of her ham on rye and pointed the crust at Roger.

"The shipment of beakers that came in this morning—who authorized them?"

Hastily he choked down the minuscule piece of his own sandwich that he'd just bitten off, and went into one of his by-now-familiar coughing fits. "I imagine I did," he said apologetically when he could talk. "Why, is there something wrong with them? I ordered from the same supplier we've always—"

"They're fine." She popped the crust into her mouth and looked longingly at the dessert lineup on the nearby serving counter before firmly forcing her attention back to him. "Just checking, is all. I like to keep tabs on everything, as you know."

"Of course." Roger set his sandwich aside. The cup in front of him held lukewarm water with a tea bag floating listlessly on top. With every appearance of enthusiasm, he jerked the string of the tea bag up and down while he spoke, not noticing that the water was barely changing color. "I must say, Miss Swanson, I'm terribly glad you've taken over the reins, so to speak. The supervisory position only fell to me because no one else wanted it, but I'd much rather be behind a microscope. I'm afraid I not only lack your head for detail, but I can't seem to control the staff with as firm a hand as you do. Why, just yesterday Sir William demanded to know why he hadn't been consulted about the extra personnel that had been hired. He hardly believed me when I told him we had the same number as always, but that you'd lowered the boom on the break times the technicians had been taking."

"I went out the back door the first morning and saw every last man jack of the British staff sucking away on cigarettes," Dawn said acidly. "I told them if they wanted to smoke themselves into early graves that was fine by me, but they could do it on their time, not Sir William's. Plus I made sure they cleaned up the mountain of old butts they'd dropped. As I told Sir William from the start, I'm not here to win a popularity contest. I'm here to smooth out any problems that might hinder his work."

She reached briskly over and took the tea bag from

the bespectacled Englishman. "That's as good as it's ever going to get, Rog," she said, not unkindly. "Now tell me, do you think Sir William's pleased with me?"

"Pleased? Dear Lord, he's ecstatic!" He blew unnecessarily on his cold tea. "When you discovered that the reason his mutation experiment had been compromised was because the cleaning staff had been wiping down the petri dishes with glass cleaner every night, he was beside himself. The experiment's going well now, by the way."

"Yeah, great," she said distractedly. "But listen—how do I get close to him? I mean, there are things I need to discuss, but whenever I try to set a time for a meeting he simply tells me he can't be disturbed and that I'm to do whatever I think best for the running of the lab. I suppose that's a compliment, but there really are a couple of decisions I need his input on."

"I had that very problem myself," Roger commiserated. "But never fear—I finally found out that the one time of day you can be sure of pinning him down is just around teatime. He always retires to his rooms and has a proper British tea, with paste sandwiches and anchovy toast and on special occasions, baked beans and egg." He glanced down at his unfinished meal and weak tea with a noticeable diminution of his earlier gusto and then looked up at her, his expression brightening. "I say—why don't we drop in on him now? He'll probably ask us to join him, but since it's to help you I don't mind fibbing and telling him I haven't eaten yet."

"Four o'clock is teatime? I thought this was a late lunch," Dawn said, pushing away her chair and waving him back into his seat as he began to stand. "No, Rog, I wouldn't dream of dragging you away from your marmot sandwich." He coughed in quick consternation, but she rushed on, "I'll find Sir William myself and talk with him. Thanks for the advice."

She made her way to the lunchroom exit, not forgetting to glower meaningfully at a table of technicians who by her watch should have finished their meal break and been back in the lab a few seconds ago. Five pairs of thick lenses magnified five suddenly guilty gazes as they jumped to their feet, gathered up their trays and practically fell into one another as they deposited their litter in a nearby bin before hastily heading back to work.

Their reaction went unnoticed by Dawn. She'd been in place for over four days, she thought grimly, and except for her first night here when she and Sir William had had their nocturnal conversation, she'd barely laid eyes on him. *And as for getting any closer to finding out where he keeps his notes, forget it,* she told herself in disgust. *If I don't make some serious progress soon, I'm going to have to change my tactics. Time's running out and I can't count on my symptoms remaining in remission like they have for the past few days.*

The possibility of her headaches returning was never far from her thoughts. Equally dangerous, though, was the likelihood that Asher might dig up another fragment of her Lab 33 past more damning than the partial print he'd already discovered, and make the decision to turn her in to the authorities.

She'd expected him to show up in person the night she'd escaped from him and made it back to her room, but instead he'd sent Keifer. The young lieutenant had obviously been uncomfortable with his mission; even more so when Dawn had answered his tentative knock at her door dressed in brown flannel pyjamas and with a drab robe firmly cinched around her waist. She'd squinted disgruntledly at him, as if he'd awoken her from a sound sleep, and at his halfhearted query as to whether she'd been out and about on the grounds during the past hour, she'd given him a full dose of Dawn Swanson indignation.

"Are you accusing me of conducting some kind of clandestine rendezvous with a *man,* Lieutenant?" she'd demanded, snatching her glasses from her robe pocket and angrily jamming them onto her face. "Because if you are, my opinion of you just sank as low as my opinion of Captain Asher. I might have expected this kind of harassing accusation from him, but not from—" She'd stopped and glared at him. "He sent you, didn't he?" she'd asked furiously.

"The captain said he'd seen someone who might have been you roaming the restricted area a few minutes ago, yes," Keifer had said awkwardly. "It was an honest mistake, I'm sure."

"Are you?" Dawn had leveled a disbelieving look at him. "I'm not. I think your commander made a fool of himself the day I arrived, and since then he's tried his best to make his ridiculous suspicions seem justified. From the first it struck me as odd that a senior SAS officer should be assigned to a lower-level posting like this, but now I'm beginning to realize there's a reason he's been shunted out of more active duty."

This last had been merely the kind of cutting remark Dawn Swanson would have delivered, but to Dawn's interest, it unexpectedly roused a defensive response from Keifer.

"I consider it an honor to serve in any capacity with Captain Asher," he'd said stiffly. "I'm well aware of the details of his military career, and if the man has any fault at all, it's that he's gone above and beyond the call of duty at times." He'd clamped his lips together, as if he'd said more than he'd meant to, and with a formal nod and an apology for disturbing her, had taken his leave.

Dawn's curiosity had been piqued, but when she'd closed the door behind Keifer and sat down on her narrow bed, her own hidden history rather than Des Asher's had been the main thing occupying her mind.

Accidents happened, she thought now as she turned down the hall that led past the lab to the staff's living quarters. Not every eventuality could be foreseen. But Lee Craig, for all his faults, had been the best black-ops teacher a girl could possibly have, and he'd drummed into her the vital importance of leaving nothing of herself behind when she completed an assignment. For those missions that had necessitated her going undercover, naturally it had been harder to obliterate all trace of her often weeks-long presence at a given scene, but even then it had merely been a matter of caution and discretion. For instance, she reflected, take the glass she'd just drunk milk from in the cafeteria. Within minutes it would be entering a dishwasher and her fingerprints on it would be cleaned off. But when she'd taken consignment of the beakers that had arrived this morning, she'd been careful not to touch any of them. They would be here and possibly still unused long after she'd left, and plastering her prints all over them would simply give her one more thing to wipe down before she went back to Lab 33.

She would have sworn Donna Schmidt had been as scrupulously careful as Dawn Swanson, but apparently that wasn't the case, she told herself in chagrin. In her persona as Fräulein Schmidt she'd possibly neglected to wipe a desk drawer or the space bar on her computer keyboard or maybe even one of the Spode china coffee cups she'd handed around during the many meetings between the Swiss banker and his business associates. It didn't matter where the authorities had lifted the partial thumbprint. It just mattered that it was on file.

And it also mattered that Carter Johnson had assured her it hadn't been.

It's SOP—standard operating procedure—for those pencil pushers on Aldrich's payroll to run us through the computers every once in a while, Dawnie. One of Lee Craig's earliest lectures on tradecraft came back to her. Turning down the corridor that led to Sir William's rooms, Dawn frowned but didn't push the memory away. *That's how they justify making the big bucks, while us dumb schmucks who put our lives on the line are lucky if we get our expenses reimbursed.* He'd winked, and a thirteen-year-old Dawn had winked back at him, feeling as if she and her beloved Uncle Lee were in an exclusive club of two. He'd ruffled her hair, but then his grin had disappeared and his tone had sobered. *Standard procedure or not, when you're about to leave on assignment, you insist the bastards make one last check on your cover identity, your prints, the whole enchilada. Shit happens, and even the best of us can get pulled over for a broken taillight or some pissant infraction like that. You don't want to hand your license to some Smoky to call in, and then look in your rearview mirror to see the son of a-bitch holding his gun on you as he walks back to your vehicle.*

Like everything Lee had told her, she'd taken that advice as gospel, Dawn thought. Before each mission it had become her own standard operating procedure to have

Lab 33's Identities Department give her one final assurance that her cover ID was clean, her weapons were untraceable and she herself didn't exist as far as the outside world was concerned. She'd stood over Carter as he'd conducted his computer sweep with the sophisticated software that enabled him to tap into every data bank in the world, no matter how closely firewalled and guarded, and she hadn't left his side until the program had run its course and delivered its all-clear message.

Or had she?

She came to a stop in the middle of the deserted hallway, her mind racing as she mentally replayed the scene: Carter seated in front of his computer but angled slightly away from it as he talked with her, only occasionally turning back to the monitor to type in a command. He hadn't bothered to hide his boredom at what he obviously saw as an unnecessary precaution on her part, had even gone so far as to drag his skateboard out from under his desk and had been restlessly propelling it back and forth with one foot to emphasize his irritation. At some point he'd shot the board too far forward and it had gotten away from him, flying into the path of old Henderson from Lab 33's counterfeiting department and nearly tripping him. She'd been the one to go over to Henderson and smooth his ruffled feathers before retrieving the skateboard, Dawn remembered. Her attention had only left the monitor for a minute or so…but a minute would have been plenty of time for Carter to hide any message he hadn't wanted her to see, if that had been his ploy.

She was suddenly glad she hadn't acted on her first impulse and used the clandestine bookstore phone number to contact Lab 33 the morning after Asher's revelation. Yet another of Lee Craig's truisms had been that information was only a valuable weapon as long as your opponent didn't know you had it.

The door to Sir William's suite of rooms was in sight. Slowly she began walking toward it again, her feet in their grubby Dawn Swanson sneakers making a squeaking sound against the tiled floor with every step she took. Had Carter deliberately tried to sabotage her mission? If so, why? *He'd have to have one hell of an incentive to risk the consequences of Peters finding out,* Dawn thought. *I should know—it took one hell of an incentive, courtesy of the Cassandras, for me to go up against Aldrich. But if that little weasel's playing two sides, somehow I don't think his motive is to do his part in the fight against evil.*

But was that really her motive? Hadn't she agreed to help the Cassandras for her own reasons—reasons that primarily included the icy desire to extract some kind of payback from Aldrich Peters, some kind of revenge for the lie he'd made of her whole—

About to raise her hand to knock on Sir William's door, she never completed the motion. Pain slashed through her head, immediately robbing her of her strength and her senses. It felt as if she was being bludgeoned—as if a giant pickax was being raised repeatedly and smashed down to sink into her very brain.

She fell to her knees, her head hanging limply between her braced and trembling arms. Nausea rose in her and she felt her stomach gather itself to violently eject the meal she'd so recently eaten.

"So the rumors are true…you *aren't* invulnerable anymore. Interesting." The harsh whisper—in her disabled state Dawn found it impossible to tell whether it came from a man or a woman—penetrated her consciousness just enough for her to attempt to look at the speaker. Her head felt as if it weighed a ton, her neck barely able to support it. Painfully she opened her eyes…and saw nothing but blackness.

"Blind, too?" Mockery tinged the voice. "The mighty Dawn O'Shaughnessy certainly has fallen, hasn't she? I can hardly believe it."

It was the voice's mockery that lit a feeble spark in her. She was in danger, Dawn thought through the fog clouding her senses—mortal danger. The owner of the voice was amused to see her this way, which could only mean that he or she meant to take advantage of her temporary vulnerability. Dredging up the last of her resources, she wiped the back of her hand across her mouth and forced her lips to lift in a cold smile as pain stabbed unendurably through her.

"Don't believe it. Because even in the state I'm in I'm *still* your worst nightmare."

As she rasped out the last words she rose to her feet and blindly launched herself in the direction of the voice. Her grasping hands closed around a neck, and, operating on sheer desperation and will, she began to tighten her grip.

"You *freak!*" The voice was no longer a whisper; it was a strangled gasp. "Someone should have killed you a long time ago!"

The pain rose to its highest pitch. She had to hang on, Dawn told herself as she began to lose consciousness. Even if only for a few more seconds, she *had* to hang on long enough to vanquish this unknown, unseen opponent. Because if she didn't—

She knew as soon as the searing agony went through

her that her fears had been right. Whoever her opponent was, he or she was her mortal enemy…and this enemy knew her one vulnerability.

It was a race between her impaired regeneration abilities and her inability to draw oxygen past the blood that was pouring in a choking flood into her lungs, she realized dazedly. And whether she lived to fight again, or died in the next few minutes depended solely on the outcome of that race.

Her unknown enemy had just shot her in the throat.

Chapter 8

"Can you hear me, lady? If you can, say something, okay? Dammit, sir, she's not responding. I think we should get her to the infirmary right now."

She was flying, Dawn thought, a little ripple of delight passing through her. Now *this* was a superhuman gift worth having! Why in the world hadn't Aldrich told her he'd given her the capacity for flight along with the rest of her enhanced abilities?

Maybe because you can't fly, O'Shaughnessy. You've been lifted up into someone's arms, you numbskull.

The caustic voice inside her head swept away her delight and brought with it a full awareness of the situation. Immediately she ran over the salient points in her mind.

One: she'd been shot. Two: she'd apparently survived and the wound in her throat had healed, judging from her unrestricted breathing. Three: her headache had vanished, which was probably why her regenerative powers had come back in time to save her; and four: she'd been found unconscious and lying on the floor by at least two people—whoever was now holding her in his arms and the person he'd just addressed as "sir."

Those were the facts she knew. It was the ones she didn't that could endanger her.

Had she healed before she'd been found, or had the process of regeneration been witnessed by anyone? And was the man who hadn't yet spoken her would-be killer, interrupted in the act of watching her die and now having to pretend to have stumbled innocently upon her prone body?

"No need to have those quacks you military types call medics probing and prodding her if she doesn't need it. It looks to me as if she simply keeled over outside my door and bloodied her nose in the process of falling. I might even have heard her hit the floor if I hadn't been listening to the end of an Elgar symphony on the phonograph." The irritated English accent was unmistakably Sir William's, Dawn realized, which relieved her of one of her worries. His pronouncement had relieved the other. If his off-the-cuff diagnosis was fainting and a nosebleed, then he couldn't have seen anything out of the ordinary…like someone trying to kill her.

Cold anger flared inside her. The killer had known her real name, had known of her abilities and the one way she could be killed. Who fit all those criteria? She thrust the question aside for the moment. Whoever her attempted killer had been, she would find him or her, and when she did, the owner of the mocking voice would learn he or she had picked the wrong damn woman to try to kill. Her would-be assassin didn't know it yet, but he was as good as dead.

Her attacker's death would have to wait, though. Right now she had a more immediate matter to deal with.

"But, sir—" The soldier who had her in his arms was trying to argue with Sir William. She felt like advising him not to waste his breath, but that fact promptly became self-evident.

"What's it say on your name tag? Reese, is it?" Sir William gave an unimpressed grunt. "Right, then, Reese. Instead of standing there like a bloody statue, bring my lab supervisor into my rooms and set her on the sofa. She's getting some color back into her face, so I think we can safely say she's off the critical list."

You might have known, O'Shaughnessy. She was almost startled into a smile. *Of course you're doing the fainting-damsel thing with Lover Boy. The poor guy seems fated to save your butt on a regular basis.*

She'd been about to open her eyes anyway, but now she had a good reason, she thought in amusement.

"Where am I?" She intended to milk this situation for all it was worth. She let her lashes flutter upward, only realizing as she did that her glasses were sitting askew on the bridge of her nose. Hastily she pushed them straight and gave Private Reese her best helpless-female look as he lowered onto Sir William's sofa.

Firm jaw. Indigo eyes. Those thick dark lashes and the sexy mouth she'd noticed on their two previous encounters. Dawn sighed.

"*Damn,* but you're gorgeous, Reese," she muttered. The indigo eyes widened momentarily, then lit with faint humor. "The name's Terry, and you're obviously still delusional, angel." He grinned at her.

"Is she lucid?" Sir William's testy question broke the moment. Reese fixed a quick frown on his face and looked up at the older man.

"Barely, sir. But I think she'll be all right in a minute or so. Should I call the infirmary anyway?"

"And have them put Miss Swanson on sick leave just when I've finally found someone who keeps my lab running smoothly so I can concentrate on my work? Not bloody likely, soldier." Sir William glowered at Reese. "Although you're a Yank, you report to my nephew, I suppose?"

"Lieutenant Keifer's in command of the Rangers, sir, but Captain Asher's in overall command of this facility, so yes, I guess you could say I ultimately answer to him," Terry Reese answered with formal courtesy. "He's really the reason I'm here right now. The captain wanted me to convey a message to you." He hesitated. William London snorted.

"Spit it out, man. I doubt that any message Asher has for me is so top secret Miss Swanson can't hear it. If he had his way, I daresay he'd rule me a security risk, and if I had mine I'd do away with half of those cumbersome regulations of his that always seem to be impeding me."

Reese glanced down at her and then back at the scientist. "Then the captain's latest pronouncement won't come as a surprise, Sir William. As of immediately, he's implementing a twenty-four/seven tracking of all personnel, including your people and yourself. That means that whenever you leave an area you're supposed to log onto the nearest computer and input your destination, how long you anticipate being there, and what the reason is for changing location." His smile flashed into a rueful grin. "All I can say is don't shoot the messenger, sir. I'm just passing on what he told me to tell you."

"Of all the damned cheek!" Sir William exploded. "You mean if I decide to go to the loo I've got to tell the whole world how long I think I'll be? Not on your nelly, lad. Take a message back to my tight-assed SAS nephew. Tell him I have no intention of complying with his dictatorial pronouncements, and I'm specifically instructing my lab staff to ignore them, too. And if he doesn't like it, he can damn well lump it!"

"Damn well lump it," repeated Reese solemnly. "Yes, sir, I'll tell him. But you don't want me to let him know what happened to Miss Swanson, do I understand you correctly?"

"Captain Asher has a problem with me, so no, please don't bother letting him know I fainted." Dawn sat up on the sofa and swung her legs off. She placed her sneakered feet tightly side by side and clamped her knees together. Time to bring the Swanson chick back, she thought regretfully. Her absence up until now could be attributed to her temporarily dazed condition, but not even Terry Reese's indigo eyes were excuse enough to continue acting out of character. "Luckily, unlike you I don't have to have to answer to him, but to his uncle." She gave the wild-haired old Englishman a stiffly apologetic nod. "I'm sorry for disturbing you like this, Sir William. By the time I remembered to have lunch I realized this would be a good opportunity to speak with you on some matters and I decided to eat later. I should have known better. Sometimes my blood sugar drops when I miss a meal."

God, now the gorgeous Terry not only saw her as

dowdy, but in need of regular hearty sustenance to avoid crashing onto her face, she thought with an inner amusement. She suddenly remembered her massive plate of barbecue ribs at the juke joint, the three Danishes she'd scarfed down for breakfast this morning, the more-than-adequate ham on rye she'd had for lunch, and her grin vanished. *Hey, the days of Scarlett O'Hara starving herself to attract a beau are over,* she thought in irritation. *Besides, this is one undercover assignment where I can't afford to indulge in any extracurricular activities, no matter how tempting.*

"Then when I ask you out I'd better feed you." Reese kept his tone low, but there was no chance of Sir William overhearing him anyway. The older man had moved impatiently to the door, obviously eager to have his reply to his nephew conveyed as soon as possible. Reese lifted one eyebrow inquiringly. "It also might help if I knew your name."

She stared in disbelief at him. "Dawn," she said flatly. "But since you're a babe who probably has to fight off supermodels everywhere you go, I don't think I'll hold my breath for that date, Private Reese."

"Seven o'clock tonight. East exit of the building. I'll be waiting, angel." He sketched her a sloppy salute, turned it into a snappy one as he passed Sir William, and left before she could think of a suitable Dawn Swanson put-down.

"Well, if you must pass out from hunger, you couldn't have picked a better time and place to do so." William London closed the door and turned energetically to Dawn. "You're in for a treat, my girl—I was just about to sit down to a real English tea. Ever tried Marmite sandwiches?"

* * *

"Asher was a fairly inoffensive child. He was born to my youngest sister later in life and Daphne was rather taken aback to find herself a mother at forty, but as she'd hired a nanny for Destin she only needed to take three weeks away from her groundbreaking work on the Victorian poets, and her husband Charles didn't need to ask anyone to fill in for him at Cambridge." Sir William scowled. "But I must say that as a grown man Asher's certainly turned into a bloody officious—"

"Destin?" Dawn interrupted. "Des isn't short for Desmond?"

By the time she'd politely choked down two sandwiches and three cups of tea, she'd realized that her hopes of maneuvering the conversation around to where Sir William kept his notes was a lost cause. Reese's message had incensed him, and all he wanted to talk about was his nephew and how Asher's security precautions were hampering his work. It wasn't wasted time, she reflected. The irascible Englishman had let down his guard with her during his tirade, and she had the added bonus of learning more about the man who had vowed to stop her from accomplishing her mission. Information on an opponent, no matter how trivial, was always worth having.

William London looked at her in surprise. "Desmond? Don't tell me you don't recall Tredhope's lines. 'Lo, t'was sweet night were Destin's ally—for in the end, his love's fingers prove'd rosy dipped in his blood; false lady be no friend.' Edgar Tredhope? Minor but influential poet who died of consumption in the 1890s?"

"Nope, 'fraid not," Dawn answered politely, hoping her inner thoughts weren't showing in her expression.

Well, well, she told herself, *who would have guessed Mr.
SAS was named after a character in a sappy poem written by a third-rate Victorian poet? Now all I have to do
is think of some way to casually bring that up in conversation the next time we talk.*

She glanced around the room, taking note of the features for future reference. Sir William had succeeded in
converting a sterile and featureless room in a desert-
based government facility into a fairly close approxima-
tion of an Oxford study. The armchair she was sitting
in was comfortably shabby and the large velvet-cur-
tained window behind his desk must have been demanded especially by him, since all the other windows
in the facility were small. Books spilled from every
available surface, and on the corner of the ancient oak
table upon which the remains of their recent repast were
spread, incongruously sat the small skull of some long-
gone and hapless rodent.

London was shaking his head. "Good Lord, what
kind of education do you colonials receive over here?"
He poured himself another cup of tea, topped up hers
before she could decline, and returned to his rant. "Of
course, when he was five he was packed off to board-
ing school and I didn't see much of him while he was
growing up, but still, you could have knocked me over
with a feather when I learned he'd gone into the military. Could have knocked his parents over with a feather,
too," he added thoughtfully. "Daph and Charles pride
themselves on their liberal views, but to have a son
wearing a uniform, especially a Special Air Services
uniform? Not the kind of career they'd hoped he'd have
chosen," he mused, "especially after the fiasco he was
involved in last year."

Her antenna pricked up. "Fiasco last year?" she said carefully. "Is that why he was transferred to this particular posting?"

For the first time since he'd started venting, London hesitated. Dawn turned her attention to her tea to dispel any impression that she was waiting eagerly for his answer. Finally the old man spoke, his tone no longer indignant, but now pained.

"My nephew and I don't see eye to eye on many things, but I refuse to believe he was responsible for what they say he did. The boy I once knew might have become a hard man but he's not a murderer, and that's what it was—sheer murder. I'm not talking so much about that group of thugs who called themselves a palace guard, although from what little I've learned they'd laid down their weapons and surrendered, so killing them was against all rules of war. But there were civilians involved, too—women as well as men. Their deaths are indefensible." Under bushy eyebrows his gaze became steely, and for a split second Dawn saw a trace of his nephew's implacability. "And the one man who didn't deserve to live walked out of that bloodbath unharmed, by God, and at this very moment is instructing his high-priced legal eagles in the lies he's put forward as a defense for his years of atrocities."

There was only once incident that Sir William could be describing. Dawn's mind fixed in revulsion on the scenes she'd heard sketchily described in news bulletins and insufficiently reported upon in the few articles that had been written for the papers before censorship regulations dammed up even those meager trickles of information.

Sir William had called it a bloodbath. From what little she knew, his description was an understatement.

Hassad Al-Jihr's long dictatorship over the tiny Middle
Eastern area known as Bah'lein had been marked by
years of torture, death and the disappearance of thou-
sands of citizens, but those well-documented evils had
been overshadowed by the events that had occurred during the defeat of his regime. While being held pending
his trial on crimes against humanity, Al-Jihr was coun-
tercharging that the western liberation forces sent in to
remove him from power had unleashed a savageness
much worse than anything he'd been accused of. The
handful of photos and reports that had briefly been made
public seemed to bear out his incredible assertions.

She'd seen her share of violence, Dawn thought with
a shudder, but even she'd been sickened by the pictures
of slaughtered palace servants and their families. The
unknown SAS officer allegedly behind the butchery
had been dubbed by the world's press as "The Wolf of
Bah'lein." It was a shock to learn she knew that wolf
under the name of Des Asher.

Although, according to Sir William, she realized as
he continued, she didn't.

"It's criminally unfair. Since no official charges have
been laid against him, Asher hasn't been allowed to defend himself and the damn fool is so loyal to his bloody
SAS that he didn't even lodge a complaint when some
idiot at Whitehall tried to have him suspended. I raised
merry hell when I heard about it, I can tell you." London gave the same sharklike grin Dawn had seen tightening his nephew's features. "So I made them an offer
they couldn't refuse, as I believe the phrase goes. At the
time I was ready to jump ship and work exclusively for
the Americans. I hate hamburgers and no one over here
seems to know how to make a decent cup of tea, but

when it comes to coughing up the money needed to properly fund research like mine, you Americans have it all over my penny-pinching countrymen. I'm on the verge of something unimaginably big—the reversal of genetic aging itself. Even the discoveries I've made so far could change the way our bodies regenerate from accidents or illnesses. Your government immediately recognized the importance of my research—and how dangerous it could be if it fell into the wrong hands."

"You said there was a deal," Dawn prompted after a heartbeat's stunned silence. She needed to keep him talking, she told herself tensely. He'd just confirmed Aldrich Peters's belief that this wild-haired, bad-tempered old man whom some had dismissed as past his scholarly prime had made a breakthrough that would undoubtedly win him his second Nobel Prize…and in the process, save countless lives. *Including mine, Faith's and Lynn's,* she thought exultantly. *Sir William's main aim seems to be aging-reversal, which for an elderly man isn't surprising, but right now the regeneration process he's already discovered is a whole lot more relevant to me. Dammit, his notes might even be somewhere in this very room!*

"Ah, yes, my deal," London said with grim satisfaction. "I told the bastards at home that I'd insist this be a joint British-American venture…but only if Ash was put in charge of security here, instead of being left twisting in the wind while the Bah'lein affair was sorted out. They had no choice but to agree."

"You think when the facts come to light during Al-Jihr's trial Asher will be cleared?" She couldn't keep the faint note of skepticism from her voice. Sir William glared at her.

"Damn straight, as you say over here. And even if he's never officially cleared I won't believe he gave the order to murder those people. He's no more capable of acting dishonorably than you are of—of—" He sputtered to a stop. She supplied the rest of his sentence for him.

"Of being a cold-blooded assassin?" she suggested quietly.

He looked suddenly tired. "You think I'm a fool who refuses to face facts, don't you?"

She stifled the impulse to lean forward and clasp his hand. Dawn Swanson wouldn't make such a gesture, she reminded herself. Normally she wouldn't, either, but for some reason Sir William's staunch defense of his nephew had moved her.

That's touching, O'Shaughnessy—real touching. Go ahead and get all misty-eyed if you have to, but don't forget why you're here. The old man's got something you want…and no matter what you have to do to get it, you're not going back to Lab 33 without it.

Her inner voice was right, Dawn thought mutinously, but that didn't mean she couldn't offer some crumb of comfort to the troubled man sitting across from her.

"Of course I don't think you're a fool. My uncle always took my side in a fight, too," she said swiftly. "He used to tell me that even if it cost him everything he cared about in the world, he wouldn't ever stop fighting for me."

She halted, her lips still parted from the rush of words that had poured from some part of her she'd thought she'd cut out months ago. And she *had,* she protested with inner vehemence. The day she'd learned Lee Craig's real role in her upbringing, she'd unhesitatingly excised her life-long adoration of the man who'd pretended to care for her.

He'd vowed to protect her the best way he knew how, she thought, angrily quenching the pain that welled up in her. Had he thought he was keeping his vow by killing the mother she'd never known?

"That's how I feel about Asher." London raked a bony hand through his white hair, disarranging it still further. "Not that he'd thank me if he ever found out about my little deal." He laughed suddenly, and Dawn realized that the young Oxford genius in the famous photograph from so long ago still lurked below the surface of the respected and honored scientist he'd become. She pushed her own thoughts aside as he continued, an ironic gleam in his eyes. "He hates this assignment. Thinks of it as some kind of baby-sitting detail that he has to make the best of, which is probably why he's driving me up the wall with all his intolerable security measures. It would be like rubbing salt into a wound to tell him I arranged the whole bloody thing. Here, take a look at this."

He jumped from his chair with an alacrity that belied his years and hastened over to one of the oak book cases that lined the wall. Dawn surfaced from her somber mood of a moment ago. Whether he knew it or not, William London had already discovered the secret of not growing old. He had the mercurial enthusiasms of a child, and under that testy exterior was a boyish sense of humor. She liked him, she thought slowly. If she'd met him under different circumstances, this odd companionship that seemed to have sprung up between them might have developed into friendship.

"Where in damnation is Jancwiez's *Drosophila melanogaster Magnus: A Revolutionary New Look at the Sex Life of the Fruit Fly?*" muttered Sir William, running a finger impatiently along a row of volumes on one of the bookcase's shelves. "I chose that particular piece of drivel specifically because I knew I'd never take it down to look through it, and yet now it's not—ah, yes, here it is."

Roger's advice had paid off, Dawn thought as she watched London reach for the book. Even if she hadn't had the chance to bring up the subject of his notes, the rapport she'd established with Sir William made it possible to suggest they make these teatime meetings a regular occurrence. As his trust of her solidified over the next few days, he might actually let down his guard long enough to voluntarily reveal where he kept the research he wasn't yet ready to release to the world.

She hoped it worked out that way, she told herself uncomfortably. Because if it didn't, her only option would be to break into his rooms during his absence and search for the information Aldrich Peters had ordered her to—

Her worried thoughts came to a halt as she stared at Sir William. He'd placed the book she'd assumed he'd wanted to show her on a table beside him, but he was still standing with his back to her, his reaching hand moving counterclockwise inside the bookcase where he'd found the volume. Her keen hearing caught the faint but unmistakable *click* of tumblers falling into place, and then the old man gave a grunt of satisfaction.

"Here we are." He withdrew a slim metal box from the depths of the bookcase and turned to her. "I suppose Asher would have a fit if he knew about this photograph, too, but when he's been particularly officious it reminds me that he wasn't always that way."

As he spoke he opened the folio-size box and extracted from it a small snapshot. She took it from him, but although she kept her focus on the picture of a very young Destin Asher seated on a pony and bending forward to pat the animal's glossy neck, she was remembering another photograph, kept along with all else he valued, by a man who was now dead.

Sir William London and Lee Craig, the hit man known as Cipher, were two very different types. But it seemed likely that they had at least one trait in common, Dawn told herself. Just as Lee had secreted bearer bonds and cash and untraceable passports along with the picture of herself in his hidden safe, she was willing to bet that the photo of Ash wasn't the only treasured thing his uncle kept in the metal box now sitting on the table in front of him.

She'd found out where Sir William kept his notes on the regeneration process. Now all she had to do was steal them.

Chapter 9

Status: nine days and counting
Time: 0101 hours

"Hey, O'Shaughnessy, what're you wearing?" From the plastic bud nestled securely in Dawn's ear came Carter Johnson's voice. Dawn pressed her lips together in exasperation.

"Chanel No. 5. Eat your heart out, skater boy. Now put Kruger on again."

"Sorry about that, Dawn." The usually stolid-sounding tones of Hendrix Kruger were edged with irritation. "Five by five my end. How are you receiving me?"

"Same here. Five on the volume scale, five for clarity," Dawn answered, keeping her voice low. "Tell that jackass standing beside you that if he pulls any more stunts, I'm aborting this operation right here and now."

"One of my men is escorting the *moegoe* out as we speak." Kruger had never lost his South African accent or the habit of lapsing into Afrikaans slang when annoyed, although circumstances had forced him to leave Johannesburg years before. Dawn knew from Lee Craig that those circumstances included being the alarm-bypass member of a team that had pulled off a legendary heist of diamonds worth millions—a heist that should have eliminated the need for Kruger to practice his particular criminal specialty ever again, except for the fact that one member of his gang had hired a hit man to take out the others immediately following the caper.

Hendrix had escaped with his life, but not his share of the diamonds. Lee Craig had warned Dawn about him.

That big Aryan bastard's got it in for anyone in our profession, Dawnie. He might say he doesn't hold a grudge over the way things turned out, but take a look at his eyes sometime. They're as cold as the grave—and I think that's exactly where he'd like to put you and me if he ever has the chance. Keep it in mind when you work with him.

Like I don't have enough to worry about right now, Dawn thought as she pulled on a pair of black leather gloves. She flipped up the turtleneck of the zip-fronted black top she was wearing so that it covered more of her neck, bent to adjust her pants over her ankles, and slipped on the thin, rubber-soled shoes that were another recent and clandestine addition to her Dawn Swanson wardrobe. Finally she cast a quick glance over the tools attached to her hip belt and then tugged a face-and-hair-concealing balaclava over her head.

"Locked and loaded, Hendrix. I'll be in the air shaft for the next ten minutes, so when I get to the electrical room I'll check in with you again."

"Understood." There was a faint hiss of static in her ear, and then all sound from the tiny bud ceased as her contact with Hendrix Kruger and Lab 33 temporarily broke off.

She'd been a busy girl in the four and a half days since her conversation with Sir William London in his study, Dawn reflected as she hoisted herself up into the now-familiar shaft. Her first order of business had been to dial the number of the antiquarian bookstore that connected her to Aldrich Peters and inform him she suspected she'd located London's findings on the regeneration process. Peters's reaction had been predictable.

"Get solid confirmation that he keeps his notes in the box. Then kill him and come back here with them."

Her reply had been casual. "No problem, Doctor. It's not the way I thought you'd want to play it, but you're the boss. I'll probably see you late tomorrow—"

"Explain." Peters's one-word command had been icy. She'd injected a faint note of surprise into her voice.

"The buyback, of course. I assumed that once our people had a chance to study William's papers, you'd find a way to inform the government you'd sell them back to them. But you've got other plans, right? I mean, the feds might play ball with a thief, but not when a world-renowned Nobel Prize winner's been killed while he was under their protection."

There had been a moment of silence on the line. When Peters had spoken again his voice had been thoughtful. "You have a point. Since you're the agent-in-place, what alternative do you suggest?"

"Well…" She'd feigned dubiousness. "I suppose I could screw something up in the lab one evening and then bring it to the old man's attention. Knowing him, he'll stay there all night trying to figure out what went wrong. But, hell, your way's better, Doctor. The SAS prick who runs the security here does everything but land-mine the corridors after curfew each night. For one thing, there's a video monitor in every hallway to record all comings and goings. The only reason the cameras aren't live twenty-four/seven is because the old guy dug his heels in, said it was a gross violation of his staff's privacy. Asher had to be content with them going on at midnight, but even if I didn't have to worry about being seen on the monitors I'd still set off an alarm as soon as I tried to get into London's rooms. The lock works on a facial-features scan, plus a number code as soon as you're inside. I tell you, Des Asher's precautions make Fort Knox seem like the petty-cash box at a church bazaar. I'll pull off the job tomorrow afternoon when I have my next meeting with Sir—"

"The simplest solution would be to knock out the electrics and emergency power backup to the whole facility for the relevant time period," Peters said crisply. "I'll have Hendrix Kruger talk you through the procedure. You'll need equipment and communications, so I'm afraid it'll be necessary for you to make a brief trip to Lab 33 to collect everything. Shall we say the night after tomorrow? That will give Kruger time to gather information on the facility's system so that he can brief you beforehand and we'll schedule the actual operation for the night following your visit here."

Which might explain why I'm so damned sleepy that even this freakin' air shaft looks comfy to me right now, Dawn thought disgruntledly as she stifled a jaw-stretching yawn. *Sneaking out last night and jogging cross-country to where Peters had one of his people stash that ultralight plane for me, flying the little sucker to Lab 33 and staying there long enough to be briefed by Kruger before flying back again and slipping into my room just before daybreak didn't leave me with a whole lot of nap time.*

Just ahead of her the duct branched into two, and she was fleetingly tempted to take the branch that led to the roof and eventually to the delicious Private Reese's bed. She smiled ruefully to herself as she took the other branch. All other considerations aside, she would be drummed out of the female population of the world if she crawled under the covers with a babe like Lover Boy, only to waste the opportunity by promptly falling asleep.

Terry had surprised her. He'd been waiting for her at the east exit of the staff building sharply at seven o'clock on the day he'd spoken to her in Sir William's study. She hadn't shown herself, but instead had remained hidden behind one of the handy boulders dotting the grounds that she'd utilized previously. He'd been holding a second motorcycle helmet by its strap in his hand, and just for a moment she'd toyed with the reckless notion of giving the Swanson chick a night she'd never forget, but common sense had reasserted itself. After half an hour of waiting, Reese had looked at his watch with a wry smile, tossed the helmet to a red-haired female private who was going off duty, and with his lucky companion seated behind him on his Harley had peeled out of the gates a few minutes later. Dawn had wandered back into the building and had consoled herself with a couple of Marmite sandwiches in the cafeteria before heading back to the lab.

Since he hadn't tried to contact her since, it looked

like she'd blown it with Reese, she thought as she noise-lessly slid aside the vent cover that gave access to the electrical room. Within an hour or so she would be leaving this place behind, so it was unlikely their paths would ever cross again, but she would never forget him.

"And not just because of those dreamy indigo eyes of his, either," she murmured to herself as she set the vent cover aside, being careful not to strike metal against metal as she did so. "The man probably saved my life, showing up when he did. Although I guess it's really Asher I should thank," she added grudgingly, "since it was his message Terry was delivering to Sir William."

Unconsciously her hand went to the back of her neck. Was it her imagination, or was there still a tiny raised area from the massive exit path of the bullet that had torn through her throat? Although her regenerative powers had come back just in time, maybe they were no longer capable of completely removing all traces of a wound. She felt a sudden chill at the thought but, with an effort, pushed her fears away. From what Aldrich Peters had said, Lab 33's genetic team was only missing one critical part of the solution to her gene breakdown, so it wouldn't take long for them to make the serum once they had William London's notes in their possession. *Instead of worrying about your symptoms, try figuring out who the shooter outside Sir William's door might have been,* she told herself sharply. *He knew all about you, so he has to be someone you've gone up against in the past, someone who hates you enough to want you dead. The only other possible explanation is that he's what you once were—an assassin who's working for someone else. But whose hit list could you—*

About to lower herself through the vent, she suddenly

froze, words she'd read more than nine months ago
searing their way through her mind.

Subject actively working against the Cassandras;
must be considered extremely dangerous...

"*No.*" The instant denial came from her lips in an almost inaudible whisper. "The Cassandras couldn't be
trying to kill me. Not after they showed me the truth and
persuaded me to work on their side. Kayla Ryan treated
me as a friend, dammit—I can't believe she was lying
to me. I *won't* believe—"

I promise I'll always stay strong enough to keep them
from owning you—even if staying strong costs me ev-
erything I care for in this world.... When the man she'd
thought of as her uncle had made that vow to her, she'd
believed him, Dawn thought slowly. She'd unquestioningly believed everything Lee Craig had told her, and
some damned important things he'd told her had turned
out to be lies. If she'd learned one bitter lesson from the
experience, it had been that no one could be trusted.

And yet she'd given her trust to a group of women she
hardly knew—a group of women who had sent one of
their own to eliminate Lee Craig and who might well still
see her as an enemy whom CIA agent Samantha St. John
should rid them of. Again denial flashed instinctively
through her. She forced herself to focus on the facts.

There was a hit out on her—a hit that had come chill-
ingly close to success three days ago. The Cassandras had
reason to want revenge for the actions she'd taken against
them at the time when her loyalty had been to Lab 33. And
except for Aldrich Peters and a handful of his people, the
women who had professed themselves her friends were
the only ones who knew she was here—Dawn had told
Kayla where to look for her if there was an emergency.

And finally, the Cassandras included Sam St. John, a trained operative who was one of the few professionals whose lethal talents might prove to be a match for her own. They'd been a match for Lee Craig's.

But now wasn't the time to analyze the possibility that she'd been betrayed by those she'd trusted, Dawn admitted coldly to herself. She was in the middle of an operation that would require all her skill, nerve and attention, and if any of those necessary components were lacking during the next hour, there was a good chance Des Asher would have her behind bars before the night was over.

It's almost a pleasure going up against Mr. SAS, she thought grimly as she gave a cautionary glance into the small anteroom below her before dropping silently to the floor. *At least he's never made any secret of the fact that we're on opposite—*

"Amber? With a sexy name like that, I bet you're a real knockout, right? So, uh, what are you wearing, Amber?"

What she was hearing from the room just beyond her was so much like an echo of Carter's earlier infantile query that for a split second Dawn was confused. Then she reacted.

"Kruger! Are you reading me, Kruger?" she asked hoarsely as she dodged down behind some metal shelving. "I've got a situation here, do you copy?"

"I copy, Dawn." Hendrix Kruger's accented voice sounded in her ear. "What kind of situation?"

"I'm in the outer entrance to the electrical room," she answered tersely. "You know, the electrical room that isn't supposed to have anyone in it at this hour? Well, guess what—it's got an occupant, and from what I can hear, said occupant's a lonely soldier on a phone sex line. I'm going to have to try again tomorrow night, dammit."

Too late she realized how out-of-character her agitated pronouncement would sound to the South African. Hastily she tried to think of some acceptable reason for her decision to delay, but before she could, Kruger's voice was in her ear again.

"Why not simply kill him now?" There was an edge of puzzlement to his tone, but it was shadowed with something else she couldn't immediately define. "That's what you assassins do, don't you? You kill people. Then you wash the blood from your hands, fall into bed and sleep as soundly as if you had merely swatted a fly. That's what your *onkle* Lee taught you. That's what he did until the day his own blood ended up being spilled, am I right?"

She knew what was in Kruger's tone, Dawn thought, a sliver of anger piercing her worry. It was hatred. Lee Craig had been right—Hendrix Kruger, Lab 33 criminal that he was himself, had been glad to see the Cipher killed and he would be equally glad to witness her death…as long as he could protest to Aldrich Peters that he had nothing to do with it. She controlled her sudden revulsion and answered him evenly.

"You got that right, buddy. Say, I never did hear what happened to that diamond-heist pal of yours who tried to have you bumped off. He got away with the whole score, didn't he? Is he living the life of Riley in some tropical paradise, with servants and yachts and beautiful women, while you're still working like a dog to make a dishonest buck, or what?" She heard the South African's indrawn breath, and put a shrug in her voice. "But hey, that's your business and you probably don't like talking about it…just like I'm not real crazy when you talk about my business. You catch my drift, Kruger?"

"You talk like your uncle." His voice shook slightly, and then steadied. "Yah, I understand. We stick to the job at hand from now on, agreed?"

"Agreed," she answered flatly. "And like I said, we've got a problem with the job at hand. Aldrich Peters doesn't want anything screwing up his chances of making a deal with the government after Lab 33's finished with the material I'm here to steal, and killing anyone who crosses my path is the fastest way to screw up I can think of. I guess I'm just going to have to put Mr. Lonelyhearts temporarily out of action."

"Don't forget there is a time line on this op, Dawn," Hendrix warned stiffly. "Every hour on the hour an outside probe automatically checks the systems. There is nothing I can do to circumvent that, so if the power is still down at two o'clock the secondary override response will be deployed. It's now—" he broke off briefly, and Dawn realized he was checking a chronometer "—now 0114 hours."

"And here I was thinking you didn't care," she drawled. "Don't worry, I'll be quick as a bunny."

Once again the plastic disc in her ear went silent as Kruger abruptly switched his end of communications into receive-only mode. Rising from her crouching position behind the shelving, she moved to the door that led from the anteroom to the electrical control room. It was open a crack. Carefully she pushed it open a little more and peered through.

"A college student? Gee, it doesn't seem right, you having to do this type of work just to put yourself through school. What are you taking?"

Dawn felt a twinge of compunction for what she was about to do. The young Ranger sitting at the electrical console with his back to her and his cell phone clutched to his ear had to be straight off the hay wagon if he was falling for the old "co-ed trying to get an education" ploy, she thought pityingly. On the other hand, she was probably doing him a favor, she reflected, opening the door enough to slip through. Not that she had firsthand knowledge, but it was her understanding that 1-900 calls racked up big bucks on a credit card pretty darn fast…and from what she'd heard of the conversation so far the poor guy certainly wasn't getting his money's worth.

"Nursing, huh?" Oblivious to her stealthy approach behind him, the Ranger sounded suddenly intrigued. "So are you wearing, like, a nurse's uniform right now? You know, the white stockings, one of those cute little nurse's caps—"

"I gotta hand it to you, buddy, you certainly have a healthy imagination," Dawn said dryly as she lowered his unconscious body to the floor. "Tell you what— imagine that the karate chop I just gave you was a love tap, and maybe you'll get a good dream out of this whole incident. Remember—hot nurses, white stockings held up with frilly garter belts, you're the husky patient getting a sponge bath." She retrieved his cell phone from where it had fallen beside him and started to tuck it in his pocket, but on impulse she brought it to her ear. "You still there, college girl?" she asked perfunctorily. "Don't look now, but I think your tuition just got cut off."

She terminated the call and dragged the Ranger to the far side of the room, propping his limp body against the wall before returning to the console he'd been seated in front of. She swiveled the chair he'd been using so that it faced the console. A bewildering array of knobs and dials and switches confronted her, and she took a deep breath.

"Tower, the pilot's just had a heart attack and I don't know how to fly this thing," she said under her breath. "You'll have to talk me down, do you hear? You're gonna have to talk me—"

"I don't copy you, O'Shaughnessy." Kruger's voice coming over the earpiece sounded confused. "Who had a heart attack and what do you mean, I must fly down? If you are calling for Lab 33 reinforcements, I should contact Dr. Peters before authorizing a team to—"

Besides being a vengeful jerk, the man had zero sense of humor, Dawn thought in disgust. She sat forward in the chair, surveying the console. "Don't mind me, Hendrix, I just had a lapse into disaster-movie mode for a second. Now, what do I do to shut down the power to this place without a whole bunch of alarms suddenly going off?"

Sense of humor or not, when it came to his own specialty Kruger was the best, she told herself six minutes later. He'd walked her through every step of the complicated procedure as easily as if he'd been sitting beside her, his answers to her occasional worried questions patiently unruffled...up until now.

"Wait!" There was an edge of nervousness to his command.

She paused, the pair of wire cutters she was holding poised to snip through a final connection. "What's the problem? You said cut the red one, right?"

"Repeat the sequence to me once more. Green, red, yellow—"

"Yellow, then two whites, a kind of mauve wire, and

one that I guess I'd call tan." She squinted at the tangle of wires. "Or maybe olive? Some kind of blah shade, anyway, but I'll go with tan."

"You described the wire after the two white ones as mauve." For the first time since he'd started giving her instructions Kruger seemed less than confident. "Mauve is pale orange, yah?"

Dawn felt beads of sweat pop instantly out on her brow. "Negative, repeat, negative, Hendrix. Is this a language thing or a guy thing? Mauve is pinky-purple. Pale orange is freakin' pale orange. Any other decorating questions?"

"Then the sequence should have been yellow, two whites, *lilac* and olive," he said, his tone a clear indicator that he was mopping his own brow. "Lilac everybody understands. It's like the flower. Cut the yellow wire."

Gingerly she opened the jaws of the wire snips and released the casing of the red wire. Her jaw set, she moved the tool to the yellow wire, tightened her grip and paused.

"You're absolutely sure this time?"

Kruger's confidence had returned. "Of course I am sure, Dawn," he said expansively. "Go ahead and cut."

She held her breath and cut. At the exact moment the blades in her hand sliced through the wire, the brightly lit room plunged into blackness.

Chapter 10

Status: nine days and counting
Time: 0122 hours

"Did it work?" Hendrix Kruger's query was tentative, and at it, Dawn snapped.

"Did it *work?* What the hell kind of question is that, dammit? Yeah, it worked—the lights are out, anyway."

"…eight, nine, ten." Seemingly oblivious to her irritation, he followed the last number with an expectant pause. "The backup system hasn't come on?"

"Did you hear me say *oh crap, what now?*" she asked impatiently. "No, the backup system hasn't come on, Kruger. That means the alarms are disabled as well, right?"

"For another thirty-seven minutes and eleven seconds," he informed her. "Don't forget, at two o'clock—"

"Yeah, at two o'clock all hell breaks loose." She pulled on the night-vision goggles slung around her neck and adjusted the refracting lenses. The room became visible again, although everything around her looked greenish and ghostly, including the still-unconscious Ranger in the corner. "Since I won't be needing your help for the rest of this operation, I'm closing down this comm-channel now. Been swell doing business with you, Hendrix."

Not, Dawn thought with a grimace as she moved surefootedly past the Ranger and into the adjoining anteroom. She opened the door to the main corridor and glanced out before setting off with a frown toward the part of the building where Sir William's rooms were.

Whether or not the Cassandras had betrayed her, they'd done her one massive favor: they'd given her a reason to break free of Lab 33 and the people she worked with there. Kruger was far from being the worst of the lot, but her interaction with him tonight had shown her just how alienated from her former profession she'd become.

"Which leaves me with the question of what I'm supposed to do with the rest of my life," she muttered as she came within sight of her destination. "I don't think I have what it takes to be a kindergarten teacher or a librarian, and with my résumé the federal agencies wouldn't want to touch me with a ten-foot pole, much less offer me a job. But retiring at twenty-two sucks, dammit. I've got at least fifty more years to go before I'm ready to start lining up for early-bird bingo."

And those fifty years depended on her movements in the next thirty minutes, she reminded herself as she came to a halt in front of Sir William's door. Just inside was her only chance for survival—his notes on the re-generation process, secreted away in his bookcase safe. As luck would have it, when she'd shown up on some pretext yesterday afternoon London had been perusing them, and although he'd hastily gathered them up and returned them to the safe when she'd walked in, she'd seen enough to get the confirmation Aldrich had required. Dawn reached for one of the smaller items on her belt, a tool that would be enough to land her butt in jail if she were ever caught with it in her possession, and squatted down to work on the lock.

It was a tedious job, made more so by the unwieldy night-vision goggles. During her brief visit to Lab 33 the night before, she'd decided against using a penlight; her reasoning being that a beam of light, no matter how minuscule, would be too dangerously noticeable in a pitch-black building.

She cursed as the pick slipped for the second time in as many minutes. A penlight would help, but it would be visible if anyone happened by. So far she'd only had a near miss with two lab technicians who'd almost blundered into her in the corridor on her way to London's office. Still, she couldn't be too careful.

Presumably the military personnel had been roused to post extra guards while they tried to get the power up and running again, but at that time of night most of Sir William's staff were asleep. In fact, the old guy was probably all alone in the lab right now, cursing the darkness and trying to figure out how his latest experiment got contaminated.

Behind the goggles her gaze darkened briefly in compunction. In the short time she'd known him, she'd grown to like William London and, despite his irasci-

bility, she knew the feeling was mutual. Now she was
about to betray him by stealing his research and handing it over to Lab 33.

"What option do I have?" Angrily she maneuvered
the pick into the lock mechanism. "Walk up to him and
say, 'Oh, by the way, I happen to be a genetic mutant
and I could sure use your regeneration method right
about now, mind if I borrow these notes?' Nice old guy
or not, there's a damn good chance his scientific curiosity would get the better of him and the next thing I'd
know, I'd be waking up strapped to a table with a bunch
of white-coated freaks shoving needles into me. So this
is the only—"

Her muttered diatribe broke off as she felt the pick
lift the tumblers inside the lock. Unconsciously holding
her breath, she delicately turned the doorknob.

The door swung open.

Replacing the pick in her belt, she rose from her
squatting position and strode into Sir William's deserted
study, making sure the door locked again behind her as
she entered. It had seemed cozy and untidily comfortable the previous times she'd been here, she thought
with a frown. But the greenish hue from the night-vision lenses robbed the room of its familiarity and turned
its shabbiness into unsettling disorder.

"And if you were here to do a *While You Were Out*
makeover that might actually be relevant," she said
under her breath as she circumvented the oak table with
its resident rodent's skull and made her way to the wall
of bookcases. "But this is a B & E, in case you've forgotten. All you need to worry about is cracking that safe,
finding the information that's going to save the lives of
you and your sisters, and getting the hell out of here

within the next—" she glanced at her watch "—twenty-four minutes. So focus, dammit."

Her time limit had dwindled to thirteen minutes when she finally set the folio-size box in which Sir William kept his treasures on the oak table. She took a moment to roll her shoulders free of the tense kinks that had settled in them during her unexpectedly prolonged efforts to break into the safe. *Who would have guessed an eccentric old Englishman would even know such a thing as a Rose-Jackman Commander Mark IV existed, let alone have one installed,* she thought in outrage. *R-J's are the crème de la crème of unbreakable safes, and most of the stuff London keeps in it could be stored in a discarded cigar box, for God's sake. What do you wanna bet the ever-meddlesome Destin Asher insisted on the Mark IV?*

But Asher hadn't counted on a woman with super hearing listening for the Rose-Jackman's normally inaudible clicks as she spun the safe's dial, just as he hadn't counted on her bringing down his whole security system so that the keypad and scan features of the entrance into his uncle's study were useless. He hadn't been the challenging opponent she'd anticipated he'd be, Dawn thought with passing regret as she set aside the photo of a young Ash on his pony. And she'd never had the opportunity to go one-on-one with him as she'd hoped.

"Not that I've got any doubts as to what the outcome of that little tussle would be," she said out loud, leafing quickly through documents, newspaper clippings about Sir William's investiture, older clippings about his Nobel Prize win. "But it would have been interesting to see how the SAS trains its men to fight. Being English, it wouldn't surprise me if they stick to no hitting below the belt, no kicking, no—"

Experimental Results and Conclusions on Tissue and Life-Support Systems Regeneration in Humans. The title of the thick sheaf of bound and typewritten notes she was holding said it all. Dawn felt a curious tightness in her chest, and for one stricken moment she wondered if it signaled the onset of her symptoms. Then she gave a shaky laugh.

"You're just excited, O'Shaughnessy, and for good reason. What you've got here is a revocation of three death sentences—yours, Faith's and Lynn's. No wonder your heart's going pitty-pat."

She glanced at her watch. Eleven minutes remaining. It was ample time to make her escape from the building, avoid the extra guards that would be posted around the temporarily out-of-order electrified perimeter fence, and be well on her way before the power came back on. She began to close the box preparatory to returning it to the wall safe, and then froze.

"…questioned him like you said, but the kid swears he doesn't know anything more than he's already told us. He'd been working in the electrical room yesterday, he found he'd lost the St. Jude medal he wears, and he went in there to see if it had fallen onto the floor by his workstation. When everything suddenly went dark he slipped and hit his head."

The low voice was Keifer's and it was coming from halfway down the hall. Impatiently Dawn removed the plastic communications device from her ear. Without the tiny blockage her enhanced senses could now pick up the sound of three pairs of booted feet heading her way.

"Oh, crap, what do I do now?" she muttered, echoing her earlier comment to Hendrix. The pace of the approaching boots was too sure and swift to be the sound

An Important Message
from the Editors

Dear Reader,

If you'd enjoy reading romance novels with larger print that's easier on your eyes, let us send you *TWO FREE HARLEQUIN INTRIGUE® NOVELS* in our *NEW LARGER-PRINT EDITION*. These books are complete and unabridged, but the type is set about 25% bigger to make it easier to read. Look inside for an actual-size sample.

By the way, you'll also get a surprise gift with your two free books!

Pam Powers

eel off Seal and

Place Inside...

THE RIGHT WOMAN

she'd thought she was fine. It took Daniel's words and Brooke's question to make her realize she was far from a full recovery.

She'd made a start with her sister's help and she intended to go forward now. Sarah felt as if she'd been living in a darkened room and someone had suddenly opened a door, letting in the fresh air and sunshine. She could feel its warmth slowly seeping into the coldest part of her. The feeling was liberating. She realized it was only a small step and she had a long way to go, but she was ready to face life again with Serena and her family behind her.

All too soon, they were saying goodbye and Sarah experienced a moment of sadness for all the years she and Serena had missed. But they had each other now, and that's what ed

She held

PRINTED IN THE U.S.A.
Publisher acknowledges the copyright holder of the excerpt from this individual work as follows:
THE RIGHT WOMAN Copyright © 2004 by Linda Warren. All rights reserved.
® and TM are trademarks owned and used by the trademark owner and/or its licensee.

YOURS FREE!

You'll get a great mystery gift with your two free larger-print books!

GET TWO FREE LARGER-PRINT BOOKS!

YES! Please send me two free Harlequin Intrigue® romantic suspense novels in the larger-print edition, and my free mystery gift, too. I understand that I am under no obligation to purchase anything, as explained on the back of this insert.

PLACE FREE GIFTS SEAL HERE

199 HDL D4CJ

399 HDL D4CK

FIRST NAME

LAST NAME

ADDRESS

APT.#

CITY

STATE/PROV.

ZIP/POSTAL CODE

Are you a current Harlequin Intrigue® subscriber and want to receive the larger-print edition?

Call 1-800-221-5011 today!

Offer limited to one per household. All orders subject to approval. Credit or debit balances in a customer's account(s) may be offset by any other outstanding balance owed by or to the customer.

▼ DETACH AND MAIL CARD TODAY! ▼

(H-ILPS-03/05) © 2004 Harlequin Enterprises Ltd.

The Harlequin Reader Service™ — Here's How It Works:

Accepting your 2 free Harlequin Intrigue® larger-print books and gift places you under no obligation to buy anything. You may keep the books and gift and return the shipping statement marked "cancel." If you do not cancel, about a month later we'll send you 6 additional Harlequin Intrigue larger-print books and bill you just $4.49 each in the U.S., or $5.24 each in Canada, plus 25¢ shipping & handling per book and applicable taxes if any.* That's the complete price and — compared to cover prices of $5.24 each in the U.S. and $6.24 each in Canada — it's quite a bargain! You may cancel at any time, but if you choose to continue, every month we'll send you 6 more books, which you may either purchase at the discount price or return to us and cancel your subscription.

*Terms and prices subject to change without notice. Sales tax applicable in N.Y. Canadian residents will be charged applicable provincial taxes and GST.

If offer card is missing write to: Harlequin Reader Service, 3010 Walden Ave., P.O. Box 1867, Buffalo, NY 14240-1867

BUSINESS REPLY MAIL
FIRST-CLASS MAIL   PERMIT NO. 717-003   BUFFALO, NY

POSTAGE WILL BE PAID BY ADDRESSEE

HARLEQUIN READER SERVICE
3010 WALDEN AVE
PO BOX 1867
BUFFALO NY 14240-9952

NO POSTAGE
NECESSARY
IF MAILED
IN THE
UNITED STATES

of men picking their way through the dark, so Keifer and those with him obviously had a flashlight. They would see her as soon as she exited this room.

"Uh, Lieutenant?" If she didn't get her butt in gear, there was a possibility she might get one final meeting with Lover Boy after all, Dawn thought as she recognized Reese's voice. She pulled up her sweater, jammed Sir William's notes into the waistband of her pants and hastily began shoving the rest of his papers into the box she'd taken them from as Reese went on. "Private Jones had a cell phone on him. I checked the last number dialed to see if he'd used it to call the guard shack when the power went out. Uh, it looks like he was on one of those phone-sex lines at the time whatever happened to him occurred, sir."

"Bloody hell."

Dawn's heart sunk. The third man *would* have to be Mr. SAS, she thought, closing the box and hastening to the open safe at the back of the bookcase. That eliminated any hope that Keifer, Reese and Asher were only passing by Sir William's study on their way to another part of the building. If Asher was heading this way, it wasn't coincidence, it was because of his single-minded determination to carry out his mission of keeping William London's work under his eagle eye. Any minute now he would come through the door and she would be caught like a rat in a trap.

Only if this rat tried to get out of the trap the same way she came in, she thought as she quietly closed the safe and gave the dial a random spin. *Luckily, I don't have to.*

"He tells you he went into the electrical room to look for a religious medal when the truth is he went in there to get his rocks off. Lying about one thing means he's probably lying about everything, Keifer." Asher's growl was disgusted. "Since Jones swore up and down he fell and knocked himself out after the lights went off, we've been assuming this power outage was a systems failure, but now we'd better proceed on the possibility he was coldcocked before the grid went down."

"Sabotage?" Keifer sounded alarmed.

"That's what I want you and Reese to look for evidence of," Asher confirmed grimly. "How much longer till the outside failsafe kicks in, ten minutes?"

"Eight, sir." The reply came from Reese.

"That's too long." Asher's footsteps paused. Dawn crossed the study to the heavy velvet draperies and pulled them apart. A large, fairly narrow picture window stretched nearly from floor to ceiling. She grasped the window's lever-style iron latch. "Keifer, take Reese and head on back to the electrical room right away. Here, you'll need my flashlight. I'll join you as soon as I tell Sir William what's happening."

Dawn paused in the act of easing up the latch. Her supposition had been wrong. Asher wasn't coming in to check that the safe was secure, he was just here to let his uncle know what was going on, unaware of the fact that London wasn't in his rooms. After a perfunctory check he would guess that the old man was in the lab, and leave.

Still, to be on the safe side I'd better follow through with my plan of leaving by the window, she told herself with a shrug. *It's only a two-story drop, and it'll cut my escape time in half.* She put slightly more pressure on the latch, not wanting to force it in case it gave way with a crash.

"Don't worry, I've got a penlight." There was faint impatience now in Asher's tone. "If it was sabotage, I want to know as soon as possible, Keifer."

Dawn didn't listen to the Ranger lieutenant's response. The damned latch was painted shut, she realized in exasperation. One quick jerk would release it, but the sound of screeching metal would be a pretty good tip-off to Asher that someone was in London's study. She adjusted her grip and began to try again as Keifer's and Reese's footsteps receded down the hall and the jingle of keys came from outside the door.

The latch remained stubbornly in place. She heard the sound of a key turning in the door. The tiny beam of a penlight suddenly appeared at the threshold of Sir William's study and SAS Captain Des Asher stepped into the room.

Immediately he headed for the adjoining bedroom, but as he drew level with the oak table he came to an abrupt halt, swinging the penlight's beam across the carpet, up to the table, over to the bookcases. The bright pinpoint jumped suddenly to the velvet drapes at the window...but Dawn was no longer there.

Your freakin' light's nearly blinding me, buddy, Dawn thought testily from her vantage point near the ceiling. *For your information, I'm wearing night-vision lenses and they're magnifying that penlight until it's like staring straight at an eclipse. How long do you intend to keep flashing it around, dammit?*

As if he'd heard her complaint, Asher turned on his heel and continued on his way to the bedroom. She took the opportunity to quickly strengthen her foothold on the slim molding that ran along the top of the wall and brace her arms more rigidly on the smooth surface of the ceiling, but her adjustments didn't make the position any more comfortable. It was with a feeling of relief that she saw the bobbing beam of the penlight precede Asher out of the bedroom.

This time she was ready for it, squinting through her lashes to cut the dazzle. Her half-closed gaze caught the expression of annoyance on his face as he passed diagonally below her, but it took a second for her to realize what had caused his frown.

Then she understood. The penlight's beam faded from white to yellow to a dim amber, and died completely.

"Crap, what now?" Asher muttered in the dark.

He was a man after her own heart, Dawn thought with a rueful smile. He even reacted the same way she did. It was a damn shame she was going to have to take him down, but she'd run out of options. Her window of opportunity was dwindling to a handful of minutes, and she couldn't afford to use them up waiting for him to find his way out of this room.

As she'd noted the first time she'd seen him, he had the longer reach and superior height. She had the advantage of surprise, and the best way to utilize that advantage would be to eliminate his edge over her from the start. *Dropping down onto the desk takes care of the height thing and also puts me up close and personal with him right away, so his reach actually works against him,* Dawn calculated. *The last thing he'll feel before he wakes up a couple of hours from now is the edge of my hand instantly numbing the main pressure point at the back of his neck. It'll be quick and easy, O'Shaughnessy, so let's rock and roll.*

He was fumbling in one of the pockets of his fatigues, but his slightly bent position didn't affect her game plan. She felt the familiar pump of adrenaline surge through her the way it always did before a burst of action, and then she was launching herself downward like a tensely coiled spring that had suddenly been released.

The thin rubber soles of her shoes made contact with the desktop. Asher's head jerked up and for a fragment of a second she saw his eyes widen as he saw the goggles-wearing apparition that had materialized in front of him. Her hand started to slice through the air to make contact with the exact spot near the base of his skull that would instantaneously fell him like a tree crashing to the ground, and then all at once everything went terribly wrong.

"Arghh!" As the scream tore from her throat Dawn's palms flew involuntarily to her face to shield her eyes from the supernova that had just burst into existence in front of them.

"What the—" Asher's hoarse shout was almost as explosive as the searing greenish white light that streamed from his hand.

She couldn't see! Acting on desperate instinct, she twisted her body into a semi-pivot, jackknifing her right leg close to her torso as she turned. As her spin reached its apex, her leg shot out heel first, aiming for the core of the agonizing light. She felt her foot connect like a sledgehammer with Asher's clenched hand, and a burning image sketched its way in an arc across her tightly closed eyelids.

"—hell?" Asher finished in shock as he fought to keep his balance.

He'd broken open a phosphorescent light-stick, Dawn told herself. It hadn't been a supernova, but dammit, it had appeared like one through the ultrasensitive lenses of the goggles she was wearing. Her kick had sent it flying from his grip halfway across the room where seemingly it had rolled to rest under a piece of furniture, because her closed eyelids were no longer seared with the image of a blazing core. But with the afterimage branded onto her retinas, it was still impossible for her to do more than lift her lashes just enough to see what Asher was doing.

Although the stick itself was somewhere out of sight, the room was filled with a sickly white light that hit her eyes like acid. Without thinking, she reached for the goggles to wrench them from her face.

"Right, then, you bastard." Asher's tone was savage. "Let's get that bloody contraption off you and see just who the hell you are…and then we'll proceed to the part about what you're doing here, shall we?"

He hadn't guessed her identity. The realization came to her with his words, forcing a lightning-swift decision upon her: to rid herself of the now-hampering goggles so her sight could return to normal at the cost of revealing her eyes to Asher; or keep them on and fight him without the benefit of total vision. He was going to know who'd stolen Sir William's notes as soon as her absence from the facility was discovered anyway, she told herself, again reaching for the strap around the back of her head.

This business we're in isn't like a rigged horse race, Dawnie. Lee Craig's voice flashed through her mind before she could push it away. *There aren't any sure bets. So the only way to even the odds in your favor is to have a contingency plan, because you never know when it might save your butt.*

She was going to get out of here, no problem…but

what if she didn't? She needed to keep the Dawn Swanson persona intact, she thought in resignation. Which meant she was going to have to keep the freakin' goggles—

"Kwa-sah!" The phrase exploded from her in a hissed whisper as Asher's hand clamped around her left leg to pull her off the desk. Dawn's mind instantly emptied to allow pure instinct to take over…instinct honed from childhood onward by years of dedicated training received from some of the most exacting masters of the art of battle. *"Hai!"* She grunted out the exclamation as she allowed her trapped leg to be jerked forward, at the same time using the SAS man's grip as a platform from which to propel herself into the air. *"Che-sah!"*

As the last whispered syllables left her lips, the rubber sole of her right shoe smashed brutally into Asher's chin, snapping his head back and breaking his hold on her. She didn't wait for his reaction. Letting the upward momentum of her kick continue, she arched her body into a midair flip that took her backward past the desk. She landed lightly on the floor behind it and went unhesitatingly into a crouch, her outstretched fingers closing around the thick oak edge of the desktop. She rose again, this time using her momentum to tip the heavy piece of furniture forward and hurl it at an advancing Asher.

It should have crashed into him. *Oh, you're good, sweetie,* she thought in reluctant admiration as she saw the big man throw himself sideways, the desk merely grazing his thigh as he hit the floor in a paratrooper-style roll. *But right now you're down. Sorry, but I'm going to take advantage of that.*

She needed to get past him to the door. She knew it and he knew it, and as soon as she tried to rush him he would be ready for her, so she did the exact opposite of what she assumed he was expecting.

"Consider yourself under military arrest, mister," Asher growled as she took a step back. "If you resist any further, I'll be forced—"

She hit the wall beside him running, and kept running up it. Just as gravity started to claim her and she felt her rubber soles begin sliding down the wall again, she twisted her body so that she was no longer facing the ceiling, but for a second seemed to be defying all laws of physics and standing straight out from the wall.

But only for a second. Thrusting herself from the wall, she brought both feet up as her leap projected her within reach of him, intending to knock him back down as he struggled to his knees with a variation of her earlier kick.

"Hell, do you think I'm so bloody stupid that you get to use the same trick twice?"

Instead of trying to stand, he'd unexpectedly dropped to the floor like a man doing push-ups. Dawn heard his mutter but she was too busy attempting to correct her trajectory to take it in, now that the solid wall of Des Asher that she'd counted on to halt her wasn't there. She failed. Her balance compromised, she landed awkwardly on the floor, tumbled once, and slid to a jolting stop against the leg of the round oak table just in time to see him spring to his feet and face her.

He'd outmaneuvered her. The realization disconcerted her for a moment, but disconcertion was a luxury she didn't have time to indulge in, she saw immediately. Asher's booted foot was already swinging in a brutal chopping arc toward her, with enough power behind it that if she allowed it to connect, it would send her halfway across the floor.

No hitting below the belt? No kicking? Boy, was I wrong about the training these SAS bastards get, she thought, illogically aggrieved. *He fights like me, dammit!*

She spun out of the way of his boot, feeling a rush of air as it passed over her. Now he was the one temporarily off balance, and she wasted no time in using his momentary vulnerability against him. Lightly jumping up, she again instantaneously assessed all the possible moves he might expect from her and chose the one he would consider least likely.

Her rush forward took her to within inches of him—which was a whole lot like running straight into the path of a Mack truck, Dawn thought as she experienced the fleeting impression of his muscular bulk looming over her before she back-slammed a braced elbow up and under his rib cage. She heard the harsh exhalation of his breath somewhere above her, but already she had grabbed the gleaming leather of his military-issue belt and was jerking him closer. Even as his hand began to clamp around her wrist she was twisting free and moving slightly to one side of him, using her grip on his belt to wrench him more off balance as she brought her knee crashing into the base of his spine.

No shame in crying uncle now, buddy, she told him silently as she heard the whistle of pain that escaped his tight lips. *I know what you're going through, believe me, because it's happened to me once or twice in a fight. There's a whole bunch of nerve endings right there, and every single one of those little suckers feels like it's on fire, doesn't it? So if you want to call it a day, I'll understand. If you don't, all your stubbornness is going to buy you is a couple seconds' more punishment.*

"Bloody hell, that *does* it!" Pain thickened his voice,

and even with her inadequate vision Dawn could see the same pain carved deep into his features. His gaze blazed with fury, and like a bear tormented beyond endurance, he swung one big hand toward her, his knuckles bunched into a fist.

She had plenty of time to dodge back out of reach. She began to do so, felt something solid impede her and realized that with the goggles hampering her depth of field she'd miscalculated her location in relation to the oak table. Quickly she tried to change her step back into a slip sideways. It all took just a fraction of a second too long.

Asher's uppercut hit her like a battering ram, catching her under the point of her chin. Her head snapped back on her neck with the force of his blow, and the sharp, coppery taste of blood immediately filled her mouth. She felt her feet leave the floor, felt herself start to fall backward, began windmilling her arms desperately to regain her balance.

"Nothing fancy, but it gets the job done," Asher said, his voice hoarse with anger. "Although I wouldn't want you to think that exotic crap you go in for is beyond me, you sorry son of a bitch, so before I finish this off by unsportingly pulling my gun on you, I'll give you a demonstration."

The words were still leaving his lips as he pivoted so that he was no longer facing her, but turned side-on toward her. At the same time he drew one booted foot close to his body, his palms now rigidly flat and held close to his chest. The leg he had drawn up shot out like a piston just as Dawn found stability. As it blurred toward her she stiff-armed it aside and lunged at him.

Now I'm mad, she told herself. *My lip's split wide-*

open, I nearly fell on my keister like a kid trying on her
first pair of skates, and to add insult to injury, he has the
nerve to let me know that he's held off using his gun be-
cause it's not sporting! The man's un-freakin'-believable!

She drove her first punch directly into his solar
plexus, her second and third finding the same target. As
Asher doubled over, her gloved fists moved upward, one
blow glancing jarringly off his right cheekbone. But by
then he had her rhythm. Blood streaming from a cut over
his eye, he waded in toward her and wrapped one heavily muscled arm around her shoulders, dragging her
close to him as if they were engaged in some deadly and
antagonistic kind of dance.

"Tea party's over, mate," he ground out. His mouth
was only inches from her ear, and his breath felt warm
against her skin. Dawn let herself go limp, felt his hold
relax, and then brought her knee up in a deliberately un-
sporting move. Her aim was true but he twisted at the
last moment, and her kneecap jarred achingly against
his thighbone. Asher's one-armed bear hug became
crushing, his free hand going swiftly to the Sig Sauer
strapped to his hip. "Like I said before, you're under
military arrest, not civilian, so don't hold your breath
waiting for me to read you your bloody rights. All I have
to tell you is this gun's pointed straight at you and my
finger's on the trigger, so put your hands on your head
and slowly—"

He hadn't needed to spell it out for her, Dawn thought
angrily. She could feel the muzzle of his Sig jammed
into her rib cage and if she flicked her glance downward
she could even see it, his finger on the trigger as he'd
promised. She could see his watch, too, the dial worn
on the inside of his wrist, the little hand pointing at two,

the big hand almost straight up, the sweep hand count-ing the few seconds remaining until—

Until her mission could be considered officially blown. The sweep hand's countdown was at ten... nine...eight... Exploding into action, she made a grab for the gun, felt her gloved hand wrap around the cross-hatched grip and began to wrest it away from Asher.

At the six-second mark it went off and a nine-milli-meter parabellum slug tore through the outer wall of her heart.

Chapter 11

Status: nine days and counting
Time: 0159 hours

Everything seemed to be happening in slow motion, even to the passage of the bullet through her body, Dawn thought dazedly. She could feel it continue on its way, knew it had missed her spine by a hairbreadth, felt it punch through her back. Then it was out of her but still moving. Two wings of velvet briefly enveloped her and fell away—Sir William's heavy draperies, she guessed, billowing out at the sides in reaction to the force of the projectile that had slammed through the center of them. At the same time she heard the icy sound of glass shattering as the window she hadn't been able to open earlier was blown out. She looked down at herself. She could see perfectly now, she realized, which meant that the light-stick had finally sputtered and died, giving her this final split second of darkness.

This is the experiment Aldrich always wanted to conduct, the one experiment Uncle Lee threatened to kill him over if he ever tried to carry it out on me, she thought, seeing the dark stain spreading rapidly across her shredded sweater and the thick globules dropping to the floor, some of them spattering the edges of the sheaf of papers that had fallen from the waistband of her pants when she'd been shot. *Peters wanted to know if I could survive a bullet to the heart. In a moment I'll have the answer to his question.*

"Dammit, man, it didn't have to end this way!" Asher's expression was appalled, his tone stricken. "What the hell were you thinking, going for my gun when I told you—"

She could feel it deep inside her. The process had already begun, her tissues beginning to knit themselves perfectly together again. The answer to Aldrich Peters's question was *yes*. Lab 33's lab rat could survive a shot to the heart. But could Lab 33's lab rat escape the trap she was in…the trap that was about to spring shut right about—

Now! Dawn ordered herself sharply.

Even as she wrenched off the goggles and threw herself backward, time began speeding up again, fast-forwarding so rapidly that everything seemed to occur at once. The study was suddenly flooded with light. She had a freeze-frame's glimpse of Asher's drawn features, thought she saw a flicker of shock pass over them, and then she was falling through the cool night air, her arms outstretched and her body limp. She hit the ground with a jarring thud, but knew immediately that her lack of rigidity had saved her from any broken bones.

She'd taken the fast way down, she thought grimly. Mr. SAS was going to have to take the stairs. Her contingency plan could still be put into operation…if her mobility returned in time.

It was a pretty big *if.* She heard shouts, then the Klaxon-like bursts of an alarm. The military contingent of the facility had obviously gone to code red at the sound of a gunshot and any minute now they would be converging on this area. Sir William's velvet drapes were hanging on the outside of the now-destroyed window, and while Asher was racing down the hall and taking the stairs three at a time to get to the body of the intruder he'd thought he'd killed, she had no doubt he would be barking out orders to whomever he passed.

She couldn't wait any longer. Awkwardly she got to her feet, grimacing at the blade of pain that thrust through her but ignoring its warning. *Yeah, I know I'm not healed yet, okay?* Under the circumstances, Dawn thought light-headedly, it seemed eminently reasonable to have a dialogue with her own body; after all, she was going to be asking a lot of it in the next few minutes. *But I don't have a choice here. You want to end up with me being the poster girl for a bunch of curious scientists, monitors shoved up my wazoo and so many tubes coming out of me that I look like an octopus, go ahead and wimp out. If you don't want that, you're going to have to get me to my room, and pronto, dammit.*

Her pep talk had the desired effect. Putting one foot clumsily in front of the other, she prodded herself into a stumbling run, clutching the edges of her destroyed sweater together to slow the telltale trail of blood she was leaving as she headed for the building she'd just left so precipitously. Veering drunkenly toward the nearest entrance, she suddenly realized what she was doing and hastily ducked back into the shadows.

Asher burst out of the building, his boots hitting the path so violently that gravel sprayed up behind him as he tore by her hiding place. With less speed than he'd exhibited, she forced herself to sprint up the same path, slipping in between the doors he'd just exited before they had a chance to swing shut.

Right in front of her were the stairs that led to the staff's rooms, Sir William's among them. Carpeted in a utilitarian beige, they appeared to rise ahead of her like the various base camps of an Everest ascent.

"And me without my Sherpa guide," she muttered, exhaustion rolling over her like a fog. "Maybe I should take the elevator instead."

But there was too much of a risk that it wasn't working properly after the power outage. It would take time to get all systems back online, and although the elevators would be a high priority since a few of the scientists and technicians were wheelchair-bound, the odds were good that Asher's people were working first on the security features that had gone down...like the hall video monitors.

As the thought occurred to her, Dawn glanced in alarm at the camera situated above her. It was still dead, the red light that would have been glowing if it was operational not yet showing, but the mere sight of it served as a stimulus to get her up the stairs. With the balaclava still obscuring her features, she wouldn't be recognizable on camera...but the fact that her masked figure had entered Dawn Swanson's room would damn her just as thoroughly.

"Talking about systems coming back online, it feels like mine are beginning to return to normal," she said under her breath as she entered the hallway that ran by Sir William's rooms. As she'd expected, Asher's departure from the study hadn't been so hasty that he'd overlooked locking the door behind him, and for the first time since the fiasco that had resulted in her obtaining and then losing Sir William's notes, the full impact of her failure hit her.

She'd committed the cardinal sin of her profession, she thought bleakly as she turned down the corridor that led to her room. She'd let her emotions take over at the expense of the mission. There'd been a point during her fight with Asher when she could have turned tail and run, but since the day she'd arrived there had been a personal edge to their infrequent interactions, and tonight had been no different.

"Face it, O'Shaughnessy, you wanted to whip his ass," she berated herself. She let herself into her room and went immediately to the window, taking care not to turn on the light. Searchlights crisscrossed the grounds and the voice of Lieutenant Keifer was clearly audible as he directed a group of soldiers to search the area nearer the gates. "Instead, you got blown away by Mr. SAS, and in the process you not only screwed up this assignment, you insured Sir William's notes will be kept under even tighter security after tonight. With your anticipated life span now down to a week and two days, you've put yourself back at square one."

No one likes screwing up on a job, Dawnie, but sometimes it happens. When it does, the best plan of action you can have is to make it to safety, regroup your resources, and figure out how you're going to fix your mistake.

"More pearls of wisdom from a dead man," Dawn said bitterly, turning from the window and entering the bathroom. She stripped off her pants, the balaclava and the ruined top, bundled them into a blood-soaked ball and a moment later had tossed them into the air shaft with the rest of her clandestine possessions, including the gun she'd liberated from Reese and had decided not to take with her tonight—another mistake that Lee Craig would probably have a handy bromide for if he were alive, she thought dismissively.

Clad only in a plain black bra and pants, she paused in front of the mirror. *Yessir, step right up and see the amazing regenerating woman.* Lightly she touched the edges of flesh and skin that had been torn apart less than five minutes ago and were now almost knit together, before twisting the washbasin's taps on full blast and running hot water over a washcloth. The water swirling in the sink ran crimson, then pink and finally clear as she automatically scrubbed the drying blood away, her attention still on her reflection. *Break her bones and she'll bounce back. Shoot her full of holes and she heals right up. Is she a freak, a lab rat, a monster? Why, she's all of those things, ladies and gentlemen, and a fool besides, because the one part of her that won't heal is her heart—not the organ but the feelings she once had for the man who lied to her all her life. Come on, folks, let's give the little lady a big round of—*

"Shut up!" The washcloth fell unheeded as Dawn grasped the edges of the sink and brought her face to within inches of the mirror. "Shut up, shut up, *shut up!* I *have* healed! I'm perfectly fine! Sure, I loved you, you bastard—I loved you so much I used to pretend you weren't my uncle but my real father! I loved you and I believed your lies and I thought—I thought—"

The woman in the mirror opened her mouth in a silent rictus of grief. Her gold-green eyes were red rimmed and her face was wet with tears. Behind her there seemed to be a ghostly image—an image of a man, no longer young, with lines of experience and regret on his face and shadows of pain under his eyes. Dawn reached out and touched the ghostly reflection.

"I thought you *loved* me, Uncle Lee." Her whisper was agonized. "But that was just part of the lie, wasn't it? Because even if I could somehow overlook everything else you were and did, I can't overlook the fact that you killed my mother, Rainy Miller. Her death at your hands has to mean that you never felt anything at all for me, and knowing that has been tearing me apart, despite what I told Kayla Ryan…and despite what I've tried to tell myself."

She let her hand fall away from the reflection. Her anguish hardened. "Don't come back anymore, Lee. Your little lab rat doesn't need you. Stay dead and stop haunting me, and maybe then I'll be able to heal, you bastard."

Gripping the sides of the sink, she let her head hang between her braced arms for a moment. When she looked up once more, there was no one reflected in the mirror but herself. She firmed her lips to a straight line, swiped the back of her hand across her tear-marked face and began to reach for the drab robe hanging on the back of the door.

"Exit O'Shaughnessy, enter Swanson," she muttered. "God, couldn't Carter have given her better taste in clothes, or at least—"

"Open the door!"

The shouted command coming from the hall outside her room was accompanied by a violent pounding. Dawn spun around. Only when she was facing the door did she notice she was holding a wickedly jagged shard of glass in her hand, the remains of the water glass she'd instinctively grabbed and smashed to use as a weapon.

"I know you're in there, Swanson. If you don't open this door immediately I'm breaking it down!"

The voice belonged to Des Asher. So, presumably, did the boot that crashed into the door a second later, rocking it on its hinges. He was the last person on earth she felt like confronting right now, she thought in trepidation, the last person she could afford to confront while the bullet hole he'd put in her was still healing; but a more important issue was, why was he here at all? There was a full-scale manhunt going on outside this building, a manhunt he himself had ordered, and with all his faults Asher wasn't the type to let a subordinate shoulder his responsibilities for him.

"Last chance, Swanson." She frowned. Beneath the grimness of his tone was an undercurrent of fear, but what did Des Asher have to fear from the Swanson chick, as far as he knew? Her question was answered right away. "If you're okay, open the door and let me see for myself, because there's a blood trail leading to this floor and I think it came from you."

Damn. She'd been sure she'd stopped bleeding before she'd reached the top of the stairs, but apparently a drop or two had escaped her notice. Had she missed anything else? Tossing her impromptu weapon into the sink and shrugging into her robe, Dawn quickly checked herself in the mirror. The wound at the top of her ribs hadn't completely healed, but in a few minutes it would have. Aside from that, there were no visible marks on her face or body from the fight, since she was physically incapable of sustaining bruises or abrasions. She peered closer, using her fingernail to scrape a minuscule fleck of crimson from her collarbone before giving her reflection a humorless smile. Maybe a confrontation with Mr. SAS was exactly what she needed to get herself back on track. Anger would focus her, remind her of who she was and what she was here for. It would be a welcome substitute for the weepy doldrums into which she'd so ridiculously fallen a few minutes ago. Anger would be a release, dammit.

She cinched the robe around her waist as she strode to the door. At the very moment she judged that the man on the other side was bracing himself to break it down, she flung it wide open. She gave him a quizzical glance.

"Take a look at yourself in the mirror. It may provide an answer as to where the blood trail's coming from," she said without preamble. "What's going on outside and why was the power down a while ago? Are you here to give me the all-clear?"

Asher stepped into the room and slammed the door shut behind him. One eye was swollen nearly shut, but the other scanned her swiftly. "Take off the robe, Swanson. For God's sake, I know it was you I shot in my uncle's study. No one else has eyes that color. How you survived the free fall I'll never know, but..." His voice trailed off. Doubt crept into his eyes.

She widened her gaze. "O-kaay," she drawled sardonically. "And I'm supposed to have stabbed Colonel Mustard in the drawing room with a knife, right?" She pulled the robe closer around her, all too aware of the tight sensation near the top of her ribs that signaled the healing process was still going on. "Sorry, Asher, but this girl's not in the mood tonight."

She had to stall him a little longer. She was now almost positive the healing was complete, but she didn't want to take the chance of him witnessing the final seconds of regeneration, especially since the memory of Kayla's stunned reaction months ago still stung. She shrugged dismissively at him.

"I don't have the first freakin' idea what you're talking about. You shot me? I fell? Is that what you told the guards outside combing the grounds?" Her gaze narrowed as the flaw in her reasoning struck her. "You didn't, did you? Because if you had told them I was the intruder you caught in Sir William's study, they wouldn't be out there looking under bushes, they'd be here and I'd be staring down the barrels of a couple dozen guns." She gave him a slow smile. "Why, Ash, honey—you really *do* care…or else you think there's just a teeny chance you could be wrong and you'd be making a fool of yourself in front of—"

His voice was hoarse. "This isn't possible. I looked straight into your eyes right after I shot you! It has to be your blood on those research papers I found on the floor. You have to be wounded, for God's sake!"

Before she knew what he intended, he had closed the distance between them with a single stride, grasped the lapels of her robe, and wrenched the garment violently open. The belt around her waist gave way and the robe slipped from her shoulders to fall in a heap around her ankles.

Asher stared at her. Dawn bore his scrutiny with outward coolness.

"See anything that interests you, big guy?" she asked flippantly. She could afford the offhand attitude, she thought: a quick glance had shown her that there was nothing about the smoothly unblemished area of skin just below the curve of her bra to arouse his suspicions. The healing had run its course and whatever his speculations had been, the man standing in front of her would never be able to prove them. *Not how I'd planned this evening to end,* she thought in resignation, *but better than it could have. I'm still in place as Sir William's trusted assistant and the next time I lay my hands on his notes I won't let anything or anyone stand in the way of my delivering them to Lab 33.*

In fact, she was in a better position than she'd previously been, she told herself in satisfaction, because if Asher's stricken expression was anything to go by, Mr. SAS's faith in his own sanity was badly shaken. She couldn't resist shaking him up a little more.

"Where'd the magic bullet enter me, Ash?" She looked down at herself curiously, at the same time nudging the bottom edge of her bra slightly upward over the swell of her left breast. "Here? Or was it higher?" She bit her lip innocently. "Hey, I know—maybe I jerked your gun just as you fired and your bullet went a little lower, like about here." Negligently she slid a thumb under the narrow black strip of panty that traversed her hip and gave it a tiny tug southward. She looked up at him. "Or perhaps that's only the way it happens in your dreams, sweetie. It kind of sounds to me like you have a problem shooting your gun off before you're ready—"

"How the hell did you do it, Swanson—a bulletproof vest?" Under his tan Asher's hard features were gray, and even before he finished the question he was shaking his head in negation. "I'm not thinking straight. Your sweater was soaked with blood, the same blood that was pouring from you on your way back here, so you couldn't have been wearing a vest. But there's not a damn mark on you, so…"

"So you've got the wrong girl?" Dawn suggested. "I know how disappointing this must be for you, Ash, I really do. Right from the start you've been so hot to pin something—anything—on me, and tonight you must have thought you'd actually caught me red-handed. Darn it all, I almost wish I was standing here with my life ebbing away, just to make you feel better about all this." She turned slightly away from him and bent to pick up her robe. "Oh, well, *qué será, será,* as they—"

"Your back!" At the shock in his tone alarm bells went off in her mind and she spun around to face him, at the same time clumsily trying to force her arms into the sleeves of the robe. Asher grabbed the garment from her with one hand, his other gripping her upper arm. "Dammit, Swanson—the flesh is *raw!* It looks like—"

He froze, his disbelieving focus on her. "It looks like an exit wound," he said slowly. "Except it can't be, because there isn't an entrance wound."

Well, there was, but since it was the smaller by far of the two, it healed up a whole lot faster, Dawn thought hollowly. How could she have overlooked something so basic? she wondered, furious with herself. And how was she going to explain her way out of this?

Never apologize, never explain. For once she didn't care that the maxim had been a favorite of Lee Craig's, it was worth a try. She wrenched her arm from Asher's grasp, tore the robe out of his hand and leveled a flat stare at him as she put it on and cinched it around her

waist once more. "You're losing it, Captain. I guess
that's not surprising, given your last mission, but either
find some other way to work out the guilt that's obviously eating you up or put your past as the Wolf of
Bah'lein behind you and forget about it. Just don't use
me as—"

"Who told you about that?" At her mention of the
nickname, a visible shock had run through him, as if
she'd just thrown a switch that had sent an unendurable
current through his body. He recovered immediately, but
it was clear he was still more shaken than he wanted her
to know. "Don't tell me." His words were clipped. "My
bloody uncle, right?"

"Your bloody uncle who used his considerable pull
to get you this baby-sitting job." Her ploy was working,
Dawn thought in relief. She'd lobbed the verbal equivalent of a hand grenade at Asher, and the shrapnel from
its blast had temporarily blinded him to his issues with
her. She was under no illusions she'd thrown him off for
long, but all she needed was a few more minutes while
her back healed. She pressed her advantage. "Oops, I
guess I wasn't supposed to let that one slip, either. Sir
William seemed to think you'd be a little peeved he'd
had to intercede to get your ass out of the sling you'd
put it in, so he didn't tell you that you were part of the
deal he cut. Sweet old guy, isn't he?"

"He's a meddling bastard who knows damn well that
what happened in Bah'lein and whatever my role might
have been, the whole subject's been ruled off-limits by
an international court of law until Al-Jihr's trial." Asher's jaw tightened. "Which is why this discussion between you and me is closed as of now, Swanson, even
if you did bring it up as a smokescreen. I'm phoning

down to the infirmary. I'll let a doctor make the decision as to whether I throw you into a cell tonight after I arrest you, or cuff you to a gurney and—"

"God, we're back to that again," she said in a bored tone. Walking to the bed, she shrugged off her robe and sat back against the pillows. She waved a hand at the phone on the adjacent night table. "If you're so determined to shoot what's left of your military career down in flames, go right ahead. Better yet, I'll dial the infirmary's extension for you."

Forestalling his move toward the phone, she flipped onto her stomach and reached for the receiver. Idly raising her legs and crossing them at the ankles, she punched in the number that connected the room telephones with the facility's emergency clinic.

"It's ringing." She hummed a bar of "Rule Britannia" under her breath and frowned at her left index finger. "Broke a nail tonight, I can't imagine how. Oh, wait, someone's picking up." With exaggerated courtesy she held the phone out to him. He snatched it from her and slammed it back onto the cradle.

"Right." He exhaled sharply. "I've seen what I was supposed to see—the exit wound's gone."

"The imaginary exit wound?" She pretended to stifle a yawn. "If you don't need to use the phone, Asher, I wish you'd let me get some sleep. I'm due to be in the lab in a few hours, and I'd really like—"

"Not this soldier, love." Despite the endearment, his tone was hard. "The details of my last mission are classified, as I just said. But there's no harm in telling you something about the one previous to it, although you don't need to know specific names and locations. We were sent in to rescue hostages from an embassy that had been taken over. I volunteered to exchange places with the pregnant wife of a civil servant, and the rebels jumped at the opportunity to take a real live SAS officer as prisoner. I was kept in a cage for three months, beaten and tortured daily, and every time I fell asleep my captors would wake me up to tell me I could walk out a free man if only I'd let them videotape me denouncing my side and labeling my country and yours as evil forces. I walked out a free man, all right. I caught one of the bastards off guard one day, killed him with my bare hands, and used the gun I took off him to eliminate the others. But I never let myself be brainwashed into saying something I knew wasn't true, and I'm not going to now."

Abruptly he sat on the edge of the bed. Still lying on her stomach, Dawn felt his hand spread wide on her back and she tensed, ready to take whatever action was needed. "I know what I saw," he said with ominous softness. "I don't give a damn if it doesn't make sense. How about we play a variation on the game of Truth or Dare we were playing the other night when I caught you skulking around the grounds after dark?"

"What kind of variation did you have in mind?" She hoped the terseness of her reply would conceal the anger building in her. The man had no idea how dangerous his implacability could prove to be. If Aldrich ever guessed that the SAS commander he'd once ordered her to kill now knew she wasn't an ordinary woman, the head of Lab 33 would renew his order—and this time he would expect her to unquestioningly carry it out.

"More truth." Asher still had his hand on her. "You know I don't dare take something so fantastic to my superiors, so why not, Swanson? For example, my first question would be, how did you do it? How did you receive a bullet point-blank to your chest no more than fifteen minutes ago and not only survive, but show no signs of a wound now?"

For one reckless moment she was tempted to tell him. It had worked before, Dawn thought swiftly—she'd divulged her profession to him, and he'd found her assertions so fantastic he'd assumed she was spinning a tall tale. But then he hadn't had the evidence of his own eyes to corroborate her story.

Now he did. And she had the feeling that no matter how incredible Des Asher might find her insistence that she was genetically capable of regenerating after being shot, some part of him would believe her. The risk factor was unacceptable…so she had to come up with another course of action that would derail his suspicions of her.

They were on her bed. She was already half-undressed and he was already touching her. It wasn't rocket science, she thought edgily.

She was going to have to seduce Mr. SAS.

Chapter 12

It had been four and a half days now, Dawn fumed as she loaded her tray in the cafeteria line, four and a half *freakin'* days since her failed attempt to steal Sir William's notes and the humiliating aftermath of that failure. She stacked a carton of milk precariously on top of a brimming glass of tomato juice, jammed two oatmeal-and-raisin cookies beside the slice of peach pie she'd already selected, and pushed her way back along the line to grab a second sandwich. She was burning off calories faster than she could supply them, she thought grimly, but it wasn't action that was taking its toll of her energy, it was frustration.

Mr. SAS had proved impossible to seduce. She'd

given it her best shot, but unfortunately her best shot hadn't consisted of much more than a husky sigh and a languid stretch to unfasten her bra, because as soon as he'd realized she had no intention of answering his questions he'd abruptly stood up from her bed.

"Sorry, love, but you've screwed me over enough for one evening," he'd said. "Normally I'm as willing as the next man to take advantage of the opportunity for a quick shag, but this is just a little too cold and calculated even for me. I liked you better when you were trying to kick the hell out of me. At least then your emotions were honest."

He'd started to open the door to the hallway, but suddenly he'd halted. He'd turned back to face her, his eyes sharp. "Bloody hell, there's a link, isn't there—a link between what I saw happen to you tonight and the research you were trying to steal. You must want to get your hands on those notes pretty badly to have taken a bullet for them, am I right?"

From her prone position on the bed she'd given him a flat stare, not bothering to hide her fury. "Since it's just you and me right now, yeah, Ash, I'll admit it. I want those notes. I'm going to get them. You got in my way tonight, but that won't happen again."

"Don't be so sure." There had been the same coldness in his eyes as she knew was in hers. "From now on one of my people will be watching you twenty-four/seven. Your phone calls will be monitored. You're never going to be alone with Sir William again, no matter how much he objects. After a while, whoever you're working for will get tired of waiting for results, and he or she is probably going to blame their agent-in-place. If I were in your shoes, I'd start making plans for that eventuality." He'd hesitated. Then he'd shrugged. "The rules have changed, Swanson. In the future if I catch you in a restricted area, I'm going to have to treat you like any other intruder, so conversations like the one we had a few nights ago are a thing of the past. But before we close all communications between us, I want to make two things clear. One is that I knew my uncle pulled strings to get me this posting."

She'd been momentarily startled out of her anger. "You knew? But then why—"

"Why did I accept? Why did I let him think he'd put one over on me, why didn't I cut him out of my life when I found out what he'd done?" Asher shook his head. "He did the wrong thing, but he did it for all the right reasons. He did it because he cared. I threw that into the equation, and I realized that although I hated what he'd done, I couldn't hate him. He's family. For better or for worse, he's a part of me."

She'd felt oddly unsettled by his words and she'd covered her discomfiture with a sharp laugh. "Lordy, Captain Asher, I do believe you've brought a tiny tear to my eye. Who would have guessed the Wolf of Bah'lein was such a softie at heart?"

She'd regretted the unpleasant gibe as soon as she'd uttered it, but it was too late to take it back. Asher's expression became granitelike and his tone was equally hard as he answered her.

"You said it yourself—it's just you and me here right now, so I'll break every rule in the book and set the record straight this once. I didn't do what they say I did, but I hold myself responsible for not guessing what that evil bastard Al-Jihr was planning in time to stop him. There's definitely blood on my hands...even if it's as in-

visible as the wounds on you." He looked suddenly
weary. "As for any tears in your eye, love, I don't flat-
ter myself that I put them there. It was obvious as soon
as I walked in that you'd been crying your heart out."

Her control snapping, she'd jumped from the bed, but
even as she'd sprung toward him he'd closed the door
behind him, leaving her alone in her room. Within minutes she'd heard the heavy tread of booted feet take up
a position just outside her room, and early the next
morning she'd heard another guard coming to take the
place of the first one.

Asher had carried out his threat to the letter, Dawn
reflected as she slid her laden tray onto an empty table,
ignoring Roger Poole's hopeful glance from across the
cafeteria. Since that night, she'd had a permanent, albeit ever-changing shadow following her during her
daily routine: waiting outside her room every morning,
watching her from a corridor through the windows of
the laboratory, staying a discreet distance behind her if
she decided to take a stroll outside in the evening. If necessary, she supposed drearily, she could use her air-duct
routes to make her way through the building at night,
but they were useless unless she had a destination in
mind, and she still hadn't discovered where Sir William's notes were now being kept. Even the old scientist himself didn't know, according to a conversation
she'd had with Roger yesterday.

"He's rather miffed about it, but he sees his nephew's
point," the Englishman had confided during a tea break.
"The thug who attempted to filch his research hasn't
been caught and although security's tighter than ever,
what if he makes a second attempt? As long as Sir William's as much in the dark as anyone else regarding the

location of his notes, he can't be forced to divulge that information to an intruder."

"Although if I were Sir William, I'd rather be able to spill the beans if I was being threatened instead of having to say, sorry, old chap, haven't a clue," Dawn had replied impatiently. She'd caught Roger's crestfallen look and relented. "Sorry, Rog, I'm sure it's a good ploy."

"A good precaution," he'd corrected her with one of his apologetic coughs. "And I'm glad Asher's taking precautions with your safety, too, by having you guarded around the clock. It's well-known you're the old man's right-hand staff member, so it's possible you could be targeted as well."

His concern had made her uncomfortable. In fact, Dawn thought in chagrin, she was uncomfortable about the whole situation, which wasn't like her. Yeah, she'd come here under false pretenses and cultivated her friendships with Roger and Sir William and the rest of the scientists and technicians for her own ends. But her actions were justified, weren't they?

Her brow furrowed in thought, she pushed her empty sandwich plate aside and reached for a cookie. The moral implications of what she was doing could be addressed sometime in the future, but right now she had more immediate worries, not least among them being how she was going to make her long-overdue phone report to Aldrich.

Since Asher had made good on his vow to have her watched, she'd had to assume he'd also kept his threat to have her calls monitored. The morning after her failed theft attempt, she'd made her way to one of the pay phones in the building and had begun to dial the number of the antiquarian bookstore that served as her contact relay to Lab 33 and Peters, but even as she'd punched in the first few digits, the young soldier who'd followed her from her room had closed the distance between them.

"Do you mind?" She'd injected a full dose of Dawn Swanson irritation into her tone. The private had remained standing where he was.

"Sorry, ma'am, but Captain Asher's orders. We stick to you like glue, and if someone contacts you or you try to contact them we have to be sure from your conversation that you're not making the call under duress." He'd given her an embarrassed smile. "Real sorry, Miz Swanson, but I guess the captain's being extracautious after all the excitement last night. You go right ahead with your call and pretend I'm not here."

"Forget it," she'd muttered, hanging up the phone and stalking away.

She'd tried every day since, with the same results, Dawn thought worriedly. Last night she'd even climbed up onto the toilet tank, intending to make her way through the air ducts to a pay phone, but then she'd remembered the hallway monitors and had realized the futility of her plan. But she couldn't leave it any longer. Somehow she had to get in contact with Aldrich today.

...whoever you're working for will get tired of waiting for results, and he or she is probably going to blame their agent-in-place...

She hadn't needed Asher to put that particular fear into words for her. It had been in the back of her mind from the start, and with each day that passed, the knot in her stomach got tighter. Peters didn't countenance failure, even from a trusted employee, and from one on tenuous probation, as she was, he could well see it as deliberate disloyalty.

Unless I can convince him that I meant to screw up my first attempt at getting the notes, she thought with sudden hope. She swallowed her mouthful of cookie without chewing, her mind working overtime on the idea. It might work, she decided. It would take all her persuasive skills, but it just might work—if she could get to a phone and contact Lab 33.

"You. Me. Food. Hot damn, I think I finally got that date with you I was hoping for."

Jerked from her thoughts by the voice coming from beside her, she looked up quickly to see Terry Reese, a corner of his delectable mouth lifted in a wry grin. He was carrying a cafeteria tray, and, seemingly oblivious to the unhappy glare Roger Poole was directing his way, he set it down on the table and took the seat across from her.

"This time if you skip out on me, I've got orders to follow you," he informed her as he twisted the cap off a bottle of sports drink. He shrugged. "Hey, it's not how I planned to get to know you, angel. But like you told me in Sir William's study a few days ago, my supreme commander seems to have it in for you."

"No, he doesn't," she lied swiftly. "At least, maybe he does, but he certainly isn't having me guarded for any reason other than my own protection." She gave him a prickly Dawn Swanson look from behind her glasses. "Don't tell me you soldiers are under the ridiculous impression you've been assigned to watch me because I'm under suspicion."

"Nope." Terry Reese sank strong white teeth into his BLT. He chewed and swallowed. "Everyone else believes what you just said, because that's the official line—the captain's told us that since you're pretty damn close to the old English guy, you could be in danger of being snatched for any information you might have. I'm the only one who thinks that's a crock, if you'll pardon my French."

"Sometimes French is the only language that'll do, especially when you're discussing Mr. SAS," Dawn muttered. The indigo eyes watching her lit up with quick humor, and she gave Terry a reluctant smile. "Okay, you're right. For reasons only known to himself, Asher's convinced I blew the power the other night after coldcocking some husky private, broke into Sir William's study, cracked the safe and was about to take off with some research notes when he walked in on me. Apparently I then engaged him in hand-to-hand combat that only ended when he pulled his gun on me."

Terry nodded, his manner perfectly serious. "Lucky for you those horn-rims you wear didn't get lost during the fight. That's something most lab assistants don't consider when they're planning a violent crime." His smile broke out again. "Now you're handing me a crock, right?"

"I wish I was." Dawn sighed, but inwardly she felt a faint stirring of excitement. Reese had unwittingly helped her out twice before. There was no reason why the old adage of "three's a charm" wouldn't apply to her gorgeous guardian angel, was there?

"But that's insane." The humor had left his eyes. "It's no secret that the thief Asher surprised in London's study was shot and fell out of a second-story window. How does Asher explain away the fact that you're all in one piece, for crying out loud?"

Dawn looked down at the tabletop. "It was pretty humiliating," she said in a low tone. "He—he insisted on checking for himself. His realization that there wasn't a scratch on me didn't seem to make any difference to his opinion, which is why you're here right now, I guess." She raised a drawn face to Terry. "The thing is, I was offered another job at the same time I heard of this position, and there's a chance I could still get it. I'd like to. As much of an honor as it is working with Sir William, his nephew's attitude toward me has made it impossible for me to continue on here."

"That's pretty damn understandable," Terry said, his anger apparent. "So where's the problem—just leave. After the way you've been treated, you don't owe anyone anything in the way of notice."

"I said there was a chance the other job's still available," she reminded him. "If it's not, I'll have to stick this one out, because I can't afford to be unemployed. But with all my calls being monitored, I can't phone the other lab to find out if they've filled the post or not. Sir William's going to know I'm looking elsewhere for a job, and he'll see that as a breach of loyalty and give me my walking papers."

"Which would be okay if you had somewhere else to go to, but not if the alternate job's been taken in the meantime." Reese frowned. "You asked me once why I wanted a date with you, honey, when I could have my pick of supermodels. I still say you were giving me too much credit, but are you interested in hearing my answer?"

Not really, Lover Boy. On pins and needles waiting to see if her ruse had worked, Dawn had a hard time keeping her tart reply to herself. *You're a babe and actually a really nice guy, but my main concern right now isn't us making beautiful music together, it's getting to*

*a freakin' pay phone and talking my way out of a world
of trouble with my boss. Either you can help me with
that, or I've got to find another solution to my problem.*

Her smile was slightly strained. "I remind you of
your sister? That's what most men tell me just before
they pull out a wallet photo of the gorgeous girl who
broke their heart. Don't worry, Terry, I'm used to—"

"Will you shut up and give me a chance here,
honey?" There was sharp frustration in his tone. "You
don't remind me of my sister, because I don't have one.
You remind me of a girl I used to sit behind in biology
class. Mandy was the smartest kid in school and she had
a wicked sense of humor, but I was a jock and all I knew
was she wore glasses and didn't treat me like a god the
way all the other girls did. I never dated her, but guess
what? All these years later, she's the only one I remember from my high-school days. She had pride and class
and independence, just like you do, Dawn. I guess I've
grown up a little, because that's what I look for in a
woman now."

"Oh." Her response was inadequate, she knew, but
her throat had constricted so tightly that for the moment
it was all she could manage. Terry Reese was a simple,
decent human being and she was using him—just as
she'd used Roger, just as she'd used Sir William, just as
she'd used everyone else here who'd made the mistake
of offering her friendship. *About the only person I
haven't manipulated is Asher,* Dawn thought bleakly,
*but that hasn't been for lack of trying, it's just because
the man's the male equivalent of me…so closed off from
everyone that it's impossible to slip under his guard. But
even Asher's held on to a faint connection to the world
through his uncle.*

Who was she connected to? Not Lee Craig—not anymore. He was dead, but the severance between them went far deeper than death. She didn't know about the Cassandras. In the past they'd seen her as an enemy, and for all she knew their position hadn't changed. Which left her with an unthinkable, undeniable conclusion.

Aldrich Peters had created her. Aldrich Peters was her sole chance of survival. The man she hated with every fiber of her being was the only person she had a link to.

Which didn't alter in the least her intention of killing him as soon as—

Darkness. Coldness. A terrible sound filling her ears, like the rage-thickened snarls of a dozen dying men. And *pain*...pain that transcended pain, that went beyond agony, that escalated past the point of sensation and became an element around her and in her, as pervasive as air, as choking as water, as searing as fire.

"...guess what I'm trying to say is that I think you're pretty special, Dawn, and if I can help you out in this situation, I will. There's a pay phone just down the hall from the cafeteria, isn't there?"

She'd had another attack, Dawn thought dazedly. It was over now, and since Reese's tone held no alarm it seemed apparent that he hadn't noticed anything out of the ordinary while it had taken her over, but it had been the worst yet. *I survived it,* she told herself fearfully, *and I just might be able to survive another of this magnitude. But they're tearing me apart a little more each time they occur. I can't hold out much longer against them.*

"Between here and the lab," she said through lips so dry they felt cracked. She moistened them and tried to focus. "Why?"

"You need to make a private call. I need to find out why the joker who was supposed to relieve me at one o'clock hasn't shown up yet."

"Maybe he hasn't shown because it's only quarter-to," she began, but Terry shook his head.

"Your watch must be wrong," he said as he fiddled with the knob on his and then extended his wrist toward her with a frown. "See—ten past already. While you're using the ladies' room next to the phone, I'll probably wander back this way, see if my relief's looking for me here. God, the losers they let into the military these days!"

"I think they let some pretty great guys in," Dawn said, comprehending what he'd just implied to her. "And Reese—I'm sorry."

"For what, honey?" He gathered up their trays and stood from the table as she pushed her chair back.

For stealing your gun, for ambushing you on your Harley, for seeing you a couple of minutes ago as just a gorgeous guy with a killer smile whom I could use. She gave a shrug as they exited the cafeteria. "For standing you up last week. It wasn't very nice of me."

"Don't apologize, I probably came on a little too strong anyway, hitting you up for a date just minutes after you'd fainted." Reese suddenly patted his pockets. "Which reminds me, I meant to give you this when I saw you. I picked it up in the hallway outside Sir William's study when I left and realized it had to be yours. Now, didn't you say you needed to powder your nose before heading back to the lab?"

Looking up from the object Terry had pressed into her palm, she saw that they were standing directly outside the entrance to the women's washroom. Beyond it was a small alcove with a pay phone. Dawn responded to his conspiratorial wink with a wooden smile, entered the washroom, turned around and came back out into the hall again.

Her gorgeous guardian angel was halfway down the corridor, heading for the cafeteria. She was alone. She walked to the alcove and picked up the telephone receiver, but her stunned attention was still on the small gold object Terry Reese had found in the hallway after an unknown killer had come far too close to assassinating Lab 33's ex-assassin.

A lapel pin in the shape of a small shield, it bore the Latin motto *Audent Fortuna Juvat,* which she recognized as meaning Fortune Favors the Bold…and below the motto was written *Athena Academy.*

Had the assassin who'd shot her truly been Samantha St. John, and had she inadvertently left her calling card?

"I see." Was it her imagination, or had the frost that had been in Aldrich Peters's voice for the first minutes of their telephone conversation thawed slightly? Dawn wondered as she gripped the receiver with tense fingers. He went on, and this time his tone left no doubt that the cold fury he'd displayed moments ago had abated somewhat. "You should have alerted me to your plan. I'm willing to overlook your breach of protocol this time…but only this time. Do we understand each other?"

"Yes, Doctor." It wasn't hard to keep her response subdued. She was on autopilot, Dawn thought as the sharp edges of the Athena Academy pin bit into the clenched palm of her free hand, but perhaps that was a good thing. She'd presented her case to Aldrich unemotionally, her earlier trepidation at his possible reaction no longer her prime concern, and apparently her cool manner had been more convincing than an impassioned explanation of her actions.

"Good. That being said, I commend you on a masterful strategy, Dawn, and one worthy of your late uncle. By deliberately aborting the first attempt to steal London's papers—an attempt that as you say can hardly be laid at your door when Captain Asher is looking for a suspect with a gunshot wound—you've laid a highly pungent red herring across your trail. When you and the papers actually do disappear from the facility tonight, Dawn Swanson will be assumed to be a victim rather than the perpetrator. You've covered your tracks superbly."

"I intend to spill enough of my own blood in my room to make it seem impossible for Swanson to have survived long after being forced to help her attackers locate the safe where the papers are now kept, and then apparently being taken as a hostage by them when they left," she added tonelessly. "When the authorities don't find her they'll assume her body was dumped and buried somewhere in the surrounding desert. She'll enter the books as missing, presumed dead."

"And with a carefully chosen middleman brokering my deal to sell London's research back to the government, my involvement in this mission never comes to light, Lab 33 receives a healthy influx of cash into its coffers and you escape the death sentence you're living under," Peters said thoughtfully. "All because Lee Craig taught his protégé how to play a double game so well."

Dawn frowned. "I wouldn't call it a double game, Doctor. That implies my loyalties are divided. It's more accurate to say that I'm throwing up a smokescreen."

"Which you're also superb at," he said without hesitation. "My apologies, Dawn, I'm afraid I have a shaky grasp of the terminology of your profession. Well, then, can I expect your arrival at Lab 33 within the next twenty-four hours, barring any unforeseen complications?"

"There won't be any complications, unforeseen or otherwise," she said with finality. "And if there are, I'll take care of them the way Lee Craig taught me to."

Even as Peters terminated his end of the call, Terry Reese rounded the corner from the cafeteria and began heading her way. Dawn raised her voice slightly. "I understand, Ms. McGrisken. I really couldn't expect you to hold the position open indefinitely. Please keep me in mind if anything else comes up." She hung up.

"I can see it wasn't the news you were hoping for," Terry said as he reached her. "I wish we had time to talk about what you're going to do now, angel, but we've got to put some distance between us and this phone. I think I saw Mr. SAS in the cafeteria, and what's worse, I'm pretty sure he saw me. Your next stop is the lab, right?"

"I'll be there all afternoon." She fell into step beside him, thankful for his assumption that her manner was due to disappointment over not getting the fictional job. *When really I'm acting this way because I'm encased in ice,* she thought with detachment. *Except instead of feeling cold on the outside, the cold's coming from deep inside me. I wonder if I'll ever feel warm again...and I wonder if I'll ever care whether I do or not.*

Because right now she didn't. Having ice in her veins meant she felt nothing over the Cassandras' possible betrayal. It meant she could shut herself off from the events she would have to set in motion tonight. It numbed all feeling, gave her cold strength, turned her back into the woman she had been before her world had been ripped apart by an earlier betrayal.

You've been trying to be someone you weren't, O'Shaughnessy, Dawn told herself, barely noticing Reese's concerned glance as she left him and the soldier who had just arrived to relieve him at the door of the lab. She strode sightlessly past a group of scientists and technicians, coming to a halt at the back of the room where a row of wire cages lined the wall. *You thought you could make amends for the things you did, maybe one day be accepted by the Cassandras as one of them. But you were raised to be the Cipher's protégé, a genetically altered killing machine, Lab 33's lab rat. You'll never be able to put the past behind you, so you might as well accept what you are.*

She unlatched the first wire door, lifting it open with one finger. The two creatures inside cowered momentarily at this unexpected interruption to their routine but excitement overrode their caution. They scurried to the threshold of the cage, hesitated for a second and then ran out along the table. Dawn wasn't watching them. She was already unlatching the second cage, and then the third and fourth ones. Only when the tenth cage had been opened and its occupants released did she stand back and look at them as they scurried down the table and across the floor.

"It feels like freedom, doesn't it?" Raised voices and a few nervous shrieks came from the room behind her, but she kept her eyes on the excited ex-prisoners and addressed her low words to them. "You think if you run fast enough and far enough they'll never catch you…but you're wrong, little brothers and sisters. You'll never be free. You'll never escape. And just when you think you have, those bars will come slamming down again, stronger than ever."

It would take the lab a long time to round up all those rats and get them back in their cages again.

"And I know how long," she said aloud. "Nine months, fifteen days and fourteen hours. It doesn't take much time at all to put a lab rat back into her cage.

"All you have to make her understand is that it's the only place she belongs…the only place where she'll *ever* belong."

Chapter 13

Dawn Swanson was dead. Dead, buried and never to be resurrected, Dawn thought as she stared at herself in the full-length mirror on her bathroom door. "Ain't gonna miss you, babe, that's for sure," she said softly. "You cramped my style way too much. And I really, *really* hated wearing your clothes."

Not that the ones she had on were what she would have chosen had she a choice, she told herself with a grimace. She'd soaked the stains from the skintight zipped top she'd been wearing the night she'd been shot, but there had been nothing she could do about the blasted-out hole in the fabric at the top of her rib cage and the exit hole at the back, and try as she might, she hadn't been able to totally clean the blood from the left sleeve. The former two problems she could live with. The latter she'd solved by hacking off both sleeves with a pair of scissors. Her shoulders were now exposed in the cutaway garment, but the impromptu tailoring had given her greater ease of movement.

Her army-issue boots laced up well past her ankles and had been filched a few hours earlier from the bedside of a sleeping female soldier, a feat she'd accomplished by using her air shaft mode of travel one final time. A quick detour to the men's quarters on the way back had resulted in the bowie knife that was now strapped to her thigh, unwittingly supplied by a Ranger whose overheard nickname of "Blade" had suggested to her that he might have an interesting collection of unofficial weaponry in his locker. It was a supposition that had proved correct, since besides the bowie knife she'd relieved him of a wristband-mounted switchblade and—Freudians would have a field day with this one, she thought wryly—a short, scabbarded sword that came with its own spring-release back-holster.

All in all, the Swanson chick had definitely received last rites, along with her baggy sweats, her cumbersome bottle-lens glasses, and best of all…

"Is it true blondes have more fun?" she muttered to her reflection, taking in the honey-colored braid that started high at the back of her head and swung halfway down to her waist. Several shampooings had eliminated the brown rinse from her hair. "Or is that just an urban myth, like a woman's favorite weapon is poison? The rest of this arsenal might come in handy, but give me a gun any day." She checked Reese's Beretta, shoved the pistol into the snug waistband of her black pants and pulled her top concealingly over it.

She looked like what she was, she thought assessingly—Lab 33's assassin, the protégé who had inherited the position Lee Craig had so abruptly vacated when Samantha St. John's bullet had taken him down last October. The woman in the mirror was leanly muscled, armed to the teeth and clad all in black. Eyes the arctic green of pack ice stared unblinkingly out of an expressionless face. She exactly fit the description that had been circulated in the urgent and confidential e-mail Kayla Ryan had shown her months ago.

Her immediate objectives hadn't changed. She still needed to get Sir William's notes to the scientists who could utilize them to save her life—hers and her sisters', whether she could trust the women sworn to avenge their biological mother or not.

Crossing swiftly to the bathroom, she reached above the sink and felt behind the frosted glass shade of the light. She unscrewed the bulb enough to break the connection and the light went out. She moved back to the bedroom, stepping onto the bed to reach the overhead fixture.

Her actions in the lab this afternoon had been regrettable but not disastrous. She'd implemented a hasty plan of damage control. Sinking to her knees, she'd covered her face with her hands and let her shoulders heave in silent sobs, only raising her head when she'd felt Roger's tentative arm around her.

"I'm sorry," she'd gulped, throwing an appalled glance at the scurrying rats around her. "I don't know why someone would do this! Ever since the break-in I—I—"

"You're suffering from stress," Roger had said with uncharacteristic fierceness. "And it hasn't been helped by having an armed guard follow you around everywhere you go, either. Is it really necessary to have your people dogging Ms. Swanson's every step, man? Can't you see the toll it's taking on her?"

His angry questions had been directed at Asher, who was watching her performance with an unreadable expression on his face. Aqua eyes held hers for a moment, and before turning on Roger.

"I see that something's taking its toll on our Ms. Swanson," he said evenly, "although I'm willing to bet my security precautions aren't to blame. I'll have one of my people escort her to her room where she can regain her composure."

At that point Sir William had arrived on the scene. In the middle of his bellowing tirade against the loose rats and then his nephew's high-handedness Asher had walked away, and a few minutes later Dawn, with a gruffly solicitous Sir William at her side and a guard ten paces behind her, had headed for her room.

"His methods are overbearing, I agree, but he means well," the old scientist had said awkwardly as they'd paused outside her door. "When I learned he'd assigned a security contingent to you I thought it would reassure you, but I should have realized how unsettling it might be." His veined hand had rested on hers and he'd lowered his voice to a confidential level. "I'm telling tales out of school again, I suppose, but maybe it will put your mind at ease if you understand why there's no chance of any thugs coming after you for my notes. Asher's locked them away in his own office safe. Knowing my nephew, he probably stands guard over them all night himself. Does that make you feel any better about this whole situation?"

"More than you know, Sir W," Dawn said under her

breath as she unscrewed the lightbulb and dropped it onto the bed. "I thought I was going to have to use you as my hostage to force Asher to lead me to the notes and hand them over. I didn't want to do that, and the woman I was twenty-four hours ago wouldn't have been able to, but to spell it out in terms you'd understand, I've regenerated. I'm back to who I was before I'd ever heard of a group called the Cassandras, much less put my trust in them."

She passed by the dresser, swept her hand across its surface, and gave a good facsimile of a muffled and cut-off scream as assorted toiletries and a clock-radio crashed to the floor. Almost immediately she heard a sharp knock on the room's door.

"Everything okay in there, ma'am?"

Unlike Reese and the hapless private whose phone-sex conversation she'd so abruptly terminated four nights ago, her guard this evening had looked to be in his mid-thirties, she recalled, and presumably his extra years had taught him extra caution. Although Terry had taken pains to assure her that Asher's briefing to her guards hadn't raised their suspicions about her, some of the more experienced Rangers had treated her like a possible hostile rather than a civilian in jeopardy, including the one who was even now unlocking her door.

"Stand away from the entrance, ma'am," he ordered from the hall. "I'm coming in."

Suspicious or not, he thought he was dealing with the Swanson chick, she reflected as she saw the door begin to open. He would take an unwary second to hit the light switch and then she would—

He stepped in, hesitated in the doorway as she'd predicted.

From her position behind it, she gave the door a powerful kick. It slammed against the Ranger, who stumbled back a pace over the threshold, and before he could recover his balance she leaped from her hiding place, wrested his weapon from him and brought its stock crashing down on his skull.

He crumpled to his knees to fall face forward on the floor. Swiftly she reached down to the pulse at the side of his neck.

It was slow but steady. He would live, although for the next forty-eight hours he'd have one mother of a headache, Dawn decided as she dragged him farther inside the room.

She stepped away from him, and as she did she caught a shadowy glimpse of her reflection in the dresser mirror. For a moment she felt oddly disoriented, as if she had nothing to do with the grim woman who had just taken out one of her own country's soldiers so emotionlessly.

What the hell am I doing? Whose side am I on here? This is all—

The frantic voice inside her head was abruptly silenced as the ice that surrounded her choked it off. Dawn made her way to the door with a frown. She was on no one's side but her own, dammit. Her affiliation with Lab 33 was a thing of the past and, if her assumption about the appearance of the Athena Academy pin was true, her alliance with the Cassandras had been broken by their actions, not hers. She would use both organizations for her own ends and then dispose of them before they could dispose of her. Her frown smoothed out into blankness and she edged a glance around the side of the door.

The video camera was mounted high on the wall at the end of the hall, its gleaming lens sweeping slowly from left to right and then back again as it scanned the width of the corridor. Taking only a split second to assess the speed of its tracking rhythm, she jerked her head back into the room and slipped the bowie knife from its sheath on her upper thigh as the lens swiveled her way again.

For the space of a heartbeat she waited. Then she made her move.

She stepped fully into the corridor, noting as she did so that the camera was temporarily pointed away from her. Her arm came up and her wrist bent back in a fluid throwing motion just as the lens was nearly facing her again. The bowie knife left her grasp smoothly and flew like the deadly missile it was straight for the camera's lens.

It hit dead center, shattering the glass and penetrating the body of the camera. Like some lumbering beast that didn't know it was mortally wounded, the camera kept slowly tracking back and forth, the knife's wickedly long blade quivering from it.

Walking to the end of the hall, she grabbed the hilt of the knife and pulled it out of the camera before sheathing it again and pushing open the door to the stairs.

Ten minutes later, after disabling the camera on the ground floor in a similar manner and taking out the two soldiers posted at the entrance to the military building, noiselessly Dawn closed the door to Asher's office behind her. Contrary to what his uncle had said, he didn't stand guard over Sir William's locked notes all night, she realized, remaining very still and letting her glance travel around the shadowy room. He didn't have to.

Because the whole area, starting from where she was standing just inside the door, past the metal, paper-strewn desk six feet away and continuing right up to the steel safe that was positioned behind the desk, was criss-crossed with glowing red beams that looked like strands of silk from some radioactive spider. The place was wired to the max with infrared trip-alarms.

"Crap." Her lips barely moving as she spoke, she made rapid calculations based on the scene in front of her. She took a shallow breath, tucked her braid into the neckline of her top so that it wouldn't swing free and began contorting her slow way through the maze of in-frared beams.

The summer she'd been fourteen she'd accompanied Lee Craig on a mission that had taken him to Prague. To her adolescent fury, as soon as they'd arrived he'd informed her that he intended to work the job alone and that he'd made arrangements for her to take specialized training during the time he would be occupied. Her fury had lasted only until he'd dropped her off at the small, family-run circus that was to be her home for the next two months.

"Papa Wisznewski thought those grueling eight-hour gymnastic sessions he put me through were to teach me how to walk the high-wire like I'd been born to it," Dawn breathed as she carefully lowered her torso under a beam while balancing on one leg. She lowered her-self full-length to the floor and kept her eyes on another beam only millimeters above her face as she slid below it. "Wonder what he'd think if he knew how I was put-ting them to use right now."

By the time she made it to the desk she could feel a thin sheen of sweat coating her limbs and trickling down between her shoulder blades. She hesitated for a second, then began the last phase of her journey to the safe—a distance of only three feet, but bristling with a barbed-wire effect of red beams. Her worst moment came when, her head down and both her hands splayed out on the floor for balance, she felt her braid slip free of her collar. As it swung by her face she caught it in her teeth before it interrupted the path of one of the red lines of light.

Then her ordeal was over and she was standing in the blessedly clear area in front of the safe. Spitting the tail of her braid out of her mouth with a sense of relief, she hunkered down in front of the combination lock, laced her fingers together and stretched them out until her knuckles popped, and then got to work.

Compared to the high-end Rose-Jackman model in his uncle's study, Asher's safe had been about as hard to break into as a cigar box, she thought with a frown a few minutes later. In fact, if it hadn't been for the infrared sensors that had made it so hard for her to make her way across the office in the first place, she would have suspected a trap...or at least considered the possibility that Sir William's papers were secreted somewhere else. But they weren't. They were right there in plain view as the safe's door swung open.

"Bingo," she whispered hoarsely as she grabbed them up and began to unzip her top to secure them next to her body.

The red sensors suddenly shut off, and as she turned quickly around, the room's bright overhead lights went on.

"Checkmate's more like it, love," replied Asher from beside a filing cabinet near the doorway. He took his left hand from the light switch and closed the small metal door of an alarm panel, the Sig Sauer in his right hand never wavering from her. "I suppose I could have collared you as soon as you walked in, but it was a real education watching you beat the sensors. Besides, I've got a fatal weakness for green-eyed blondes, as I think I might have mentioned to you when your hair was a different color...especially if they're wearing skintight black instead of baggy sweatshirts and pants." His tone hardened. "You're damn good, Swanson. Drop the papers, put your palms flat on the desk and spread your legs as wide as you can."

"Sorry, I never go that far on a first date," Dawn said with a cold smile. She shook her head. "I've got no quarrel with you, Ash, but believe me when I say if I have to take you down to get out of here with these notes, I will. All you have to decide is whether we're going to do this the hard way or the easy way."

"And all you have to decide is whether you want to risk another gunshot wound over a pile of papers that are absolutely worthless to you." His grin was tight. "Hell, Swanson, did you take me for such a fool that you thought you had the real thing in your hand? The introduction's the same, but after that it's all scientific rubbish, cobbled up by the ever-obliging Roger at my request. Even the artistic blood spatters on the first few pages are faked. They're not yours from the other night, they're mine, courtesy of a deliberately careless shave the morning after your first robbery attempt. You've been set up. Don't worry, though, you're in good company. My uncle's also under the impression that this is where his notes now are. I was counting on him letting the cat out of the bag to you, and it seems I was right."

"This document's a fake? You set me *up?*" Dawn heard her voice rise, but she was powerless to control it. Somewhere deep inside her a volcano seemed to be erupting, its furiously hot lava boiling over and melting the protective ice that had kept her together. She stared at Asher, trying and failing to read him. "You're lying," she said in shaky anger. "If these papers were worthless you wouldn't have bothered with the security system."

"And you would have waltzed in here, realized it was all too easy and guessed it was a trap," he replied with a shrug. "The real document's safely back in the Rose-Jackman in the old man's study, which makes this a double-bluff, love. I thought you of all people would appreciate the irony of—"

"Without those papers I'm *dead,* damn you!" As she shouted out the accusation, Dawn hurled the bound pages straight at him. Instinctively he moved as they fluttered by his face, and that was all the advantage she needed.

The bowie knife sliced through the air and shuddered to a twanging halt, its razor-sharp blade gleaming cruelly and the first inch of its tip pinning the skin between Asher's thumb and index finger to the wall behind him. As his hand spasmed in agony the Sig Sauer fell to the floor and Dawn closed the distance between them to kick it away, pulling Reese's Beretta from her waistband as she did.

"I need the freakin' notes, Ash," she said harshly. "I intend to get them, and I'm taking these as well just in case. But if this really was a trap and these papers are worthless, you wouldn't have left the real document lying unprotected in a safe I'd already cracked once. Who's standing guard in Sir William's study?"

Aqua eyes blazed at her. "You know what I've learned to appreciate about Americans?" Destin Asher asked, ignoring her question. His smile was a grimace of pain. "The colorful phrases you come up with for the most ordinary sentiments. *Bite me.* Now that's one of my all-time favorites, *love.*"

His booted foot came up as he snarled out the last word, taking her unawares as his heel smashed the Beretta from her hand. *Careless, O'Shaughnessy,* Dawn warned herself. *Whatever you do, don't let his free hand get close enough to the handle of the knife to pull it out.* But her body was ahead of her thoughts and already she was pivoting to deliver a high sideways kick to his left shoulder.

He feinted out of range, ducked up again and grasped her ankle as she tried to retract her leg. With both hands he used her momentum against her and flipped her backward into the air.

She crashed ignominiously onto her rump and stared up at him in shock. Asher, his right hand dripping blood from where he'd torn it away from the bowie blade, rushed toward her.

"What the hell do you mean, you're dead without those notes?" he growled as he threw himself at her.

She rolled out of the way at the last minute and had the satisfaction of seeing him wince as his shoulder made violent contact with the corner of the iron desk. "You wouldn't believe me if I told you," she grunted, rolling back and slamming a braced elbow into his ribs. She saw his Sig under the desk where it had slid when she'd kicked it from his grasp, and made a dive for it.

"Try me, Swanson." Just as her fingertips brushed the gun's grip, she felt him yank her away, his hand securing a hold in the bullet-shredded back of her top. She heard a tearing sound and then she was free. Asher dropped the strip of black fabric he'd been left with and clamped a hand around her left wrist as she stretched full-length on the floor for the Sig again. "Bloody hell, what are you packing in that scabbard you're wearing, anyway?"

"Nothing, I'm just happy to see you," Dawn ground out, releasing the button on the wristband she was wearing on her right arm and closing her fingers around the handle of the switchblade as it jumped into her hand. She flipped onto her back and brought the stiletto's blade to his throat. Asher froze instantly, his face inches from hers.

"You're a one-woman commando raid, love," he said in a strained tone, his gaze slanting once at the knife and then meeting hers again. "Swords, knives, guns…and a whole bag of back-alley tricks when the weaponry runs out. It was the truth, wasn't it?"

She didn't bother to pretend she didn't know what he was talking about. "The assassin thing?" she said through gritted teeth. "Yeah, it was the truth. And I'm telling you the truth now when I say that I'd prefer not to kill you if I don't have to."

"I don't know how to break this to you, love, but you're awfully damn close to killing me right now," he gasped.

She didn't allow the blade to shift. "Close only counts in horseshoes, Ash. And grenades," she added dryly.

Incredibly, he managed a smile. "You don't have any of those tucked away in a back pock—"

Two things happened at once to prevent him from finishing his sentence. The lights went out, not only in the room but outside in the hallway, Dawn realized as she saw the line of brightness under the door disappear.

And from somewhere outside came a quick burst of automatic gunfire.

Slowly she withdrew the blade from the vicinity of Asher's throat and heard him exhale.

"Not your arrangements?" he asked, his lips so close to her ear that his breath was warm on the nape of her neck. She shook her head in the dark.

"No, not mine," she said. "But I'm pretty damn sure I know whose arrangements these new developments are…and if I'm right, we're both in a world of trouble."

Chapter 14

Status: four days and counting
Time: 1007 hours

Dawn began to get to her feet, but Asher's tight grip on her arm stopped her. "Wait," he directed her tersely.

The habit of command might die hard, she thought, but die it would. Circumstances had apparently made them temporary allies, but he needed to understand that she didn't take orders from him.

"For what, teatime?" She let an edge of impatience shade her tone as she shook off his hand. "If I'm right and we're under siege by the people I think we are, we've got to strike back immed—"

The lights went on again; not to their former level of brightness but with a dim yellow glow that created sickly shadows instead of a clear view of the room. It was better than nothing, Dawn conceded.

"It's teatime now," Asher said. He stood and crossed to the desk. Picking up the phone's receiver, he listened for a second and then set it down. "There's been a few changes made since you came close to crippling this facility four nights ago, although unfortunately a backup phone system's not one of them. I gave higher priority to setting up the firewall precautions that now make it impossible to shut down the auxiliary power system when the main one's tampered with. Anything else you'd like to challenge me on, Swanson?"

He was pulling rank on her, dammit. She gave him an unimpressed look. "You weren't sure it was going to kick in, were you?"

"My heart was in my mouth," he answered unhesitatingly. His teeth flashed briefly in the gloom, and she felt her own lips curve reluctantly up in response before she tightened them again.

"Ground rules," she said sharply. "You cover my back, I'll cover yours. We hunt in a pack, got it?"

"Not quite." Asher bent to retrieve his Sig Sauer, but then paused. "Getting my gun, Swanson. Am I going to feel that pigsticker you like throwing so much between my shoulder blades as soon as I turn away?"

"We're on the same side for now." She strode to the wall behind the desk and pulled the bowie knife out with a tug. Without thinking, she wiped the tip clean on her pants before thrusting it into the sheath strapped around her thigh. She glanced up to see Asher watching her.

"I'd be more convinced by your offer of solidarity if it weren't my blood you just cleaned from your knife," he said dryly. Another short burst of gunfire came from outside and he grabbed up the Sig. "Sorry, Swanson, but I can't trust you're not on the side of whoever's out there trying to take over this place. I'm cuffing you and leaving you here while I—"

"I was on Lab 33's side once," she interrupted him impatiently. "Now I think I'm on its hit list—just like you are and just like any of your people who try to stop them will be."

"Lab 33?" Asher shook his head before she could answer. "Forget it, there's no time. Just fill me in on the important things, like how many, their level of training and armament, what their objective is."

"Probably no more than twenty if it's the usual Lab 33 covert ops force, trained like you wouldn't friggin' believe, armed ditto," Dawn said as she spied the Beretta in a corner and retrieved it. "I was sent here to steal Sir William's notes on the regeneration process by a certain Aldrich Peters, and my guess is that he's gotten tired of waiting for results and decided to take a less subtle approach. Since I didn't deliver, I'm expendable." She checked her weapon, avoiding Asher's gaze. "You warned me of just such a contingency, as I recall. I should have given more weight to your advice."

"You're not the first to be left twisting in the wind when a superior decides not to back you up. I ignored the warning signs in my own situation, which is why I'm here," he said curtly. "Right, then. We work as a team for now, Swanson, but that doesn't mean I'm not going to arrest you after this is over, understood?" As he spoke he flung open the door and flattened himself against the wall while she did the same on the other side of the opening. Acting as one they both moved into the doorway at the same time, Dawn crouched slightly down in front of him, her Beretta held in a two-handed grip; Asher behind and above her with his Sig at the ready.

"*Try* to arrest me, you mean," she corrected as they moved from doorway to doorway down the hall to the entrance of the building. "I assume we're heading to Sir William's study?"

"One of your American bank robbers once said that he robbed banks because that's where the money was. If your Lab 33 people are after my uncle's notes, it stands to reason at least some of them are on their way to his room while the rest of them create a diversion." Asher kept his tone low and raised a cautionary hand as they neared the end of the hall. Swiftly he looked around the corner and jerked his head back.

"Evers and Chase were on security detail at the entrance tonight. They must have been taken out already, damn—"

"By me, not Lab 33," Dawn said, moving past him. She anticipated his response and forestalled it. "They're alive, just unconscious in the bushes, okay? Come on, follow my lead."

She hadn't really expected him to, she thought without rancor as the two of them raced side by side through the dimly lit foyer and kicked open the doors to the outside, in unison holding back for a moment before rushing the exit and hitting the walkway in twin paratrooper rolls. *Like me, he's probably used to playing a lone hand when he can,* she told herself as Asher, showing the same low profile as herself on the other side of the walkway, kept pace with her on their way to the building that housed the lab and civilian quarters. *But with a Lab 33 black-ops team as our opposition, right now both of us could use a partner...and although I hate to admit it, Des Asher's almost as good at this as I am.*

"You're almost on a par with me at broken-cover reconnoitering, Swanson." Asher had crossed the walkway and was at her side, his whispered words of approbation accompanied by a distracted nod. "We'd better decide on a plan of action before we go in—"

"We see a Lab 33 team member, we kill him. There, now we've got a freakin' plan," Dawn said in irritation. She took a deep breath and forced a more even tone to her voice. "One thing we should get clear—don't put yourself in danger for me, Ash. If you can prevent me from taking a bullet at no risk to yourself, be my guest. I don't like getting shot any more than the next girl, but as you saw the other night, I can take a licking and still go on ticking."

Her flipness was a cover for her sudden apprehension. The man had some idea of what she was, but there was a big difference between having some idea and knowing for certain. *Face it, O'Shaughnessy, no one feels real comfortable around a freak, and that's what you are—a freak, just like those Lab 33 guards said so long ago,* she told herself.

"So I saw what I thought I saw the night I shot you?" His question was tense, and her heart sank. She concealed her reaction with sharpness.

"Your friggin' bullet blew a hole in me and I healed right up? Yeah, that's what happened, Ash." She lifted her shoulders dismissively. "Aldrich Peters manipulated my genes before I was born in order to create a super-assassin, and one of my enhanced abilities is the capacity to regenerate after being wounded. I'm a lab rat... Lab 33's lab rat, to be exa—"

"Don't finish that sentence." Without warning he pulled her toward him, so close that she could see the anger in his eyes. "You're one hell of a fighter. You're a risk-taker with nerves of steel, a covert ops expert who doesn't know the meaning of quitting and a soldier who deserves a better leader than this bastard Peters you mention. You're the most formidable opponent I've gone up against, not to mention the only one I've ever wanted to—" He stopped abruptly. Dawn exhaled.

"If you were going to say *shag,* then the feeling's mutual," she said. "It's been driving me crazy since the first time I—"

He was already bringing his mouth down on hers. Mr. SAS kept shattering her misconceptions about the British, Dawn thought in surprise as she felt his tongue flick impatiently against her vulnerable inner top lip and then move deeper. She'd always thought the English were restrained, but there was nothing restrained about the way Des Asher was kissing her. Come to that, there wasn't anything remotely restrained about the heat that immediately flared up inside her as she kissed him back, either, she admitted dazedly. *Why didn't we do this sooner, dammit?* she asked herself as she felt his hands, hard and urgent, tugging at the zipper on her top and then pushing her bra up. With equal urgency she began unbuttoning his shirt before impatiently tearing it open and letting the tips of her fingernails bite lightly into his chest. *It's not like we haven't had the opportunity. Hell, the man was actually in my bedroom a few nights—*

She pulled away from him, so suddenly that it took a moment for him to focus. "If you've wanted me since we met, how come you walked out on me the other night?" she demanded, yanking up the zipper on her top.

"I walked out because I didn't fancy being used by you." His eyes met hers steadily. "I'm not the hearts-and-flowers type any more than you are, love, but I had the faint hope it might mean something if we ever got together. I still have that hope. Am I a bloody fool to hang on to it?"

His directness was disconcerting. She blinked at him, her anger fading. "Probably," she said quietly. "I've lied to you from the start, Ash, but I won't lie to you about that."

"Fair enough." His wry smile belied the sudden shadow that crossed his features. He held her gaze for a heartbeat longer and then looked away, his manner once again coolly professional. "So you can take a bullet and keep going, is that what you're telling me?"

Dawn nodded, not trusting her voice. *Oh, I can heal from a bullet, all right,* she told him silently, looking at the strong line of his jaw, the burnt-pewter of his hair against the tan of his skin, the broad strength of his shoulders. *What I'm not sure of is how I'm going to get over what I just did. You're the first man I ever met who's as tough as me, but who sees past the toughness to the person I am underneath…or the person I might have been if Aldrich Peters and Lab 33 had never existed. And I've just warned you not to put your trust in me.*

She thrust her thoughts aside with an effort. "Except to the throat," she said, hoping her tone conveyed nothing of what she'd been feeling. "I can be killed if my air supply's cut off, so if it takes too long for me to heal up enough to begin drawing in oxygen again, I'm in trouble. But since that's only happened to me once before, I'm not worried." She jerked her head at the building in front of them. "I go in low, you go in high?"

"Sounds good," Ash said as another sharp burst of

gunfire erupted from somewhere on the grounds. He half rose and paused, his glance at her unreadable. "You know, one of the lab rats that were so *mysteriously* released wasn't found. It got clean away and made it to freedom. You might want to remember that when the time comes to make a decision, love."

"I've already made—" *Damn* the man, Dawn thought as he swiftly stood and began a zigzag sprint toward the building's entrance. She overtook him a yard away from the door and dropped into a crouching run as he kicked it open and they burst across the threshold. Out of the corner of her eye she saw a blur of red race over him and then race back to the middle of his chest.

"Five o'clock *low!*" she barked out, swinging the Beretta in her hand to her right and firing instinctively.

Both Asher's and her rounds caught the darkly clad figure. The man fell instantly, obviously dead before he hit the floor. Dawn ran over to the body and knelt beside it.

"Thanks for the heads-up, Swanson." Asher's smile was brief as he relieved the dead man of his weapon. "You think the bastard realized he got the two-for-one special?"

"Maybe." She scanned the shadows. "But I doubt he appreciated it. I recognize this shooter, Ash, so my guess was right—this is a Lab 33 operation, courtesy of Dr. Aldrich Peters." She stood, her expression grim. "The stairs, or cover this floor first?"

"This floor. Then we won't have to worry about any nasty surprises coming after us when we do get to the next level."

He made the decision without hesitation, and just as unhesitatingly, Dawn followed his lead down the darkened hallway. This was the kind of situation his SAS experiences had trained him for, she admitted. Whereas she had more often been in the position of melting into the shadows to escape those searching for her, Ash was accustomed to taking the offensive in any search-and-destroy operation. Their talents were different but complementary, she thought with a frown. It was too bad that at some point they would have to go up against each other—

"Bloody hell!"

The reason for his whispered curse was immediately apparent. She shrank back against the wall, just out of sight of the open doorway to the cafeteria, the scene she'd glimpsed making her want to swear, too.

"I counted four gunmen," she said in a low tone. "Dammit, Ash, they must have rounded up most of the lab staff and herded them in there. Roger…" She swallowed hard. "Roger's on one of the tables, bleeding from the head."

"And one of the female techs is lying dead or unconscious over in the far corner of the room." Asher's jaw tightened. "Any ideas on how we take out the Lab 33 contingent without risking further civilian casualties?"

"We need a diversion," she answered slowly. "You provide it here by the entrance, I'll go in from above." She saw his momentary puzzlement and nodded upward at the almost-invisible air grate in the ceiling. "The ductwork. By now I know it like the back of my hand. Don't ask."

"I don't want to," he muttered, locking his fingers together to give her a boost up. "Dammit, that was next on my security to-do list."

What she'd told him was true, Dawn reflected as she

hoisted herself into the shaft, the ductwork was now as familiar to her as if it were her own personal and hidden freeway through the building. But the previous times she'd crawled through it she hadn't been acutely aware that only a few feet of space separated her from an alert enemy below. *Plus those other times you weren't festooned with enough hardware to sink a battleship,* she thought edgily, *not to mention wearing a pair of thick-soled combat boots that'll make a sound like a kettledrum against the metal walls if you put a single step wrong.*

Dead ahead was one of the louvered grates that looked directly down into the cafeteria, marked only by the slight lessening of the darkness in the shaft from the half-power lighting coming from the room below. Scrunching forward on her elbows and knees, she maneuvered herself to where she could squint through it and found herself staring straight into the open eyes of Roger, still lying on the table.

There was no way he could see her. His glasses lay shattered on the floor a few feet away, and his eyes were so clouded with pain that she doubted he was even aware of his surroundings. As she watched, she saw his right fist come politely to his mouth, and he gave one of his patented apologetic coughs, this one ending in a spasm of choking.

A terrible anger filled Dawn. "Gonna get you out of there, Rog," she said in a shaky undertone. "Hang on just a few seconds longer, pal. Me and Ash are going to take down every last mother of those bastards who did this to—"

A sudden burst of gunfire erupted suddenly from the direction of the cafeteria's entrance. From her vantage point she saw the four Lab 33 guards jerk their weapons away from their captives and toward the doorway, and instantly she acted.

Shoving the grate aside and dropping down into the room, she landed on the table beside a barely conscious Roger and saw a flicker of dull hope cross his features. Then she was focusing her attention on the nearest Lab 33 operative.

He was standing with his back to her, but at the sound of her boots hitting the floor he whirled, bringing his rifle into firing position as he did. Supremely aware of Roger lying behind her in the operative's line of fire and the frightened group of scientists behind him who could be hit by a stray bullet of hers, Dawn didn't hesitate.

The bowie knife left her hand as the gunman's finger began to squeeze his weapon's trigger. It flashed toward him like a silvery bolt of lightning and found its target before he could get off a single shot.

"Jolly—jolly good, Miss Swanson. It *is* you, isn't it?" Roger's weak voice came from behind her as she placed a booted foot on the operative's chest and pulled the knife from his chest. Dawn looked swiftly over her shoulder and saw the shy Englishman attempt a smile. "That's the ticket. Right…right through the murderous heart of that son of a bitch, as you Americans might say…"

A spasm of choking racked him, and a look of apology crossed his face. Then his coughing abruptly ceased and his eyes dimmed in death.

Grief threatened to engulf her. She pushed the wave of emotion away and replaced it with cold determination. A quick glance showed her that Asher had now entered the cafeteria and had taken out another opponent

already, but as she looked she saw one of the two remaining gunmen take aim at the SAS man.

This time the Beretta was her weapon of choice, but
just as she brought it swiftly up to snap off a shot she
felt a burning sensation at the side of her neck, as if
some angry hornet had stung her. Ignoring the pain and
the sudden trickle of blood, Dawn fired at her target and
with savage satisfaction saw him throw his hands into
the air as her bullet found its mark. She turned to face
the fourth and final Lab 33 operative.

Despite the poor light there was no mistaking Hendrix Kruger's blunt features. The South African expa-
triate's pale blue eyes widened in quick alarm and then
he moved more swiftly than she would have guessed he
was capable of.

The woman he thrust in front of him as a human
shield was one of the British lab techs whom Dawn had
noticed during her time undercover as Dawn Swanson,
but had never had the opportunity to speak with. Nearly
fainting in terror, behind her glasses her mutely be-
seeching eyes held Dawn's.

"It is true what the *doktor* says, then." Kruger nodded judiciously as he realized she wasn't about to fire.
"Once Lab 33's top assassin wouldn't have let such a
small thing as a bystander's death stop her from taking out an enemy. But you have become soft, it
seems."

"I never would have sacrificed a civilian to save my
own skin," she said evenly. "I'm not about to now, either."

Kruger opened his mouth, but whatever his intended
reply would have been, it remained forever unspoken.
Asher's shot was deadly and accurate, and as the South
African crashed to the floor, the terrified lab tech took

a few stumbling steps and fell into the arms of a group of co-workers.

"Five down," Asher said curtly as Dawn joined him in the doorway of the cafeteria. He saw her quick assessment of the gaping wound on his shoulder and shook his head. "A stray bullet tore me up a little, but it's nothing that can't be stitched together later. From the gunfire we've been hearing outside, I'd say there have to be at least ten shooters scattered around the grounds as a diversionary force to keep my people from reaching this building. If your original estimate of twenty is correct, we're still outnumbered five to two."

"I've been up against worse odds. I imagine you have, too," Dawn replied with a shrug. She lengthened her stride as they neared the stairs to the second level, suddenly not wanting Asher's keen awareness on her. "Rog didn't make it," she said, her voice sounding too harsh to her own ears. "His death is going to tear your uncle…tear your uncle…"

What the hell was the matter with her throat? she wondered angrily. Had Kruger's badly aimed bullet nicked some vital cord necessary for speech? Because try as she might, she couldn't get the rest of her sentence past the odd-feeling swelling that seemed to be blocking her voice.

"I'm sorry, love." Asher's grip on her arm brought her to a halt as they reached the top of the stairs. "He'd become a friend, hadn't he? Don't try to talk about it right now while it's still so painful, but later if you want a shoulder to—"

Dawn wrenched her arm from his grip. "A shoulder to cry on, Ash? Give me a freakin' break! I mean—" she made an all-encompassing gesture at herself "—look at me! Guns, knives—I'm not exactly the girlie-girl type who falls to pieces over every little thing, dammit. Rog was a nice enough guy and he didn't deserve to die, but any friendship you thought I had with him was all part of my cover…just like the relationship I cultivated with Sir William and just like the one I tried to cultivate with you."

"Is that what you tell yourself?" His smile was tight. "Not true. You're no lab rat, you're part of the human race, and you've got all the emotions the rest of us poor mortals have. It's nothing to be ashamed of, whatever that bastard Peters may have tried to make you believe. Like I said, you're going to have to make a decision at some point, but for your own sake, know who you really are before you make it."

"I do." She kept her voice low and jerked her head in the direction of Sir William's door, now only yards away. "I'm a woman who's itching to take out some Lab 33 thugs, with or without your help. Any friendlies in your uncle's study besides the old man himself?"

He kept his attention on her. "I posted Keifer and Reese to guard his research. My uncle and my men, Swanson—so before we make our move I need to know how far you'll go to get those notes for yourself."

It took a second for her to understand what he meant. When she did, outrage filled her. "You're asking me if I'd let you help me take out Peters's men and then turn my gun on you and your people?"

"You said without that research you're dead," he reminded her in a tense whisper. "I have to assume that means you hope there's still a chance you can deliver on your contract with Aldrich Peters and have him rescind the shoot-to-kill order he's put out on you."

"Dammit, I—" *He's got every right to ask the ques-*

tion, O'Shaughnessy, Dawn thought suddenly. *A few minutes ago you told him not to trust you...and he shouldn't. But at least you can set his mind at ease on this particular point.*

"A man named Lee Craig taught me everything I know, Ash," she said quietly. "He was an assassin and a liar and if he hadn't been killed I would have had to take him down myself. But he lived by his own code, and for what it's worth he passed that code on to me. I won't betray an ally. Your men and your uncle are in no danger from me."

"Your word as a geeky lab tech?" He gave her a wry smile and she felt some of the tension ease from her.

"May I be forced to hold my hand over a Bunsen burner flame if I'm lying," she said with mock solemnity. She took a deep breath. "Ready?"

"As I'll ever be," he said, his smile thinning. "Let's party, Swanson."

They hit the door running, and without its security system in place it burst open instantaneously. Dawn got a split-second glimpse of the scene and threw herself into a roll, dimly aware that beside her Asher had done the same. They came up firing, each on opposite corners of the room, each choosing the nearest targets. She felt a searing pain claw its way through her right arm. Wincing, she tossed the Beretta into her left.

She'd been wounded, but she would heal, she thought as she aimed with cold deliberation at the black-clad operative who spun around from the open safe and began to bring his rifle into firing position. She didn't know if she could say as much for Reese, whose prone body was lying half under the desk, and she was almost certain that wasn't the case with Keifer. Ash's friend looked more dead than alive. Her quick assessment of the scene as she'd entered had shown her Sir William as being the only non Lab 33 member unharmed, although from the pallor of his face as he strained against the gag stuffed into his mouth and the cords binding him to the chair behind his desk, his health situation could become critical at any moment.

The man in front of the safe was one she'd seen dozens of times in the underground corridors of Lab 33. His eyes widened in brief recognition. "You bitch, O'Shaughnessy!" he snarled as he began to pull the trigger of his assault rifle. "This is my lucky—"

"Day?" she suggested as her bullet smashed into him, driving him back against the open safe. He slid sideways along the wall, leaving a smear of crimson, before tumbling to the carpet.

"Two and two." Asher's voice was ice, but its coldness wasn't directed at her. His angry glance swept over the bodies of the two men he'd eliminated, and then to Dawn's lifeless opponents. "Our estimate was off by one. Too bad."

She nodded, already on her way to Sir William. "I know. It wouldn't have caused me any sleepless nights either if I'd been able to take down a few more of those bastards. And it sounds as if the situation outside is under control, too." She squatted down by the old scientist's chair. "Check on your men, Ash," she said quietly. "I'll take care of your uncle."

Taking the gag off was her first priority, she realized, alarmed by the way Sir William's eyes were bulging desperately at her. It was some kind of tough nylon material, so instead of trying to untie the knot she used the stiletto.

"Now for your hands and ankles," she said as Sir William's mouth worked soundlessly. "Don't worry, your saliva's just dried up, sir. Give yourself a minute to recover before you try to—"

"Watch *out!*" Sir William shouted hoarsely.

Dawn reached swiftly for the Beretta, lying on the floor beside her where she'd placed it. As her hand closed around it she saw a red pinpoint of light race up her arm, across her chest, and then up higher where she couldn't see it…to the one vulnerable area on her body.

Fear tore through her. About to roll out of the line of fire, she saw that her only available option would place her directly in front of Sir William and put him in danger. Desperately she tried to see where the shooter had hidden himself, but as she glimpsed the barrel of a rifle protruding from behind the velvet drapes at the window, she knew her time had run out.

An unseen finger pulled an unseen trigger. A flash of muzzle fire lit up the dim room. And the round that had been fired caught SAS Captain Destin Asher as he made a flying leap to cover her.

"No!" Dawn was barely aware that she'd screamed out the denial. Asher crashed to the floor in front of her, but already she was on her feet and firing at the Lab 33 operative who had stepped forward from the curtains and was aiming at her. "You bastard, you killed my *partner!*"

Afterward, she never could recall exactly which of her shots took him down. She didn't remember standing over him, firing the last of the Beretta's fifteen rounds and then continuing to pull the trigger on an empty chamber. But at Sir William's gentle reprimand, she came to, as if she had been shaken roughly from a nightmare.

"That's enough, my dear. He's dead. And we have men here to save." She turned a blank stare toward the old scientist and saw him rise with difficulty from Ash's body. His bushy eyebrows drew together in a scowl, but his faded blue eyes were bright with moisture. "My nephew's badly wounded, but he'll survive if he gets medical attention right away. So will Private Reese, although if Lieutenant Keifer pulls through it will be a miracle, I'm afraid," he said heavily. "I'll phone down to the infirmary."

"The phones aren't—" Dawn closed her mouth as Sir William began speaking into the receiver of the obviously now working instrument. She looked down at Asher.

Beneath his tan his skin was a muddy-gray, and under the hastily tied strip of cloth Sir William had used to stanch the wound seeped a dark flow of blood. But his eyes were open and he was watching her. "One…one of them called you O'Shaughnessy," he rasped with difficulty. "It was good fighting alongside you, O'Shaughnessy. Think we might do it again sometime?"

Swiftly she bent down and touched her lips to his. She straightened and shook her head. "I don't think so, Ash. You risked your life for me, and I'll never forget that. But if I stuck around you'd just have to arrest me, and I can't let that happen." A few feet away from him on the floor was a familiar sheaf of papers. She walked over and picked them up, tucking them inside her top, before striding to the doorway.

"The truce between us is over," she said tonelessly. "If we ever meet again, we won't be fighting side by side, we'll be fighting to the death against each other."

Chapter 15

Status: nine hours fifty-eight minutes and counting
Time: 1402 hours

"I made an error in judgment, Dawn." A trace of annoyance crossed Aldrich Peters's aquiline features. "As I told you when you delivered London's notes to me three days ago, I was wrong to doubt that you would accomplish your mission and doubly wrong to suspect you might have turned against Lab 33. But now that my people have come up with the serum that will save your life, we should look to the future, not the past."

"Agreed, Doctor." Dawn nodded curtly at a passing Lab 33 guard clad in the familiar gray-and-red uniform, noting the fear that darted in his hastily averted eyes. "But I can hardly look to the future if I don't have one, and after what happened at Sir William's lab I see that as a very real possibility. I've been talking with Drs. Sobie and Wang, and they tell me that the serum has no effect on an ordinary human being. That being the case, I took the precaution of setting up a blind control situation."

Peters frowned. "I don't understand."

In front of them the hallway came to an abrupt halt at a pair of steel doors. She glanced upward at the electronic lens positioned there, pretended to hesitate just long enough for her retinas to be scanned, and then stood aside to let Aldrich Peters precede her through. The doors closed behind her as she and Lab 33's director entered the extensive laboratory facilities of the complex.

"Carter's going to be taking the serum at the same time I do. The hypos will be filled from the same sealed vial, and I'll choose which one I get and which one's injected into the director of your Identities Department. I think that's fair, don't you, Doctor?"

This was the moment of truth, Dawn thought, watching Peters's reaction. Carter was too valuable an asset for Peters to gamble away. If his chilly gray gaze showed even a flicker of hesitation she would know that his plan to have her killed hadn't been discarded but merely revised.

"To everyone but young Carter." He sounded unperturbed, and she let out a breath she hadn't been aware of holding. "If you believe there's a chance I've given orders for you to be injected with a poison instead of a lifesaving compound, your paranoia doesn't bode well for our relationship, Dawn."

"See, I would have said that your attempted hit on me had taken care of the 'not boding well' thing already," she drawled. "Like Uncle Lee used to say, it's not para-

noia if they're really trying to kill you. Do we do it my
way or not?"

· It really *wasn't* fair to Carter, Dawn thought a few
minutes later as she and Peters entered the procedure
room. Large and spotlessly gleaming, its walls and
floors were of white tile and a bank of high-intensity
lights flooded out even the faintest of shadows. Near the
high ceiling a barrier replaced the white tile, and behind
it she could see what looked like the full contingent of
Lab 33's scientific team, obviously gathered there to
witness the procedure that would take place below. Behind a glass partition stood two stainless-steel gurneys.
Strapped to one of them was the skateboarding head of
the Identities Department.

Of course, if Carter for whatever reason had deliberately failed to reveal to her the fact that her partial
thumbprint was on Interpol's files, he deserved everything that was about to happen to him, she thought coldly
as Peters conferred with Dr. Wang and Dr. Sobie. And
although neither he nor Peters knew it, getting a harmless injection would be the least of his problems today.

Her phone call to Kayla Ryan three nights ago had
been brief and to the point. "Tell your people that Lab
33 goes down in seventy-nine hours exactly," she'd said
tersely. "That'll be just after nine, three nights from
today. I'm on my way back there now and I'll make sure
that all the arrangements we agreed upon are in place
for you and the authorities."

"Slow down." Kayla's tone had held a burr of sleepiness, but her next words had proved she was anything
but fuzzy minded. "What's the matter? You sound like—"
She'd given an uncertain little laugh. "Well, if you were
anyone else I'd say you sound like you've been crying."

Anger and doubt had warred in Dawn. Could Kayla and the others really have betrayed her? It just didn't feel right, not when they'd obviously cared so much for her biological mother. Not when they'd tried so hard to find Dawn and her sisters. But she couldn't take any chances now. "What you hear in my voice might be urgency—I've broken into a gas station and I'm using its phone to report in to you as I promised I would. When the Cassandras and their backup forces storm Lab 33 they'll have no problem with the facility's air locks and retinal scans—I'll have disabled everything a few hours before. Having doors opening for them won't alert the suspicions of Lab 33's staff and guards, of course, because that's what should happen. They'll assume their retinas have been scanned or they punched in the right code for a lock. But the doors will open no matter who's trying to get access, understand?"

"I understand." All trace of sleepiness in Kayla's voice had disappeared, but the caring tone remained. "Just remember, you aren't in this alone any more. You've got allies."

You don't want to be my ally, Ryan, believe me. The last one I had ended up hating me. Clutching the receiver to her ear, Dawn had closed her eyes, trying to shut out the scene that had been replaying itself in her mind ever since she'd walked away from Asher: the disbelief in his eyes, the pain that had tightened his features, the coldness that had replaced all other expressions just before he'd lost consciousness and she'd slipped out the door while Sir William was still on the phone. Had there been another way to handle the situation? *You know there wasn't,* she thought bleakly, *not without revealing who and what you are to too many people…and in the process, revealing that Faith and Lynn are equal candidates for the kind of research that some shadowy government department would want to conduct on the three of you if your secret got out. If the price you have to pay to keep that secret to yourself is making the man who saved your life wish he'd let you die, then you'll just have to pay it.*

She took a deep breath, realizing she'd come danger-ously close to saying something she might regret. "Sorry if I sound abrupt. It's just that I've been doing a lot of thinking lately, trying to work through that healing you said I needed to do. I still have mixed feelings about Lee Craig and sometimes I blame the Cassandras for the fact that I never had the chance to confront him with his lies. It's silly, I know, but…" She'd let her voice trail off and had given a thin smile as Kayla had fallen for the bait.

"It's not silly at all." Kayla's words had been sym-pathetic—falsely sympathetic? "And you're right, it's partly the fault of the Cassandras. Instead of giving you time to come to terms with the bombshell we dropped on you last December, we asked for your help in find-ing your sisters."

"Lynn and Faith are going to be part of the raid, aren't they?" Dawn spoke sharply, her edginess based on sudden fear. "I mean—" she tried to soften her tone "—if anyone deserves to be there when Aldrich Peters has to face the music, it's them. He tampered with their lives, too." Lynn's super agility and computer knowl-edge and Faith's extrasensory skills would be helpful.

But what's more important, I'm going to have to tell them what's happening to their genes and give them the reversal serum soon after they arrive, she thought wor-riedly. *I hate leaving it to the eleventh hour like that, but*

I can't confirm the Cassandras' suspicions about my vulnerability by revealing that my sisters are facing a genetic crisis, too—not if Sam St. John is really trying to take me out.

"You couldn't keep them away," Kayla answered. "They both want to do their bit to bring down Lab 33. They told me if I was talking to you to send you their love, by the way."

Her grip on the phone had tightened. "They're doing well?"

"They're doing fine." There had been faint puzzlement in Ryan's voice. "Why wouldn't they be?"

"No reason, just sisterly concern." Relief had flooded her at the knowledge that Lynn and Faith obviously hadn't been suffering the debilitating symptoms she had. "I'd better ring off now, Kayla. As it is, Aldrich Peters is going to have some questions for me when I reach Lab 33, and I don't want to arouse his suspicions any more than I have to."

"I understand." Kayla had hesitated. "Or maybe I don't. You never did tell me what this last hush-hush mission for him was all about, just that you needed to complete it for your own reasons. One day you'll have to fill me in on all the exciting details."

She'd nearly lost it at that point, Dawn thought now as she waited for Peters to finish giving his instructions to the doctors. *Either Ryan's a way better actress than I would have thought, or the Cassandras haven't betrayed me. If the pieces didn't fit together so perfectly, I wouldn't consider that the Cassandras could be behind the assassination attempt on me.*

But the pieces did fit, not merely because the assassin had known her real name, had known her location and had been aware of her enhanced abilities, but that a professional-style execution had been attempted. That could point to Lab 33, but it could also point to the Cassandras.

The organization she'd given her life to had betrayed her—but could these special women truly be her enemies?

As Peters turned from the doctors and began walking toward her, Dawn reflected on the irony of one thing she *was* sure of—the one man who'd had no reason at all to take her side had risked his life for her safety.

"I've explained your decision to Dr. Wang and Dr. Sobie," Aldrich said crisply as he rejoined her. "Being medical people, they're not happy that you're taking your treatment into your own hands, so to speak, but they confirm what you told me about the serum being harmless to young Mr. Johnson. We'll do it your way, Dawn."

"I'd like the room cleared. I'd also like a few moments alone with Carter to reassure him, so I'll be turning off the speakers to the gallery until I actually begin the procedure," she answered, with an effort submerging her thoughts of Asher and focusing her full attention on her immediate situation. "If you could close the door behind you as you and the others leave, Doctor?"

Her attitude was close to insubordinate and from Peters's quick frown as he exited, Dawn knew he was irritated by it. She didn't care. Her time at Lab 33 would be coming to an end within hours.

Her back to the watchers in the gallery, she approached the console that controlled the lighting, temperature and speakers for the room. With a swift twist of her hand she wrenched the speaker knob completely off, and then proceeded briskly to the glassed-in cubicle where the two gurneys, only one of them as yet occupied, waited.

"Dawn! What the hell's going on?" Carter's usually laid-back manner was nowhere in evidence. His voice rose higher, cracking nervously. "A couple of no-neck goons escorted me from my office, told me they're acting on the boss man's orders, and the next thing I know I'm being strapped down like a guinea pig. Get me out of here!"

"The guards weren't acting on Dr. Peters's orders, they were acting on mine." Walking over to the nearby steel instrument table, Dawn felt an all-too-familiar stab of pain in her temples. She fought it back. The headaches had been coming with increasing frequency these past few days, but soon they would be a thing of the past. "He's now approved my decision, however. Tell me, Carter, why didn't you let me know my prints were on file with Interpol before I left on my last mission?"

As she spoke she picked up the membrane-sealed vial of serum lying on the table. She held it up to the light and then reached for one of the two hypodermic needles that had been laid out.

"I don't know what you're talking about." Carter's denial was too swift. "Dawn, babe, tell me you're not thinking of using that thing on me."

Piercing the vial's membrane with the needle's tip, carefully she drew the plunger back until the hypodermic's barrel was filled with the colorless liquid. Dr. Sobie had informed her that most of the mixture was a mild sedative, prepared that way so she would be totally relaxed while the serum did its work. Knowing that her mental defenses would be lowered for several hours had worried her until she'd hit upon the idea of disabling the sound system. It wasn't a perfect solution; there was still a chance that Peters would actually enter the chamber and take the opportunity to ask a few pointed questions to which she might mumble an answer, but at least it eliminated the possibility of a half-asleep murmur being relayed to the gallery and giving her away.

As an added bonus, their privacy right now meant she could grill Carter.

She turned to him, her eyes on the tiny stream of liquid that spurted from the needle's tip as she checked for air bubbles. "You did it for money, of course. You'll do anything for money, Johnson—even work here. Who paid you to send me out with a flawed cover story?"

"I swear I didn't know about the prints being on file, Dawn!" As the hypo drew closer to his strapped-down arm, his eyes fixed on hers with hysterical intensity. "You've got to believe me! I sent you out squeaky clean, and if someone later accessed my system and dirtied your file, I had nothing to do with it! He was just a voice on the phone and an envelope of money left on my desk afterward, dammit—I don't even know who he was! I don't deserve to be killed for walking away from my computer for half an hour, do I?"

Dawn stared at him. Weak defiance struggled with terror on his face, and the terror won. He really was despicable, she thought in disgust. He'd sold her out, and now he was justifying his actions by telling himself he'd had no option but to—

Her thoughts came to a halt. She focused on the hypo in her hand and revulsion washed over her. How different was she from Carter? For that matter, how different was she from anyone in this place, Aldrich Peters included? In front of her was a terrified man strapped to a gurney, who was convinced she was about to give him a lethal injection. She'd encouraged his erroneous belief so she could get the information she'd needed from him.

And that information had come just in time to stop her from making a terrible mistake. The voice on Carter's phone had been male, not female. Not one of the Cassandras—it had to be one of Peters's assassins.

"No, Carter, you don't deserve to be killed," she said, her voice not entirely even. "You probably deserve to be put in prison for the other things you've done, but if you'll take my advice you might even escape that." She set down the hypodermic, noting as she did that her fingers were trembling slightly, and began unbuckling the straps that held him to the gurney. "Aldrich is going to want to know why I didn't give you the serum. Tell him that the mere fact he agreed to my demand convinced me he hadn't set me up. Then go get your freakin' skateboard, tell the guards at the gate you'll be back in a few hours, and put as much distance between you and Lab 33 as you can. This particular gravy train's about to be derailed."

Despite his irritating mannerisms, Carter was no fool. He took one look at her eyes and nodded. "Okay," he said slowly. "But why are you telling me? And what's to stop me from telling Peters?"

"I'm telling you because I owe you—not only for what I just did, but for the information you just gave me. It was more important than you'll ever know," Dawn said. She undid the last strap and stood back from the gurney with a shrug. "And you won't tell Peters because if you do I'll hunt you down and kill you. Understand?"

"Totally." Hastily Carter hopped down from the gurney. At the doorway he paused and looked back at her, some of his former insouciance already visible again in his grin. "Hey, Dawn—what you said about this gravy train? No problemo, I'll just hitch myself a ride on another one. People like Peters are always looking for smart young employees like yours truly. Stay cool, babe."

The Cassandras would be furious when they learned she'd given him a Get Out of Jail Free card, Dawn thought as she hoisted herself onto the second gurney and lay back, the lights above her bright enough that she saw nothing of the onlookers in the gallery above. And that wouldn't be all they'd be furious about. Ryan, for one, would find it hard to forgive her for believing that the Cassandras could have assigned Samantha St. John to assassinate her.

But whatever it takes, I'm going to make it right with her, she told herself as she reached for the serum-filled hypo on the table beside the gurney. *Kayla is a girlfriend worth keeping, and except for my sisters, I haven't had the opportunity to make many of those.*

She felt the sharp sting of the lifesaving serum as it entered her bloodstream, and almost immediately a drowsy lassitude began to overtake her, but her thoughts continued. Maybe Kayla or one of the Cassandras could find a job for her in the legit spy world. She would be a hunter, yes, but no longer a predator. It was possible she might even have a real life with friends, a home that wasn't a laboratory, maybe a romantic interest at some point.

Asher. She would go back to him after this was all over and explain everything to him, she decided groggily. Odds were he would tell her to go to hell, but she would try anyway. *Fighting alongside him felt right, and kissing him felt fabulous,* she told herself with a slight smile. *Maybe we really* do *have a chance at that future he was talking about. Once I eliminate that bastard Peters I'll be able to—*

The headache that had been growing all day suddenly exploded through her brain. Every nerve ending in her body seemed suddenly on fire. A tidal wave of pain towered over her, crashed down on her and gathered itself for a second agonizing assault, and then a third.

She could survive this, Dawn thought desperately. Soon the serum would begin working and she would never have to go through this again. The headaches would disappear for good, her symptoms would vanish forever, and she could begin deciding what she would do with the rest of her life.

Because her foolish dreams of a moment ago would never become reality. She'd forgotten one important detail.

Once she'd assassinated Aldrich Peters she would be a woman on the run. The Cassandras would have nothing to do with her, and Asher, if he ever met up with her again, would have no option but to turn her over to the authorities.

She would get the payback she'd wanted for so long…and she would lose everything else.

Chapter 16

Status: *three hours fifteen minutes and counting*
Time: *2045 hours*

She was still unconscious. It felt as if her eyes had flown suddenly open, but they couldn't have, Dawn thought hazily. Darkness surrounded her—the darkness of oblivion, the darkness of unconsciousness, so she was still under the influence of the heavy sedative that had accompanied the serum. Drs. Wang and Sobie had obviously lied about its strength.

"They work for Peters, so you should have expected them to, O'Shaughnessy." She frowned as she felt her lips move and heard her voice—slurred but definitely her own. She couldn't be totally out of it if she could speak. But then why couldn't she make out the slightest glimmer of the harsh lighting that was suspended above her or the blank whiteness of the walls around her? She tried to raise her hand and felt it lift into the air.

Glowing green numbers came into her line of sight.

She shot bolt upright, panic sluicing through her as she focused her still-blurred vision on the luminous readout of her watch. What time was it? *What time was it?*

Eight forty-six p.m. The Cassandras hadn't stormed Lab 33 yet. She half fell, half boosted herself off the gurney and collapsed in a heap on the floor, her legs rubbery. Feeling around in the dark for the edge of the steel table, she hauled herself upright, her mind racing.

She'd told Kayla to commence the raid at nine sharp. Ryan and the rest of the Cassandras were professionals; there was no way they would shave fifteen minutes off the agreed-upon time, so the pitch-blackness all around her wasn't the result of either their attack or Lab 33's response to it, and neither was the fact that she was all alone in a deserted operating room that should have been filled with doctors and scientists.

Only one man could have put her in her current situation, and that man was Aldrich Peters. But why, dammit?

Her coordination was still as bad as if she'd spent the past seven hours tossing back Cosmopolitans instead of lying motionless on a gurney. She lurched away from the steel table, banged her hip on the console that held the speaker and temperature controls, and slammed her face into something hard and invisible. It was the glass door of the cubicle, she realized, wincing and rubbing her forehead. She found the door handle, turned it and stumbled into the main part of the room, her head tender where she'd hit it. She took two more steps and then came to a sudden stop.

Her hours-long unconsciousness had come as a release from the unendurable pain she'd been going through. Now that pain was totally gone, and for the first time in days she wasn't experiencing even the tiniest throbbing that signaled it was lurking somewhere at the back of her brain, ready to strike. The serum had worked. The degeneration of her genes had not only been halted, it had been reversed.

She fell again to her knees, but this time it was thankfulness that robbed her legs of strength. Her death warrant had been canceled…and as soon as Faith and Lynn arrived she would be able to cancel theirs, too.

Determination forced her to her feet again and propelled her unsteadily across the room. She reached the door, felt for the light switch, flipped it on.

Instantly her world went from blackness to blinding brilliance—white walls, white-tiled floor, the glittering steel of tables and gurneys. Shielding her eyes against the sudden light, she hurried back to the glassed-in cubicle, but stopped on the threshold in sudden disbelief.

There was nothing on the table—no hypos, no vials, no sign of the precious serum that had been there earlier. Everything had been removed. Everyone had gone. She had been left here alone like a rat in a trap.

"Which is *exactly* what this is!" Hastening back to the main doors, Dawn automatically glanced upward for her retinas to be scanned and then remembered it wasn't necessary. They opened in front of her and she strode unsteadily through them into the hallway, her anger growing. "Even if I don't understand what's behind all this, I know a freakin' trap when I see one. But whatever Peters has planned, he's not going to live long enough to see it through, damn him. It's going to be a pleasure to watch that bastard—"

The scream that tore from her throat overrode the rest of her sentence. Instantly her palms pressed to her temples in an instinctive but vain attempt to contain the agony that was shooting through her. The pain subsided for a moment and then came back stronger.

"All…a *lie!*" Her words came out thickly. She took a few staggering steps and fell to her hands and knees, dimly aware but past caring that a couple of Lab 33 guards were hastening down the corridor toward her. "I didn't get the serum…he never *intended* for me to get—"

"It's Dawn O'Shaughnessy, for God's sake." All she could see were the guards' boots planted in front of her, but she could hear the apprehension in the voice of the one who had spoken. Revulsion was in the second guard's voice.

"It's the freak, you mean. What the hell's the matter with her, it looks like she's having some kind of fit. Hey, O'Shaughnessy!" A pair of fingers snapped in front of her face. "O'Shaughnessy, can you hear me?" The fingers disappeared and as if from a great distance away Dawn heard coarse laughter. "Totally gone, can you believe it? If a guy ever wondered what it would be like taking a hack at that prime piece, now would be the time. I'm thinkin' that empty storage room by the elevators. You game, Lewinsky?"

"Why the hell not? I always thought she had it coming to—"

"Bad…mistake, boys." She could move despite the pain, Dawn found as she got to her feet. She swayed, caught her balance, felt rage give her strength. "Even on my worst day…more than a match for you…" For a moment her head cleared. She smashed her fist into the first guard's face and then whirled in time for her forearm to slam against the second man's windpipe. He went down clutching his throat, his eyes bulging, and she turned her attention back to the first guard as he grabbed for the pistol on his hip. Her hand came down like a blade on the back of his neck, and even before his knees hit the floor she was behind him, her grip tight on either side of his jawline.

"One quick twist and you're dead," she grated as the pain inside her head intensified. "It's what I was trained to do, do you understand...what I *am!*"

"Not anymore." The arid tones of Aldrich Peters came from the end of the hallway. Looking quickly up from the man whose life she held between her hands, Dawn saw Peters set down a briefcase and reach into the pocket of his suit jacket. "The assassin you once were wouldn't have hesitated to kill scum like that."

His hand came out of his pocket. He raised it and fired the gun he was holding. The guard kneeling in front of her gave a violent spasm and then slumped sideways to the floor. Peters fired again and the guard who had been clutching his throat kicked once and went still. The Lab 33 director dropped the gun into his pocket again and picked up the briefcase.

"You see?" he said with an austere smile. "You're not even worth the price of a bullet to me anymore, Dawn. You should have done yourself a favor and stayed unconscious a little longer."

"The serum." The hallway lights felt like knives stabbing at her eyes as she took a dizzy step toward him. "You *lied* to me! You said I would receive the serum, damn you, and then you left me to die!"

"What are you experiencing right now?" He sounded genuinely curious. "Wang and Sobie predicted excruciating headaches, maybe nausea. Were they right?"

Leaning against the wall for support, she ignored his question. "You know I need it to live, Doctor. Where is it?"

Peters looked disgusted. "Right here." He patted the briefcase. "Please don't insist on playing out this little farce to the bitter end, Dawn. I knew within days of your making contact with them that you'd aligned yourself with my enemies, and when you returned to Lab 33 professing your continued loyalty it was all I could do not to give the order to have you eliminated right there and then. But with or without your help my days at Lab 33 were coming to an end, thanks to the women of Athena Academy. Rainy Miller's dearest friends. I saw a way I could use you, and by so doing insure my retirement fund received one final influx of cash." He checked his watch before turning his cold expression once more her way. "You might be interested to know that the old man's research created quite a heated bidding war between the parties I offered it to. It's amazing the sums some of those groups of wild-eyed true believers can scrape up."

"You sold the regeneration research to terrorists?" Again the pain behind her eyes rose to a crescendo, nearly causing her to lose her balance. "Sir William said that as the formula is now, it could change the way a normal human's body heals after accident or illness. After a few years of accelerated testing your clients might well find a way to insure that every killer they send out is virtually invincible, dammit!"

"That's not my concern." Again Peters glanced at his watch. "The time, however, is. It's nine o'clock, and

according to the tap we put on that gas station telephone—one of several we installed along the route I
knew you would have to take from London's research
facility—your friends should be arriving just about—"

A muffled explosion from some far area of the complex cut across the rest of his sentence. Aldrich's eyebrows lifted fractionally. "Such militarily precise timing
could only be Captain Asher's doing. You did know that
the Athenas contacted him to lend support to this mission, didn't you? My sources tell me that your *sisters*
went to see him in the hospital where he was being
treated for the wounds he received during the action at
London's lab three nights ago. It seems he recovered far
more quickly than expected. They asked him personally
to join this fight."

"If you know about Lynn and Faith then you know I
want the serum as much for them as for myself, Doctor—and you also know I've been told the truth about
my origins and theirs." Dawn's voice was flat with hatred. "You've torn our lives apart from the moment we
were conceived, but I won't allow you to destroy us
anymore."

"I don't think you can stop me. I intend to walk out
of here by an underground escape route that no one
knows about but myself, and in your condition, there's
really nothing you can do about that."

As briskly as a man heading for a business meeting,
Peters turned on his heel and began heading down the
hall, briefcase in hand. She willed her legs to stumble
after him, but try as she might she couldn't catch up before he turned down one of the smaller corridors branch-
ing from the main hallway. Her weakness wasn't merely
a by-product of the sedation, Dawn thought desperately,

it had to be a precursor of the final stages of her symptoms. *Aldrich is right,* she told herself with grim determination. *In this condition I probably shouldn't even be capable of walking, let alone stopping him. But there's one factor he hasn't taken into consideration: how much I need to avenge myself on him. If I have to crawl through hell on my hands and knees to kill him, dammit, I'll make myself do it.* Pain lancing sharply through her head, she staggered into the smaller corridor, only to come to a halt.

It was a blind alley. No more than six or seven feet in length, it ended at a smoothly plastered wall. And it was empty.

During the past minutes the sounds of fighting had been coming closer, level by level. The shaft of the elevator was a perfect conduit for the shouts and gunfire that signaled the descent of the battle from the main entrance floor where the Cassandras and their FBI SWAT team would have gained access, down to the level directly above her. Now Dawn heard booted feet running down the hall she'd just been in and caught a glimpse of a cadre of Lab 33 guards speeding by, their weapons at the ready. In a few moments she would be caught in the middle of a pitched battle, she realized tensely. Peters hadn't vanished into thin air—there *had* to be an exit from this odd cul-de-sac.

She felt the walls for any impression, any secret release mechanism. Nothing. Quickly she dropped to her knees and ran her hands over the carpeted floor. Her fingers found what she had been looking for: an almost-imperceptible division in the shape of a square sliced into the carpet's short pile. She yanked on the fibers and the square lifted up to reveal a twisting set of stairs crudely cut into bare rock.

At any other time she would have dropped instantly into the opening, pulled the trapdoor closed above her and run down the stone steps after her quarry, but with her limbs feeling like lead and her vision blurring from the pain in her head, it took her precious minutes to make her shaky way down to level ground. Although level *underground* was a more appropriate term, she thought as she stared around her. All of Lab 33 was built below the surface of the arid and desolate area of New Mexican desert in which it was located, but this was even more subterranean than the rest of the complex. Despite the desert terrain above, it was dankly damp here, the tunnel she was in lit by sporadic bare bulbs strung along the ceiling.

"If I'm right, this eventually comes out on the far side of the canyon that's beside the main entrance to Lab 33. Peters must have built this as an escape route if the time ever came that he needed one," she said, anger giving her the strength to make her way along the tunnel. "But he never bothered to inform anyone else."

From up ahead came the sound of a heavy door closing. Dawn clapped her hands to her ears as the noise echoed through her already pounding head, but she forced herself to go on. A second door slammed just as the first one came into view, and a fierce joy temporarily overrode her pain.

Her final target was almost within reach. Everything else—the battle raging through Lab 33, the Cassandras and her sisters, even the serum itself—was suddenly swept aside by the hatred that surged through her.

She wrenched open the door and stumbled through it into darkness. As it swung heavily shut behind her, she realized she was wading through shallow water and, disoriented, she moved forward, but instead of the rough rock that the rest of the tunnel had been carved from, her feet slid on a smoothly unstable surface. She banged into what felt like a glass wall.

A brilliant bank of lights above her went on, illuminating the glass walls of the cube that surrounded her. Aldrich Peters stood on the other side of the sealed glass door ahead of her.

She looked upward just as the first icy jets of water began spurting from the massive stainless-steel head above her.

"Do you understand now, Dawn?"

Swinging her gaze back to Peters, she saw he was watching her. His voice seemed to be coming from one of the top corners of the glass cube, but she didn't bother to look. It was apparent there was some system that allowed an onlooker outside to communicate with whoever was in the glass cube, and presumably vice versa.

"That this is a trap? Yes, Doctor, I see that," she said. "And one built just for this particular rat, am I right?"

"It's been tested on others, but yes, it was built for you. Since the only sure way of killing you is by cutting off your supply of oxygen, drowning you has always seemed the most decisive method of eliminating you," acknowledged the man standing on the other side of the thick glass. "Even as a child you showed frightening promise of the powers you would grow into…and even more frightening signs that you might one day reject Lab 33 and all it stood for and begin thinking for yourself. Your doctors at the time concluded that if that happened, there would be two people most at risk from you. One of those people was myself, of course."

"And the other was Craig," finished Dawn. The water

had risen to her calves by now, and surreptitiously she glanced at the corners of the chamber where the glass walls met, hoping to discern some weakness. She had vowed she would take Peters down if it was the last thing she did, and she intended to keep that vow. There had to be *some* way she could escape, dammit.

"Don't waste your final minutes." Seemingly Aldrich had read her mind. "It's all one solid piece of glass, not tempered but of a technology my own people came up with. No seams, no joins, no place where you can break through, and the doors are triple thickness. Don't forget, it was made to withstand Lab 33's lab rat at her full strength, and you're hardly at full strength anymore, are you?" He didn't wait for an answer, but instead unsnapped the clasps of the briefcase he was carrying, extracting from it the vial of colorless liquid she had last seen sitting on the table beside the gurney in the procedures room. "I didn't totally trust the assessments of Wang and Sobie. I thought I needed to bring this along as bait to lure the rat into my trap, but the good doctors were right. In the end, the serum and the fact that it could save you and your sisters' lives wasn't what drove you to your own destruction—it was your desire to kill me. So I suppose I don't need this anymore."

His eyes met hers through the glass. He lifted the vial high and then opened his fingers, watching her intently as the container smashed into a thousand glittering shards on the rocky floor outside her prison. His gray eyes widened slightly. "Interesting. You've just seen your last hope of survival destroyed and yet you show no reaction at all, just as the psychologists predicted. I'm glad I allowed myself time to conduct this last experiment on you, Dawn. The results will be useful when

I set up my next lab and set about choosing new candidates for another gene-enhancement program."

She barely heard him. The leather of her catsuit was pressing wetly against her thighs now and her hair was plastered to her skull, soaked through by the splashing of the water pouring from the ceiling. Clumsily wading to one of the cube's corners, Dawn ran her hands along the curved edges. Peters had told the truth about that, if nothing else, she thought tensely. It was sharply curved, with no join between the walls that could be weakened by a well-placed kick. She turned her attention to the huge showerhead installation above, ignoring his words as they filtered through the speakers.

"According to the doctors' findings from the tests they ran when you returned to Lab 33, the pain in your head must be unendurable by now. It's really too bad your old mentor Lee Craig isn't here. He always told me it was him you would hate the most if you ever learned how he'd deceived you."

Her attention was temporarily diverted. "As you said a moment ago, the doctors who studied me when I was a child predicted there would be two people I'd want to destroy if I ever learned the truth—you and Craig, Doctor. You may have given the order for him to kill Rainy Miller, but he carried it out, knowing full well she was my biological mother. For that alone I wanted to—"

"Oh, no." His voice was silky with malice. "I didn't give Craig the order to kill your mother—he insisted on taking the assignment. That order was supposed to be yours to carry out."

"Mine?" The cold water rising around her suddenly felt warm compared to the icy shock that reverberated through her at his casual revelation.

Of course Aldrich Peters was capable of ordering Lab 33's lab rat to kill her own mother. He'd ordered her to kill the man she'd later learned was her father, hadn't he? And although her mission to kill Thomas King had been aborted before she'd completed it, nothing would ever take away the guilt she felt over her actions. If she'd killed Rainy Miller and later discovered who her unknown target had been, how would she have been able to live with herself?

You wouldn't have, Dawnie. That's why I took on the assignment…because I once promised you I'd stay strong enough to keep them from owning you, even if it cost me everything I cared for in this world. Thing is, kid, all I cared about was you. Lee Craig's voice had occasionally been in her head in the months since his death, but now it seemed to be reverberating through her whole being, Dawn thought wrenchingly, as if the man she'd once thought of as a father had a desperate need to communicate with her one final time. She pressed her hands to her ears and squeezed her eyes shut, but she couldn't blot out his words or stop herself from seeing his face. *But I knew one day you'd end up hating me…and that you'd have every right to. All I could hope for was that you wouldn't end up hating—*

"Damn straight I hate you, you bastard!" She didn't know she'd spoken aloud until she saw Peters's thin lips lift in chilly amusement. She tried to cover her confusion with a sneer. "If Lee Craig took over my assignment to assassinate Rainy Miller, it was because he was a stone-cold killer and not for any other reason. The shrinks were right. If he were standing here now I'd want to kill him just as much as I want to kill you!"

Still smiling slightly, Aldrich shook his head. "I'm

afraid you misunderstood me. Lee was never in the equation at all, according to the psychologists. No, the other person they knew you would want to destroy was yourself…and it seems you've fulfilled their prediction."

Dawn stared at him. Then she turned away, throwing her snarled words over her shoulder at him. "You're crazy, Doctor. Instead of using up your breath telling me more of your lies you should save it for running. Because I'm going to get out of here—and when I do it'll be payback time at long last."

She directed her attention to the ceiling again, but this time it was harder because her headache was blurring her vision. Dimly aware that she was no longer standing but keeping herself afloat by paddling, she tried to propel herself upward so that she could reach the metal conduit from which the water was gushing. She missed, and slid underwater as she fell back. Taking a deep breath, she tried a second time, and then a third and a fourth…

"Gonna…gonna see him *die*." This was better, Dawn thought minutes later. She didn't even have to jump anymore, all she had to do was put out her hand to touch the conduit. She was pushed under by the deafening torrent of water and languidly she kicked herself to the surface again, her face upturned to the glass ceiling. Her nose bumped against it. Yeah, any minute now she would be standing in front of Peters, deciding how she was going to take the bastard down. Strangling? She frowned. Too crude. She was Lab 33's assassin, after all, and she had a reputation to consider. A gun would be too fast—the moment would be over before she could savour it. She giggled suddenly and watched the bubbles float from her mouth with glee. She'd freakin' drown him, that's what she'd do! It would be perfect justice, perfect revenge, perfect...*payback.*

But first she needed to rest for a moment, and what better place to rest than here at the bottom of this incredible cube that looked as if it had been carved from ice and filled with a square of ocean. Where had she seen such a color before? It looked like beach glass, like aquamarines, like Des Asher's eyes just after he'd taken a bullet for her and just before he'd watched her walk away from him. He'd hoped they could have a future together, she thought hazily. What he hadn't understood was that she couldn't have a future—not with him, not with anyone, because she was Lab 33's assassin and Lab 33's assassin had one last hit to carry out.

A hit in which she was both the killer and the target.

"No!" A violent convulsion seemed to run through her body, and her legs, bent beneath her as she lay on the bottom of the water-filled chamber, jackknifed suddenly, shooting her up to the surface. Except there wasn't any surface anymore, Dawn thought frantically. The cube was almost full. All that remained was a sliver of space between the water and the ceiling.

She arched her neck, dragged in a shallow lungful of oxygen and felt herself sinking again. Through the wavering distortion of the water she saw Aldrich Peters's spare figure still standing on the other side of the glass.

He wants to make sure you die, O'Shaughnessy. Kind of funny, wouldn't you say—since according to him your death warrant was signed when he dropped that vial of serum. You think he knows something about your so-called gene-breakdown symptoms that you don't?

He'd said she had destroyed herself. His words had made no sense then, but now everything became chill-ingly clear—his knowledge of her symptoms, the information her subconscious had betrayed to the doctors who had assessed her upon her return to Lab 33 twenty-one days ago, Peters's anticipation of each move she'd made since she'd woken up in the procedures room tonight and gone hunting for him.

There was nothing wrong with her at all. Nothing genetic, at any rate. Just that for the past nine months she'd been methodically tearing herself in two by trying to put her Lab 33 legacy behind her while still justifying her cold-blooded desire for vengeance against Aldrich Peters. Her apparent symptoms—the crippling headaches, the loss of her abilities—had been merely the outward manifestations of her inward self-destruction. The psychological tests that had been run on her upon her return had predicted those manifestations to Peters…and his devious mind had immediately seen how he could use them to coerce Lab 33's lab rat into one final assignment.

But I'm not a lab rat anymore and I'm opting out of this experiment as of now, Dawn told herself forcefully. *I'll hand the sorry son of a bitch over to the authorities, dammit, and then go after the things I really want—like a life, a future working with the real good guys and getting to know my sisters, and maybe—just maybe—the chance to look into Des Asher's sexy aqua eyes once more.*

She shot to the surface. Dragging in a meager breath of air, she felt energy tingling like an electric current through her veins, not only recharging her strength but doubling it—no, *quadrupling* it.

"Getting outta here? Piece of cake," she muttered with wry amusement before letting herself sink to the bottom once more. Her boots made contact with the floor. Her body settled into a half crouch. Her mind shut out the man standing beyond the glass barrier, the water surrounding her, the fading oxygen in her lungs…but before her concentration became totally Zen-like, she allowed herself to notice that there was no longer the slightest flicker of pain in her head. The symptoms had gone for good.

And she and Peters had both underestimated what she was capable of. In front of her was thick glass. Dawn stared at it and visualized a spider's web of cracks radiating out from a single point in it, visualized the cracks shattering open, saw in her mind's eye the whole wall crashing outward and the roomful of water bursting out in a mighty flood.

She reached inside herself and found a woman strong enough to make all those visualizations reality.

"Kwa-sah!" The phrase exploded from her at the same time as her leg shot stiffly out from her body, her boot heel aiming for the very point in the wall where she had imagined the initial weakening. As her boot smashed into the glass the impact ran jarringly through her whole frame, but she didn't feel it. *"Che-sah!"* The spiderweb of cracks she had seen in her mind's eye were now there in front of her calm gaze, spreading rapidly from the epicenter of her kick. Her arms extended in front of her, palms flat. Dawn moved through the water and effortlessly pushed at the glass wall.

Her prison shattered and fell away from her.

Glittering shards exploded outward, propelled by an overwhelming rush of water. She held her balance for as long as she could, but then her feet slid out from under her and she was carried along with the flow, her concentration broken by a dizzying sense of joy and freedom.

I did it, Uncle Lee! Did you see me—I did it! Not the way you would have, because from now on I'm choosing my own path, my own life. But I did it, and part of the strength I needed came from you. So your little Dawnie says thank-you, Uncle Lee. Thank you...and goodbye.

The water on her face wasn't just water, it was mixed with tears. Lying on the rocky path where she'd been deposited by the now-spent contents of the tank, she dashed the tears away and with them went the last of her destructive hatred against a conflicted and complicated man who in his own way had loved her more than she'd ever known.

She could never completely erase her Lab 33 past, she thought with regret. But at least she'd put it to rest.

"You...you think you've won..."

Her thoughts had been so far from Aldrich Peters that at the sound of his voice Dawn whirled around in shock, immediately ready to defend herself if necessary. But it wasn't necessary, she saw, nausea rising in her as she took in the sight of him.

Dozens of spearlike shards of glass protruded from his crawling figure and some had sliced horrifically into his face. The water on the cavern floor around him was tinged a sickly pink, and from the paper-whiteness of his complexion it was obvious that most of his blood was now running over the wet rocks he was dragging himself across. He gave her a ruined facsimile of his former chilly smile, the nerves on one side of his face obviously severed.

"But you haven't, Dawn." Glass had also pierced his throat, and his voice was little more than a wet whisper. "I may not get out of here alive, but neither will you or the Athenas."

He was crawling toward his briefcase. Suddenly apprehensive, she strode forward and kicked it out of his reach, but too late she saw that his objective had been the small, plastic-encased rectangle lying near it. Peters's hand closed around the rectangle. Dawn heard a tiny clicking sound as his blood-smeared thumb pressed down on a button.

"Maximum...maximum body count." He didn't struggle as she snatched the unit from him. "I wanted to wait until the Athena women and the military and law enforcement agencies backing them were at full strength inside the complex. I would imagine even the stragglers have arrived by now."

"What is this?" It looked like a remote control, she thought impatiently, but it damn well didn't turn on a television. Aside from the button Peters had pushed, there was a numerical keypad and a digital readout— Her stomach clenched. "It's an explosive activator! You intend to blow Lab 33 and everyone in it sky-high, for God's sake!"

The readout showed four digits. Even as she focused on the angular red numbers, they changed from 21:01 to 21:00.

Dropping to her knees, she shoved the activator in his face, her expression etched with strain. "How do you stop the freakin' countdown? *How do you stop the countdown, dammit?*" she screamed.

"It can't be stopped once it's started." Now that he was no longer physically exerting himself, Peters's voice had more strength. "I calculated that after watching you die I would need twenty-two minutes to make my way to the helicopter waiting outside for me. I saw no reason to add a cutoff feature."

"Then where's the device?" The activator read 20:21. Dawn tasted sharp fear at the back of her throat. She grabbed Peters's shredded lapels. "You're dying—you have nothing to gain by taking others with you! Tell me where you planted the explosive!"

With a touch of his former icy arrogance, he pushed her away. "Nothing to gain? When covert government agencies that once funded me have denied their involvement and politicians whose predecessors used Lab 33's resources now pretend to be so appalled at our methods of operation that they support a group of women who want to take me down? Oh, I have something to gain, Dawn—I'll die knowing that my betrayers will pay for what they did to me."

"You want payback," she said hollowly. "So buy it with my blood, Doctor. Tell me where you planted the device in order that I can defuse it, and I swear I'll carry out the death you planned for me."

His fading gaze held cold amusement. "You're wasting your breath. Just as the activator can't be halted, neither can the device my people created be defused. Even if it could, you'd never be able to get to it. Despite its destructive power it's tiny…tiny enough to be implanted into a healing bullet hole on a man's body."

Her grasp on his lapels slid away. He slumped backward onto the rocky floor, a final gout of blood streaming from his side. "I guessed that the Athenas would enlist him in their battle, and that he would accept in the hope that he could retrieve London's research before it was sold. For a hefty sum, the doctor who attended his wounds at the hospital was willing to bend his Hippocratic oath and insert a small object in Captain Asher's bullet-torn arm before suturing it."

Aldrich Peters's voice faded. "You betrayed him, Dawn. You're the last person he'd trust now…and he'll kill you before he lets you get anywhere near him."

Chapter 17

Just ahead of her was the last curve in the rock-hewn corridor before the steps that led up to the lowest level of Lab 33. Dawn lengthened her stride, her leather cat-suit molding wetly to her body and her soaked boots squelching soddenly with each pounding footstep as she ran. Aldrich Peters was dead. Once that fact would have filled her with dark satisfaction, but now it meant nothing to her. All her thoughts and energies were directed toward one impossible goal—to somehow get to Asher in time, somehow explain the situation to him, somehow figure out a way to stop the explosive implanted in him from going off and killing hundreds of people.

Her sisters. Kayla Ryan and whichever Cassandras

might be with her today. Asher's forces and scores of women and men from all strata of law enforcement, from the lowliest part-time sheriff's deputy to the SWAT teams.

But that part of it wasn't her problem. Her problem was exactly as Peters had stated it with his final breath.

"Asher sees me as the enemy," she muttered as she took the curve. "No matter what the Cassandras have told him, he knows I wasn't up-front with them about my agenda and he'll dismiss their trust in me as misplaced…which it was," she added honestly. "How the hell am I going to convince him I'm on the side of the angels for real this time, when in the past I've—"

She skidded to a halt as she turned the corner and saw the figure of a man blocking the stairs. Then he walked out of the shadows and she recognized him.

"Reese!" The last time she'd seen Terry Reese he'd been unconscious on the floor of Sir William's study, but although she was relieved to see his injuries had been minor enough that he'd been able to join in the fight against Lab 33, this wasn't the moment for catching up. "There's no time to explain now, but I need you to help me find Ash—"

"How did it feel killing Aldrich, angel? Bet it was a real rush." He took a step forward, bringing his right hand from the side of his body. "Just like it's going to be a rush for me to kill you."

Dawn froze. The sword he'd been concealing was now held in front of him, his two-handed grip on the hilt relaxed. He was used to the weapon, she thought tensely. And in such close quarters, dodging that gleaming blade would be impossible.

"Listen to me, Reese," she said rapidly. "Whatever Asher told you about me, I'm not the same woman who walked out on him three nights ago. I'm on your side, dammit, and if I don't—"

"With Aldrich gone and his organization destroyed, stepping into your position's not in the cards anymore." Reese gave no sign of hearing her. "But the man who takes down Lab 33's top assassin will be able to name his price anywhere in the world. That's even better than having to work my way up through the ranks like Peters intended."

...some of them won't return from the test assignments I've given them...those who do will be the nucleus of Lab 33's newly formed assassination squad...each assassin has been given the name of one of the Athena Academy graduates known as the Cassandras...their missions are to kill their targets or die in the attempt... Aldrich Peters's words from their meeting at the juke joint echoed in Dawn's mind, and she drew in a hissing breath.

"I get it," she said flatly. "You were as much undercover at London's lab as I was, weren't you? Maybe you killed a Ranger who was being transferred there and took his identity, but how you got in place doesn't matter right now. You were the killer in the hallway who shot me in the throat, and when you heard Sir William coming to the door you took on the role of my savior— gorgeous Terry Reese who came by just in time." A thought struck her. "The partial thumbprint of mine that was on file. Your doing?"

"I came back here on a day off from playing soldier and beefed up Interpol's data on the mysterious Donna Schmidt," Reese said tersely. "A good assassin takes every opportunity to unnerve his target, and I knew you'd go crazy wondering how you'd been so careless as to leave even a partial print at a scene. I lifted it from a glass you'd used in the cafeteria, by the way. But having a fake Athena Academy pin made and then giving it to you later was even more satisfying. I knew from the briefing Peters gave me on you that you'd allied yourself with them, and when you let the lab rats out I really thought I'd pushed you over the edge."

His grip tightened on the sword. "I intend this to be an honorable kill, Dawn—one superb warrior pitted against another. That's why I didn't try again after our encounter in the hallway—because I realized I didn't want to take you down when you obviously weren't at your peak."

"What about when you were playing dead in Sir William's study a few nights ago?" she asked with disgust. "How honorable was that?"

A flicker of anger marred the handsome features. "Peters should have trusted me to take you down. When the attack began, I realized he'd double-crossed me as well as you, and at that point my allegiance to him was voided. Since the Lab 33 gunmen didn't know I wasn't a real Ranger, it was easy to deliberately let myself be knocked out by one of them, all the while knowing they were no match for you. As I say, our confrontation will be an honorable one. There's a sword identical to mine in a niche in the rock wall by your right hand, and I'll give you the opportunity to—"

"What *is* this, freakin' King Arthur?" Dawn exploded in irritation. "Sorry to wreck your big moment, Lover Boy, but I really don't have time for this crap."

The gun she'd collected from Aldrich's body was tucked into the back of her belt. Before Reese could begin to raise his unwieldy weapon she shot it out of his hands and then pulled the trigger twice more. The drop-dead handsome fake Ranger dropped to the floor—not dead, as was evidenced by his screams of pain, but with both his shinbones shattered.

"You know, being the world's top assassin isn't all it's cracked up to be, Reese," Dawn said, tossing the out-of-ammo gun aside and stepping swiftly over him. "But it still kind of frosts my pumpkin having wannabe's trying to take me out."

Another agonized scream was his only answer, but already she was up the rough-hewn stairs and pushing open the trapdoor. As she began racing down the hall, she checked the remote in her hand—13:59. Dammit, she'd wasted four whole minutes—minutes she couldn't afford to waste.

"And it looks like another freakin' roadblock up ahead," she muttered worriedly as she bypassed the elevator and sprinted for the service stairs to the next level. "A last-ditch stand of Lab 33 guards battling against—"

Battling against a single Navy SEAL? Dawn frowned. The uniformed man holding off the guards was an incredible fighter, but the sheer number of his opponents was wearing him down. She'd intended to bypass the skirmish if possible, but she couldn't leave an ally in the hands of the enemy.

"Got your back, buddy!" She yelled out her intention to the SEAL just as the guard coming up behind him raised the stock of his rifle to slam it down onto the man's skull. The guard pivoted to face her instead. A moment later he was out cold on the floor and she was using his weapon as a battering ram against her half of the Lab 33 contingent as her SEAL partner, his back against hers, grimly took on the ones on his side.

"Hey, buddy!" Dawn slammed the butt of the rifle into a guard's stomach. As her opponent doubled over, she dealt him a karate blow to the back of his neck. "When we're finished with this sewing circle here, I've got to find Des Asher. He's an SAS guy, tall, tanned, probably leading a mixed group of SAS and Rangers. You seen him?"

Out of the corner of her eye she saw her comrade drive a knee into a guard's groin before planting a pile-driving punch on his chin that snapped the Lab 33's man's head backward. "Main level," the SEAL grunted as he turned his attention to the next guard coming at him. "Still some pockets of heavy resistance in the entry area, although most of the lower floors have been secured. You one of the Athena women?"

"You might say—dammit, hold on a minute." Dawn expediently dispatched the two guards who were rushing her by waiting until the last moment and then ramming their heads together. They both fell to their knees and two swift kicks took them out of the fight for good. "You might say that," she continued. "Name's Dawn O'Shaughnessy. I used to work for Aldrich Peters's organization, but don't hold that against—"

"Dawn?" The SEAL threw a startled look over his shoulder at her, and for the first time since she'd come to his aid she saw his face.

Her own eyes widened. "Dad?"

"Watch your left!"

At Thomas King's quick warning Dawn saw the woven-steel garrote that was about to come looping down around her neck. Automatically she fought off the guard who had attempted to strangle her, her mind not on the physical confrontation but on the man fighting alongside her who had the same green-gold eyes and honey-blond hair as she did.

For crying out loud, O'Shaughnessy...you called him Dad? she thought in embarrassment. *You've only seen the man twice before in your life, and that's counting the time you had him in the crosshairs of a high-powered rifle. Sure, when you found Lynn and Faith, the three of you sisters had a meeting with the man who's your biological father, but even though he seemed glad to meet us he had to feel a little awkward being confronted with a trio of daughters he'd never known existed—especially since he already has a wife and a teenage son. And now you've gone and made him feel uncomfortable all over again, dammit.*

The guard slumped heavily to the floor. She turned to take on a new attacker, and then realized that the Lab 33 contingent had been wiped out by her and her father.

She fumbled for the remote activator, which she'd tucked in her belt when she'd entered the fray. "Guess I was out of line there, King," she said curtly. "Calling you that, I mean. I'm sure you'd prefer I addressed you by your rank or your last name."

"You just saved my life, Dawn." Thomas King put a finger under her chin, gently forcing her to meet his gaze. "I'd say that gives you the right to call me anything you want...but Dad sounded just fine to me."

Dawn started to blink away the stupid moisture she could feel behind her eyes, but stopped when she saw the same mistiness in her father's identical green-gold gaze. "Sounded fine to me, too," she said huskily. Wishing she could hold on to the moment and knowing she couldn't, she glanced down at the remote in her hand—10:50. Another three minutes and ten seconds had ticked by.

Panic shot through her. "Dad, I need your help. I've got to find Des Asher and I'm just about out of time. Can you run interference for me in case any more of those freakin' Lab 33 mothers try to stop us?"

"Gladly. But Dawn?" Without wasting precious moments asking for details, King stiff-armed the door to the service stairs open and kept pace with her as she took the stairs three at a time. "Stow the potty-mouth while you're with your pop, okay? After watching you in action I'd probably be taking my life in my hands if I tried to paddle my little girl's backside for trash-talking, but as a father I'd feel duty-bound to make the attempt."

"You've got to be freakin'—" He *wasn't* kidding, Dawn realized as she saw King's loving but tough expression. She swallowed. "Yes, Dad," she said meekly. "Stowing the potty-mouth directly, sir."

She'd spent most of the past six months feeling as though her insides were made of ice, she thought as she flew up the last flight of stairs. But uniting with her father had melted one of the two final frozen chips that remained. Whether or not she had the chance to thaw the last one depended on what happened in the next— tensely she glanced down at the readout in her hand— eight minutes and thirty-nine seconds.

"Those sons of bitches don't give up easy, dammit." King's blunt comment came as he and Dawn paused on the threshold of the door leading from the service stairs to the main level hallway. He caught Dawn's expression. "One of the perks of fatherhood and rank. I get to swear a blue streak when I feel it's warranted—and I'd say this warrants it."

He was right, Dawn thought as she briefly surveyed the scene, searching for a glimpse of aqua eyes, her ears alert for the sound of a British-accented command. The Cassandras and their allies had obviously seized Lab 33, but in this hallway there still remained a few dozen hard-core fanatics who refused to surrender. It was no longer a battle but a vicious brawl, with boots and fists being preferable to gunfire in these close quarters where friend and foe were so tightly jammed together.

"He's not here." She heard a strained tremor in her voice and fought to control it.

"He wouldn't be." King gave her arm a fatherly squeeze. "Despite what it looks like, this is just a mop-up operation. As one of the leaders, Asher's more likely to be overseeing things in the reception area near the entrance to the complex."

"What Aldrich liked to call the Great Room." She nodded. "But to get to it I'm going to have to wade through this."

"Piece of cake," Thomas King said confidently, not noticing the second quick glance his daughter threw his way. "We'll collect a bodyguard detail as we go. Just watch what happens if those bastards try to slow you down."

She didn't know what the hell he meant, Dawn thought as she followed him into the melee, but she was willing to trust his judgment. A scar-faced man wearing the dull gray-and- red of a Lab 33 guard saw her and immediately reached for the garrote clipped to his belt. Thomas King reacted.

"Runner coming through!" he roared, propelling Dawn ahead of him and body-blocking the guard's lunge at her. "Athena team and allies, get your runner through! Don't let the enemy delay her!"

Throughout the crowd Dawn saw determined faces

turn her way; one of them belonging to a woman of about her own age, with icy blond hair and icy blue eyes. Samantha St. John finished off the guard she'd been grappling with and instantly began making her way to their side. But Sam St. John wasn't the only recognizable figure coming to her aid, Dawn realized unsteadily. A few feet ahead was Kayla Ryan, the tough police lieutenant already clearing a path by the most expedient method possible—by using the butt of a rifle to smash aside any Lab 33 guard foolish enough to get in her way. Lynn and Faith were a little farther off, but they too were making sure that she had clear access.

"You're delivering a message? Who to?" St. John's query was curt as she slammed an elbow backward into the rib cage of a guard who was about to impede their progress.

"Des Asher, the SAS—" Dawn began, but Sam cut her off.

"SAS hunk?" she suggested, her brief smile robbing her of her ice-queen demeanor for a moment. "Saw him not more than five minutes ago in what they call the Great Hall. He was about to start questioning captured hostiles to find out if there were any booby traps around this place."

"There's one, and it's a hell of a lot closer to him than he knows," Dawn said tersely as she glimpsed a knot of Lab 33 uniforms being held at bay by her phalanx of bodyguards. "Like right under the stitches in his bandaged arm. He doesn't know it, but he's carrying an explosive device on his own body that's going to bring this whole place down within minutes if I can't somehow defuse it."

Sam St. John's naturally fair complexion went chalky.

Then her eyes blazed with a cold blue fire. "Get her through faster!" she commanded. "And I mean *now!*"

The bodies in front of them began to part as the Cassandras and their allies redoubled their efforts. Dawn found herself able to break into a jog and then a run, leaving her father and Sam St. John behind her, still doing their part in the fight. Kayla gave her a thumbs-up as she sped by. She caught a glimpse of Lynn and Faith, who shot worried but encouraging glances her way as she flashed past them.

Then she was out of the fighting and sprinting into what had once been Lab 33's so-called Great Hall, the massive room with soaring ceilings she'd always thought looked more like a bad imitation of Grand Central Station than an impressive reception area for the few highly select, ruthless clients that Aldrich Peters meant it to impress.

It looked even more like a train station now. The marble antique statues that had dotted the room had been toppled from their pedestals during earlier fighting, and those same pedestals were being used by men and women issuing orders through microphones. Stretcher bearers were swiftly loading ambulances with wounded, most of them Lab 33 guards, and several of the costly silk-covered sofas upon which Peters had once received thuggish-looking warlords had been pushed together to create a hasty triage area, their upholstery stained now with blood.

Dawn took it all in with a glance. Her gaze dropped to the remote, and cold terror washed over her—4:01. "There's no way in hell I'm going to find him in time," she said through numb lips. "And even if I do, I still have to convince the man to hustle over to that triage area, have a field surgeon extract the Lab 33 device, and then try to defuse it. It can't be *done*, dammit!"

"Bloody hell!"

The growled oath was easily audible over the noise and confusion around her. Adrenaline pumping suddenly through her, she whirled in the direction of the familiar voice.

Asher was on his knees beside a convulsing guard, trying to force the man's clenched jaws open. The guard gave one final shudder and went limp.

"Some of the bastards have suicide pills. Get that information out to the other interrogators, will you." As he rose to his feet, Asher directed his words to a Ranger beside him. The Ranger nodded and ran over to another group.

She'd found him, Dawn thought swiftly, but there wasn't time for explanations or cooperation. There might not even be time to carry out the plan she'd begun to formulate while being escorted down the hallway by the Cassandras, but it was the only option remaining to her.

"In-and-out operation, O'Shaughnessy. You've done them before," she said under her breath, taking a second to judge distances and note the exact position of the bandage on Asher's upper arm. "Only difference is, this time the stakes are a hell of a lot higher."

The night she'd walked away from him she'd predicted that the next time they met, it would be as opponents. Her prediction was about to come true.

She burst into action. Racing by the triage table, she snatched a scalpel out of the hand of a surgeon who was about to use it on a wounded guard. His outraged shout drew the attention of others, but all Dawn cared about was that Asher wasn't alerted to her presence.

An angry aqua gaze turned quickly in the direction of the commotion and immediately fixed on her as she ran at top speed toward him. The incredulous expression on his face turned almost instantly to cold fury, and Dawn's heart sank.

"Oh, *crap,*" she muttered, launching herself at him.

"I should have believed the evidence of my own eyes instead of Kayla Ryan's assurance that you were on our side," Asher growled, sidestepping her attack and making a grab for the scalpel in her hand. "What's your cover story this time—you're a surgeon with a shaky cutting hand?"

She feinted, dropped back a step and hooked her foot around his ankle. He turned his fall into a roll and was on his feet again before she could do more than slice the bandage on his bare arm.

"It's not what it looks like," she snapped. "You've got a freakin' explosive device just under the skin of your arm, Ash, and if I don't get it—"

"Come on, love, surely you can come up with something better than that. Your acting was better when you were trying to get me into your bed." His fist kissed her chin, his punch only missing its aim because she'd dodged to one side. She took the opportunity to slash again at the dressing on his arm, and this time it parted completely, revealing the neat sutures that snaked from his bicep to his shoulder.

"You're pissed off because you thought we had something going," she said in disbelief. "Dammit, you're taking this personally!"

"Bloody right I take it personally when a woman's trying to rip open my hide." His scowl turned to a grimace as she drove an elbow into his ribs. Before he could retaliate, the scalpel flashed in her hand again and the first few inches of sutures parted. "Not that I believe you, but if there really is a device, what in damnation do you intend to do with it?"

"Run like hell," Dawn grunted as she grappled with him. "If I'm still in one piece when I get outside the complex, I'm going to throw it into the canyon." She heard a clatter by her feet and instinctively looked down. The activator had fallen faceup. Its display read 1:01, but even as she watched it changed to 1:00. Abruptly she stopped fighting Asher and looked into his angry eyes.

"I'm telling you the truth, Ash," she said hoarsely. "I know I lied to you about everything else, but you've got to trust me on this or we'll all die when that readout reaches zero."

His gaze held hers for a split second. His jaw tightened. Then he was running for the entrance like an Olympic sprinter, leaping over obstacles and shoving bystanders out of his way.

"What the hell do you think you're doing?" He'd had a head start of a few dozen feet on her, and Dawn screamed the question at his back as she sped up behind him, the remote she'd retrieved from the floor in one hand and the scalpel in her other.

"What does it look like? I'm running like bloody hell!" he growled, not bothering to turn his head.

She pulled alongside him. "And then you're going to throw yourself off the cliff into the canyon?"

"Not how I'd planned to spend the evening, but yeah, that's the general idea." He reached inside his tunic and pulled out an ID hanging by a chain around his neck. The Rangers who had been about to stop them at the barrier that had been set up by the entrance jumped out of their way. Asher went on, his voice strained. "How we doing on time?"

"Thirty seconds left. Turn right where the tunnel opens up to the outside. You trust me enough to dive into thin air?"

"You fought alongside me, O'Shaughnessy." They burst out of the concealed entrance to Lab 33 and swerved right. "You're my partner. And like I said, I hoped we might have some kind of future together. So, yes, I trust you."

"Then shut up and stop running, dammit," she said furiously, sticking her foot in front of him.

He fell heavily to the ground. Swearing savagely, he began to rise again, but she pushed him back. "This is gonna hurt," she muttered, slicing down the length of his sutures.

"Damn you, O'Shaughnessy, it's reading nine seconds! Let me up!"

"This is going to hurt more," she said curtly as she pried open his healing wound and probed inside it with her fingertips.

"Six seconds." He was obviously reading the remote beside them. "Five."

"Got it!" Her fingers closed around a flat, wafer-thin disc, oddly heavy for its size. Her grip on it slick with his blood, she jumped to her feet.

"Four." His tone wasn't totally even. "I hope you don't throw like a girl, O'Shaughnessy. *Three.*"

Dawn wound up like a major-league pitcher. "I hope I don't throw like an Englishman. What the hell you Limeys see in cricket is beyond me."

"Two."

Her arm whipped forward. Her wrist snapped straight. The disc left her grasp like a fastball.

"One!"

"Oops, I dropped it. Nah, just kidd—"

"Zero!"

Somewhere in the dark well in front of her that was the yawning mouth of the canyon, Dawn saw a small, intensely bright dot of light. Confusion flickered in her and then she understood. Even as she dived for the dirt beside Asher and averted her face, yelling at him to shield his eyes too, the night lit up with a searing brilliance that turned everything to day and the canyon itself seemed to explode.

Her hands were clapped to her ears. A shock wave of sound bypassed them and punched against her eardrums, making the ground beneath her tremble like a jelly mold shaking on a plate. It receded, came back even more deafeningly a second time, receded again. Through her tightly squeezed eyelids she could see every pebble and stone in front of her where she lay, their shapes seeming to burn themselves onto her retinas.

And then it was night again.

Gingerly she removed her palms from their protective clasp over her ears and raised her face from the dirt. Beside her she saw Asher do the same. His mouth moved.

"What did you say?" She realized she'd yelled the question only as she saw him wince. She shook her head, felt her eardrums pop as the pressure in them released, tried again. "What did you say?"

"I asked if you were okay, love." The searchlights that the Cassandras and their allies had set up outside the entrance to Lab 33 had swung in their direction, and it was possible to see the tension fading in his eyes. A glint of humor replaced it. "But I suppose if you weren't, you'd pull your handy-dandy healing stunt and be as good as new in a couple of minutes, right?"

Dawn nodded. There was something wrong with her throat again, she thought in irritation. And now the tightness seemed to have spread to the vicinity of her chest, somewhere around her heart. It hurt, dammit.

But in a *good* way, she thought after a moment's reflection.

"Ash, about me walking away from you the night you took the bullet for me," she said, but he didn't let her finish.

"Ancient history, love." There was no trace of his usual growl in his tone. He reached for her hand, playing idly with her fingers as he continued. "The government is going to want to debrief you, probably for a few days. You have any plans after that?"

"I was thinking of taking a little vacation," she said unsteadily, her eyes on his and not on the soldiers who were starting to run their way. "I thought Europe, maybe a side trip to the Middle East at some point?"

"As good a place to start as any," he agreed. "The terrorists who bought my uncle's regeneration research from Peters will be trying to assemble a team of geneticists to work on the refining process. I assume you wouldn't say no if I asked you to come along with me to help find the bastards after I hand in my commission to the SAS?"

His fingers were stroking her palm as he posed the question. The damn man was always trying to get the tactical advantage, Dawn thought, which was something she would have to watch out for in the future. She tightened her hold on his hand just enough so that he'd feel it.

"You assume wrong…but I wouldn't mind having *your* help while *I* track them down. Do we have a freakin' deal or not?"

He let out a breath. "Dammit, are you this bossy in bed, O'Shaughnessy?"

"Better believe it, buddy," she said promptly as the military contingent raced up to them and she and Ash got stiffly to their feet.

A corner of his mouth lifted slowly. "Then we've got a deal, love," he said for her ears only.

"Let me through, she's my daughter!"

"And our sister!"

Dawn looked past the soldiers and saw Thomas King's broad shoulders pushing their way toward her. Behind him came Faith and Lynn, and behind them was a dark-haired man who seemed equally intent on reaching her. She recognized FBI Agent Justin Cohen, whom she'd met once at Kayla's home. His eyes met hers as they all drew closer, and to her surprise she saw a gleam of sudden moisture in them.

"And in a way, my niece," he said huskily, as King released her from a bear hug and Faith and Lynn flung themselves at her. "I believe that my sister, Kelly, was your surrogate mother. I've spent my life searching for the truth about what happened to her, only to learn she was another casualty of Aldrich Peters's manipulations. Now that I've found you it's like having a little part of her back in my life again. Like she didn't die for nothing."

"You'll tell me all about her?" Dawn said unevenly, clasping Justin's strong hands. "What she was like, the things she used to do, her dreams?"

He nodded, his grip secure on hers. "That's a promise. But for now all you need to know is my sister was

a strong woman who always tried to do what was right."
He released her and stepped away. "In many ways,
you're a lot like her," he said quietly.

Dawn actually felt tears well up in her eyes. "I'm
glad," she said. She turned toward Tom King and Lynn
and Faith, and a tear crept down her cheek.

"Hey sis, no waterworks today. I think there's been
enough of that for all of us," Lynn said and pushed a
friendly fist lightly into Dawn's shoulder.

"We've got a lot of getting to know each other to do
still," Faith added. "I foresee a lot of flying in everyone's
future." Faith's extra-sensory abilities didn't really include foretelling the future, and they all laughed. Tom
wrapped an arm each around Lynn and Faith and the
three of them moved aside, gesturing for Dawn to join
them when she could.

Justin turned away and slipped into the press of
people, but not before stopping to embrace a red-
haired woman Dawn realized was another Cassandra,
FBI forensic scientist Alexandra Forsythe. Alex and
Justin exchanged a few intimate words, and then Alex
walked toward Dawn along with Kayla Ryan and Sam
St. John. Alex flicked a sideways glance at Asher and
then raised an eyebrow at Dawn. "Saving the world
is nice, but it's even better when you get the guy as
well, huh?"

"Damn straight," Dawn said promptly. She grinned
and then sobered. "It was a group effort. The Cassandras and their allies did good, didn't we, ladies? Working together turned us into a force to be reckoned with.
Now, if you'll excuse me, I've got a gorgeous and stub-
born hunk of man to get stitched up again."

She moved to Asher's side. Kayla looked at Sam and

Alex, her expression quizzical. "A force to be reckoned with," she said slowly. "*Athena Force*. You like?"

Dawn nodded. Sam spoke for all of them. "I like. Athena Force. Kinda kicks ass, doesn't it?" She smiled. "Just like its members."

And as Dawn bullied her way through the crowd, a wryly smiling Asher following close behind her, she just made out Kayla's words. "You got that right, girlfriend," Kayla said. Dawn could feel the women's gazes on her back. "Just like its members."

Epilogue

"**Y**ou may now kiss the bride." The white-cassocked Church of England priest beamed indulgently as the handsome groom, Captain Destin Asher, formerly of the SAS, kissed his beautiful new wife, Mrs. Dawn Asher, née O'Shaughnessy.

"*Darling,* everyone's watching." Pulling away from the prolonged kiss, the bride blushed and gave her husband's hand a squeeze. For a moment it seemed as if her groom was wincing, but his expression turned into a smile as he faced the small gathering assembled in the room.

"Since there won't be a reception and Dawnie—" there was a slight rustle near the hem of the bride's exquisite lace wedding gown and Asher seemed to wince again before he went on "—Dawn and I will be leaving Venice immediately for our honeymoon in the Azores, a few words of appreciation are in order. First I'd like to thank Sir Giles Anthony, Britain's man in Venice and a close friend of my uncle's, who unfortunately couldn't be here today, for offering us the use of his beautiful palazzo in which to celebrate our special day and the fleet of gondolas that brought us and our guests here in style. Sir Giles, my *adorable* wife and I will never be able to thank you enough for—"

"Unfriendly at three o'clock, Ash! Get the freakin' padre out of the line of fire!"

Destin Asher's adorable bride reached under the masses of tulle and lace billowing around her. Her hand came back into sight holding a wicked-looking knife. As the guests' shocked gasps turned to screams, she threw it at the tuxedo-clad man by the door who was raising his automatic rifle to his shoulder.

His aim jerked up, and a deadly line of bullets thudded into the delicately hued painting on the salon's ceiling. Wrenching the blade from his arm with a cry of pain, the man began to raise his weapon again.

"Everybody *down!*" Dawn jerked her attention Asher's way at his shouted warning. Clad in a dove-gray morning suit, he reached behind the lectern the priest had been standing at before he'd been knocked aside and leveled the Sig Sauer he'd retrieved over the heads of the guests. "Lady, get *down,* dammit!" He fired off a round and the gunman at the door suddenly clutched his elbow and dropped his rifle. A few pink feathers drifted onto the upturned face of a woman wearing a towering pink hat who'd fainted dead away.

"Crap, Ash, he's *escaping!*" Dawn began to race toward the door, but halfway there she tripped on the train of her gown, sliding a few feet on her face before scrambling to her feet again. "Help me off with this freakin' thing," she said as her groom ran to her side.

Seed pearls scattering wildly in all directions, Asher ripped her bodice open, revealing a virginal white corset with push-up cups. Impatiently grabbing a handful of tulle, Dawn tore the dress down over her hips and stepped out of it.

"Take a picture, it'll last longer, buddy," she snapped at a gaping male guest. "Come on, Asher, the bastard's getting away!"

"He'll have transportation waiting down by the canal," he replied as they left their wedding guests huddled on the floor and sped out into a hallway. "No, love, take the stairs to the roof garden."

"What, are you crazy?" Despite her protest, Dawn complied, shouldering past Asher and reaching the landing a step ahead of him. "We should be following the mother, not going in the opposite direction."

"That's exactly my point." Tearing off his suit jacket as he ran, he headed up a second flight of stairs. "From the roof garden we can see which way his waiting vaporetto heads when it takes off. By the way, couldn't you find those in white?"

He pushed open the door at the top of the stairs as he spoke, his glance dropping briefly to her feet. She made a face. "The combat boots? Okay, I know they don't go with the merry widow and the frilly blue garters, but I figured they wouldn't show under that ridiculous meringue of a dress. Besides, I knew if your plan worked out there was a chance we'd be involved in a situation where combat boots would be more appropriate than satin pumps. Over by those tubs of flowers—that must overlook the front of the building, Ash."

She sped to the ornamental railing and looked down the three stories—technically four, Dawn thought, since they were on the roof—of the ancient palazzo. The beauty of Venice was spread out all around them, but her eyes were focused on the line of gondolas and motorized vaporettos bobbing in the canal just feet from the front door of the palazzo.

"After six months of always finding ourselves one step behind those bastards who bought your uncle's research from Peters, this fake wedding was a stroke of genius," she said, her attention fixed on the scene below. "Like you guessed it might, it drew one of them out of the woodwork hoping to take us both down when we didn't have our guard up. Where'd you get the actor who played the priest, Ash? He was so convincing that if I didn't know better I'd swear he was the real thing."

"Do I still get to take those frilly blue garters off later tonight?" Asher said musingly, leaning over the railing and not looking at her. "Keep the boots on, too, love. It's a kinky look, but it suits you."

His tone was too smooth. Dawn frowned, momentarily taking her gaze from the canal. "He didn't even have to refer to the book of services for the words to the marriage ceremony, I noticed. He was pretty freakin' good, Ash. Where'd you find him?"

"There's our man!"

Ignoring her question, Asher pointed to a figure stumbling onto the cobblestoned walkway that lined the canal. Another figure leaped from one of the moored motorboats, grabbed the first man by the arm and hustled him onboard. A moment later she heard the sound of not one but two powerful engines coughing to life.

"Now for the fun part," Asher said briskly as he threw

one leg over the railing and then the other. He stood on the small ledge and gave her a tight grin. "That second vaporetto's our chase vehicle, love. You up for a quick dip?"

"Are you freakin'...oh, why not. It's faster than running down all those stairs again." Dawn hoisted herself over the rail and looked at the man standing beside her. "He *was* a fake priest, right?"

"Bloody hell, O'Shaughnessy—just *jump!*" Asher grinned, grabbing her hand and leaping with her off the ledge.

* * * * *

There's more ATHENA FORCE *coming your way!*
Don't miss any thrilling moment
as the excitement continues
in COUNTDOWN by Ruth Wind
April 2005

Prologue

It was night and snowing when Kim Valenti parked at FBI headquarters in Chicago. Snow came in through the window of the stolen car—a 1971 gold Buick Skylark— that she'd hot-wired at the parking lot of the UBC television station. She'd be glad to get somewhere warmer.

Before she got out, she checked her face in the rear-view mirror. If there was blood showing, she would draw attention to herself, and someone would be concerned or alarmed, which would cause more delays. She couldn't risk losing any more time.

There was a bomb ticking away at the airport. Somewhere. Due to detonate in exactly—she checked her watch—seventy-nine minutes.

In the mirror, she saw that her lip was swollen. She'd

have a black eye tomorrow. A few scrapes, but no damage that would make her stand out too much in a law-enforcement agency.

She got out of the car and hid the gun she'd also stolen in the small of her back, tucked into the waistband of her jeans. The weight of it was comforting and cold. Her cell phone was in her hand, the cord around her wrist.

Snow fell more heavily now, and she was half-frozen from the drive through the Chicago streets in a broken-down car with a shattered window.

In spite of the cold, her torn and battered ear throbbed. She wished it *would* have frozen. At least that would make it stop hurting. Without breaking stride, she scooped a handful of snow from the hood of a nearby car and pressed the icy cold to torn cartilage.

As she approached the front doors of the FBI building, a group of men erupted into the parking lot, rushing toward cars and vans. They shouted directions to one another, pulled on gloves, carted cases and rifles.

All headed, no doubt, for the television station. Kim ducked into the shadow of a truck, watching, her mouth hard. She could tell them that their rush was futile, but they wouldn't listen to her now any more than they had earlier.

No, if she had any chance of success, there was only one man for the job—Lex Tanner, FBI explosives expert and a compatriot she'd believed in before this morning.

She spied him toward the back of the group, carrying a metal suitcase. His dark hair was cut very short, the nose surprisingly recognizable from the pictures she'd seen, and he was quite tall. At least six-four. Rangy, lean and muscled, with shoulders big enough to shelter her from the wind.

As he neared her spot, she stepped out of the shadows. "Lex Luther, I presume?"

He started, narrowing his eyes and sizing her up. Recognition washed over his features. "Valenti?" He looked more alarmed than pleased. "Where the hell have you been? I've been calling all afternoon."

"Long story. Right now, I need you to bring your little bomb kit and come with me to the airport."

"I can't. I'm on my way to UBC. There's a terrorist—"

"Yeah, yeah," she waved a hand. "Never mind. That's not the problem."

"They've stolen a bomb they're threatening to detonate—"

"It's not at the station."

"They've got hostages."

"I know." She took a breath. "Look, I don't have time to explain everything, but the drama at UBC is a smoke screen—the bomb is at the airport."

"It's not there! Don't you get it? We've been over it a hundred and forty-seven times." His exasperation might have been understandable if they'd been strangers.

If he hadn't seen that she was extremely skilled. If he didn't know better.

If she hadn't proved herself by trusting his instincts, sight unseen.

If, if, if. She shook her head. She could stand here and argue, wasting time, explaining, or she could—

She pulled out her gun, using her body to shield it from the sight of the others, and poked the barrel into his ribs. "I didn't want to do it this way, but you won't listen."

"What—?"

She glared at him. "Don't make me hurt you, Luther. I liked you until today."

"This is crazy." He glared toward the men entering their trucks.

"Don't even think about it." She jabbed the butt into his ribs, harder. "I am dead serious."

"You're going to fuck up your career doing this."

Kim met his eyes. They were extremely blue. She'd read somewhere that extremely blue or green eyes showed a highly sexual nature.

Furious was more the word at the moment.

Oh, well. "Get in the car and I'll explain."

"You won't shoot me. I know you won't."

"I won't *kill* you," she said. "But I will hurt you if you don't come with me. Now." She pushed harder.

He resisted. "Explain."

She met his eyes with an icy lift of her own eyebrow. "Walk."

He glanced over his shoulder. No one was looking at them. Kim nudged him. "I tried to go through channels, but none of you has given me the respect I deserve, and because of that, people may die unnecessarily."

"If I go against orders, I'll be fired."

"I'm not talking anymore."

For an instant longer, he resisted. His nostrils flared in fury.

"It's killing you to have to listen to a girl, isn't it?"

"No, I—"

"My mother was a nurse in Vietnam. Did you know that? She was taken hostage once for three days, and it's something that has given her nightmares the rest of her life."

"Why the *hell* would I care, Valenti?"

"Because you can trust that I am very, *very* sincere when I say that I hate the whole hostage game. I would do *anything* to free hostages—but I won't let other people die. Do you understand?"

He narrowed his eyes, the jaw still mulish. Damn. She really did not want to hurt him. She would if she had to, but it would be messier and she needed him.

"Luther, I've had a very bad night. My ear is killing me. There are a couple of bastards at that television station who may or may not kill hostages, but there are law-enforcement officials on the scene to deal with them. They also don't have a bomb at the station, and that's what I need you for."

"How is it, *Kim,* that you're so much smarter than the entire federal law-enforcement community?"

She blinked. "I don't know, *Lex.* You tell me. Maybe I'm just smart. One thing I know for sure is that I *do* know what I'm talking about because—by the way did I tell you I speak Arabic fluently?—I overheard them talking at the television station. There is a bomb or a suicide bomber headed for the airport or *at* the airport, and people will die if we don't go now. I don't know how to defuse a bomb. You do."

"You finished?"

"Yes."

"Let's go. You can explain the rest in the car."

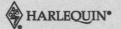

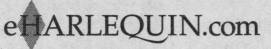

If you enjoyed what you just read,
then we've got an offer you can't resist!

Take 2 bestselling love stories FREE!

Plus get a FREE surprise gift!

Silhouette
BOMBSHELL

COMING NEXT MONTH

#37 WILD WOMAN by Lindsay McKenna
Sisters of the Ark

Pilot Jessica Merrill's risk-taking actions had earned her the nickname Wild Woman. Now she'd been charged with retrieving a powerful Native American totem from the madman who would use it to gain immortality. But Jessica's doubtful partner, Mace Phillips, was less enthusiastic about the mission. It was up to her to save the tribe—and show Mace that sometimes you had to take wild chances to get what you wanted....

#38 COUNTDOWN by Ruth Wind
Athena Force

Time was running out for code breaker Kim Valenti. She had evidence that terrorists were planning to disrupt the upcoming presidential election, but when she thwarted one attack, the terrorists made her their next target. Racing to save herself, the president and his opponent, she'd have to rely on her code-breaking skills—and the help of one sympathetic member of the bomb squad—before time ran out for everyone....

#39 THE MIDAS TRAP by Sharron McClellan

Renegade archaeologist Veronica Bright knew myths were based in truth. But her professional reputation had been torn to shreds when she'd tried to prove her theories. Now the renowned Dr. Simon Owens had handed her the opportunity to fight back—on a hunt for the legendary Midas Stone. Was this finally her chance to validate years of hard work, or was it a trap?

#40 SHOW HER THE MONEY by Stephanie Feagan

Accountant Whitney "Pink" Pearl was in trouble. She'd exposed a funny money accounting scam by one for her firm's biggest clients—and the only evidence was locked in a box with a blow-up doll! Meanwhile, someone was stalking her, and when a top executive turned up dead, she realized she had been the intended victim. Only Pink's feisty determination—and the help of one savvy lawyer—could get her out of this mess!